Terms & Conditions

Terms & Conditions

ROBERT GLANCY

BLOOMSBURY

LONDON · NEW DELHI · NEW YORK · SYDNEY

First published in Great Britain 2014

Copyright © 2014 by Robert Glancy

The moral right of the author has been asserted

Bloomsbury Publishing plc
50 Bedford Square
London
WC1B 3DP

www.bloomsbury.com

Bloomsbury Publishing, London, New Delhi, New York and Sydney

A CIP catalogue record for this book is available from the British Library

Hardback ISBN 978 1 4088 5220 0
Trade paperback ISBN 978 1 4088 5221 7

10 9 8 7 6 5 4 3 2 1

Typeset by Hewer Text UK Ltd, Edinburgh
Printed and bound in Great Britain by CPI Group (UK) Ltd, Croydon CR0 4YY

For Jemma

TERMS & CONDITIONS OF LIFE

The condition of life is a complicated one in
which the terms are rarely made clear.

My name is Frank Shaw and I write contracts for a living. I'm not proud of what I do. In my bleaker moments I believe I'm the death of an essential part of humanity. People once sealed deals with handshakes. I replace handshakes with expensive ink. I swap the human touch with cold contracts. What anti-matter is to matter, I am to trust – *I'm anti-trust*, the dark force committed to destroying life's faith, hope and wonder. Put simply – I'm a corporate lawyer.

I specialise in fine print, which places me on one of the bottom rungs of my business. I'm the legal equivalent of the guy who sweeps up hair at the barbershop. You probably didn't read my terms and conditions today, when you bought something off the internet and clicked 'Agree'; or when you signed blind some contract giving away your rights, your life, a pound of your flesh.

My masterpiece is the work I did on the modern insurance policy. I wrote it fresh out of law school when my brilliance was still radiant. Its genius lies in the fact that it's unbearably dull. Few can read it all the way through and none ever get to the small print. That's the loophole I hang you with – the policy seems to weave a golden safety net catching you as you plunge through life's tragedies but my sharp fine print rips the net to shreds. For if the devil's in the detail, I'm the devil's ghost-writer, typing cautionary tales in font so small they're rendered invisible. You can barely see them and when you do it's too late.*

I speak from bitter experience. After my car crash I learned that terms and conditions don't just govern my work – they're also the tight rules underwriting my life. However, directly after the crash – lying broken in bed – I remembered little of this; all I knew for sure was that something awful had happened.

---

* So I warn you now – read the small print.

CONDITION I

AMNESIA

TERMS & CONDITIONS OF TRAGEDY

*If some strange and terrible thing
happens to you – that's tragedy.*

*If some strange and terrible thing happens to
someone else – that's just entertainment.*

TERMS & CONDITIONS OF ME

I'm not the man I used to be.

I awoke to people – who professed to be my family – telling me I was going to be fine.

How can I be fine? I've no idea who the hell you people are!

They tried to outrun the truth, to smother reality with hope, by chanting, *You're fine, Franklyn, absolutely fine!*

Watching my forgotten family I realised that denial is like running on a treadmill with the monstrous thing you're denying waiting for you to tire, fall, and shoot back into its hairy hands. But I knew the truth – I was far from fine. The monster had me. And for a time I lay in its dark silent embrace. When I did talk, it only made matters worse.

'Who are you people?' I asked.

One of them replied, 'I'm your wife, remember?'

My second question really put a stop to them saying I was fine.

'And who am I?'

With so few clues as to who I was, it was hard to be me. I wanted to say something to assure everyone that I was the same old Frank and that everything was fine. (But I wasn't and it wasn't.) And I certainly knew when I said something wrong. Their faces leaked little rivers of worry and they'd look at me askance, as if I'd fallen out of focus, as if I'd said something unsuitable. Which was exactly the problem: I no longer suited myself. (Failure to fulfil a contract is called *impossibility of performance* and that was my trouble – I kept saying things pre-crash Frank wouldn't say.) The only thing I remembered for sure was that before the crash people just called me *Frank*. But after it they reverted to using my full name – *Franklyn*. I lost a personality but gained a syllable.*

---

* Slim compensation indeed.

TERMS & CONDITIONS OF SENSES

Mine no longer made sense.

When I saw my face I didn't recognise myself. The mirror reflected a pulped stranger: bloated eyes adrift in blood, shattered fence of teeth, gross mushroomed cheeks. And my new world wasn't much prettier either. It was a place wedged with warnings. Machines released shrill cries calling forth fast-moving medics. Signs on floors shouted, *Slippery When Wet!* Screams rose from distant corridors only to be snuffed out. My drugs came with lists of warnings as long as Russian novels. A red button declared, *Press in Emergency!*

My body was incessantly panicking, urging me to press the button all the time. Initially I did press it all the time. They disconnected it. Then I started screaming, *Help, help, I can't remember who I am!* They injected drugs, which muffled my panic below a hundred blankets where no one could get to me. I wished they'd reconnect the button. I missed it.

My terror was heightened by my muddled hormones. The accident had smashed my separately labelled jars – *Sad, Happy, Mad* – into a sloshing chaos of wild fluids. I wanted to laugh, cry and scream all at once, all the time. Also, the nerves that once ran along separate pipes to my ears, eyes, nose and mouth were plaited into a confused braid. So I saw green and tasted fish, heard screaming and saw blue, smelt cheese and heard music.

Dr Mills assured me that this synaesthesia was simply my brain's attempt to find new ways back to old memories. My sense and sensibilities were so scrambled that when Dr Mills drank a coffee I saw the steam rise like a deep bass note vibrating my tangled senses and triggering a feeling, a deeply embarrassing feeling – *a crush*. As I listened to Dr Mills' coffee, I realised that feelings are stickier than memories.*

---

* Violently shake your brain and memories float off like pollen, but feelings – they grip on like Velcro. So my first real feeling wasn't about my brothers or my wife or family – *it was about my beautiful barista.*

TERMS & CONDITIONS OF COFFEE

Its taste never lives up to the promise of its aroma.

This sticky, curly, embarrassing feeling – *this silly crush* – snagged my first real memory. I remembered that I hated coffee but I was madly in love with the coffee lady from the café in our office block. Her chocolate-brown hair poured down her face and her bosom was forever rising up towards me. I recalled spending many hours trying to think of witty, interesting things to say to her.

This one time, when it was just the two of us in the café, I said to my beautiful barista, 'Your coffees are amazing.'

She smiled. Her lips don't thin when she smiles, they fatten, and as she frothed the milk, a speck flew up and landed on her breast. It was right then that I decided to do the most impulsive thing I've ever done in my safe little life – I leant across the counter and wiped the speck away. She looked as if she was about to slap me, I flinched, she grabbed my head, pulling my face to within a whisper of hers, and in the flustered moment she covered me with espresso kisses, her breath warm, rich, full of love, her body bending towards me as her breasts . . .*

---

* Disclaimer: of course, none of this actually happened.*1

*1 My frazzled brain was blending fantasy with reality. The truth was far less Mills & Boon. In fact – if I'm remembering correctly – I barely ever spoke to her. Yet I'd return to my desk brimming with joy; but as my cappuccino cooled, a sadness settled in and every day I'd sit with a cold cup of coffee thinking, *What the hell am I doing with my life?**2

*2 And every day a tiny voice would reply, 'Not a lot.'*3

*3 This melancholy memory was the first sign that all was not well.

TERMS & CONDITIONS OF MY WIFE

Alice is my wife – allegedly.

My alleged wife, like many of my visitors, seemed very nervous when she came to see me.

Why? Were they worried I wouldn't recognise them? Maybe they were hopeful they'd be that special person – *the key* – the one whose mere presence would miraculously unlock me? Or was it that people were nervous because I'd been a complete bastard?

Was Old Frank a real twat?

I discovered early on that no one would tell me what I had really been like. When I asked my wife, she offered only the vaguest sentences; words that could have described a billion other people: 'You were, *are* . . . a nice chap and funny, really driven and . . .'

It was like that awful 'Personal Section' in curriculum vitaes – *my CV personality*. So I accepted that I was the only one who could really discover who I once was – I knew no one would ever tell me the unvarnished truth.*

But my nervous wife did drop some clues which made me realise that my memory wasn't entirely deleted. (Where my short-term memory was a burnt-out office, some long-term memories were safely backed up in a warehouse far away.) So when my wife told me I had a brother called Malcolm, two words bobbed from my amnesiac soup and I shouted triumphantly, 'Fuck this!'

She laughed, 'That's right. Malcolm liked saying that. We've tried to track Malcolm down, but he's off travelling, God knows where . . .'

My wife kept talking but I wasn't listening: I was, for a moment, mesmerised by my own hand and I could only really focus on one thing at a time. (My concentration was the most under-staffed

---

* No one would turn to me and say, *You were such a cunt-face, Frank. You hated life, detested your friends, and you were often found in parks furiously masturbating.*

department of my broken brain; it was just one guy frantically adding to an endless *To Do* list unspooling behind him like toilet roll.)

'. . . you listening, cotton-brain?' she said, but winced at what a bad thing that was to say to a brain-damaged person. 'Oscar? Your older brother? Remember? Oscar?* Tall . . . He's um . . .' As I watched her strain to describe Oscar, I realised that people knew friends and family so well that they didn't really see them any more. (Everyone becomes invisible.)

I, on the other hand, was overpowered by details. My blurred vision meant that features shot out of people's faces like caricatures – Dr Mills' bald head; Alice's black bob – but what I lacked was the glue to stick the right feature to the right person. So in my woozy underworld Dr Mills appeared with Alice's black bob, or Alice with Dr Mills' bulbous nose hanging grotesquely off her face. (Legally, *confusion of goods* describes a situation in which the property of two persons becomes inseparably mixed – I suffered *confusion of features*.)

I must have flicked in and out of sleep because Oscar was suddenly there, sitting stiffly beside my wife, as if he'd popped out of thin air, or in his case fat air, as – it turned out – he was an extraordinarily large man. The two of them were tense, sitting in silence, one fat, one slim, both watching me. I noticed that they never talked to each other directly and I sensed that they hated one another.*[1]

Oscar had a bag of plums, and he said, 'Franklyn, having another snooze, eh? Brought you these. People always bring grapes. I upped it, brought you plums. Basically giant grapes.'

And a rancid green smell oozed from somewhere.

Oscar picked the price sticker off a plum and rolled it around his fingers. I took a plum and admired it: taut skin marbled with thin crimson veins running deep into the dark flesh within – this perfect design overwhelmed me and I said, 'Can you believe this?' to which

---

* Oscar? Um? Nope, no Oscar here – try Lost & Found down the hall past the Department of Déjà Vu.

*[1] So palpable was the rage between them that I saw it as an iridescent white light.

Oscar, still staring at the price sticker, barked, 'I know! £2 for a few plums! It's daylight fucking robbery!'

I must have looked confused, because Alice and Oscar realised I wasn't talking about the price. They laughed hard and loud, forcing the tension around us into temporary submission.*

My wife said, 'That was so funny, Franklyn.'

As the laughter faded – and the tension regained its hold – I became overpowered by the foul green smell. Oscar looked at me hard as if expecting me to say something. He was ill at ease. I smiled; my shattered teeth sparked a flicker of disgust on Oscar's face as he said, 'Do you remember much about your little episode, Franklyn?'

Little episode!

My wife's hand shot across the divide between them and grabbed Oscar's knee. He jumped a little.

'What do you mean?' I said. 'What *little episode*? I was told I was in a car accident.'

My wife smiled – her hand released Oscar's knee and the gap between them flared bright – when she said, 'Nothing, nothing, nothing at all, Franklyn. You were rather tired . . . stressed and tired, before your crash, that's all . . .'

But the sharp silence that followed – which I saw as a violet scream – suggested they were hiding something from me. Exhausted by my sensory cocktail I lay back and stared up at the white ceiling. The violet scream faded, the green stench paled, and I sank into a colourless sleep.

---

* And dimming the fierce light between them.

TERMS & CONDITIONS
OF THE SPLEEN

You can live without it but it makes
life just a little bit harder.

Mornings began with Dr Mills giving me an update on my condition. It was almost comical – *were it not tragic* – the way he sat with his glasses hanging off the end of his nose detailing my grim anatomical itinerary.

'So, Mr Shaw, your bones are healing well, ribs are still loose but they'll heal, both your collar bones remain fractured. The amnesia we shall be monitoring very closely. Blood pressure is stabilising but your panic attacks are still frequent. And, finally, I'm sorry that we failed to mention this to you after the accident, it was a clerical error, and we should really have told you earlier, but I have to tell you now,' and he leaned in slowly as if about to confess something terrible and said in a solemn tone, 'you can live without it, so please don't panic, but we had to remove your soul as it was ruptured in the accident.'*

'You removed my soul?' I squealed.

'No, no, that's not my department,' he said, smiling slightly. 'Your *spleen*. We had to remove your spleen, which was ruptured in the accident. Yes, as I say, it's not an essential organ. It just means you may be a little more susceptible to infection. The spleen is a very clever little additional filter but if you have a healthy lifestyle you can survive without it. No problem at all. In fact, history shows that many great men have survived, and even thrived, without their spleens . . .'

He left the sentence hanging, so I smiled, waiting for him to list some of the great men who had thrived without their spleens, but Dr Mills merely snapped shut the file and walked off to his next patient.

---

* *Remove my soul!*

TERMS & CONDITIONS
OF MALCOLM

He was nowhere to be seen.

My wife visited, dropped off my laptop, and opened my personal email account in order to help spark my memory. I dug into my past. It was an embarrassingly shallow excavation. It seems I didn't suffer an abundance of friends. In fact, besides spam mail, the only consistent communication was from my younger brother, Malcolm, and from his sparse correspondence it was clear he was often off the grid. But his emails made me love him instantly.

From: fuckthis@hotmail.com
To: franklynmydear@hotmail.com
Subject: A Greek Tragedy

Frank – hi!

Ended up on a Greek train platform with a Scottish vagrant last night.

Missed the train and we were locked in the station.

Before he fell asleep his exact words were, *Don't worry, pal, I'm no thief – I'm just a wee bit of a murderer.*

He actually said that then fell asleep, leaving me bolt upright.

Eventually exhaustion came to collect me and I fell asleep too.

Luckily – he turned out to be a liar.

When I woke up he'd stolen everything including the sleeping bag I'd been in. *Phew!*

Love and lies,
Malc

PS Saw this on a sticker today: *The heart is a blind, hopeful organ, beating patiently, craving excitement and love. If you only feed it solitude and fear, one day it will give up on you.*

TERMS & CONDITIONS
OF HAPPINESS

Hysteria is just a hop away from happiness.

By the time I returned home my vivid panic had downgraded to anxious elation. I felt like a spy watching a stranger's life. And, man, what a life! My wife: *beautiful*. The flat: *amazing*. It's odd what you remember. I remembered exactly where the teaspoons were kept, but I still had no idea how I used to feel about this woman who was my wife. She seemed nice, though, and quite sexy.* (The only thing was, she was always watching me.)

Time and dental work had deflated my face to its original size, my eyes cleared, and all that remained was a scar on my forehead that I covered with my fringe. My senses had divorced and were independent again. And my memory was returning like the reconnection of a thousand torn fibres, an itch on your nose when your hands are occupied, screaming, *scratch me, scratch me*. I was still dopey due to the wide spectrum of anti-psychotics and painkillers but by the time I arrived home I was so happy I thought I might burst.*[1] They say that people who walk away from near-death experiences are filled with overwhelming joy. What they don't tell you is that the feeling is finite. It fades. Mine faded fast.

After a few drifting days, the first strange thing I noted about my life was that I was so completely absent from it. Like a murder scene in which someone had cleaned up all evidence of me. Was I one of those people who simply floated through life without leaving a mark? The flat was very feminine, with its white walls and profusion of cushions. So few clues. My clothes were generic, I had an ancient wind-up watch,

---

* Although we'd not had sex yet as my ribs still swam inside me like snapped bamboo in soup.

*1 Amendment to Terms & Conditions of Happiness: it transpired that my happiness was nitroglycerin. Clear and stable as long as everything was utterly calm. But shake it just a bit – and it exploded.

and most of my books were about contract law. I looked around and thought, *Where the hell am I in all of this?*

When my wife went to work I became a drowsy detective in search of myself. Under the bed I found a box. As I opened it my heart beat hard like I was about to uncover my memory, as if one simple object in this box would unblock my amnesia dam, cause a flood, and I'd drown in me. I was sorely disappointed: inside were contracts, just random ones about employment or insurance. I skimmed through them.

I did, however, know I was doing well when I, New Franklyn, spotted something Old Frank must have missed. Within the fine print of one contract was a mistake: *Term results in detriment – non omnis moriar – to the promisee.* Now I know that *Non omnis moriar**sounds like a legal term, and it slips past the eye easily. But I knew the phrase was wrong. It has no legal basis.*1

I threw the contracts back, pushed the box under the bed, then worked my way through the bookshelf where I found a book called *Executive X.* I was a bit surprised to see my wife had written it. There was a picture of her on the back looking a touch younger. The front cover image was a giant X wearing a black tie. It was a book that described a man, an executive, and for all its corporate gibberish, I could only deduce that this guy, Executive X, was a complete tosser. It was a book about how to evaluate personalities, full of asinine questions like: *Meeting someone new – a pleasure or a pain?* After reading a few pages, my hand began to shake and, before I knew what was happening, I was throwing the book against the wall and then – as if in a dream, watching myself – I was stomping on it, again and again and again, until dizziness overpowered me.

When the rage passed I was mortified.

---

* Not all of me shall die.
*1 I'll preface that by adding that odd phrases do make it into law. Latin and biblical quotes creep in. In *Donoghue v Stevenson*, Ms Donoghue drank a snail in her ginger beer and her lawyer made the court recognise that everyone – *including ginger beer makers like Mr Stevenson* – should *Love thy neighbour*, and in so doing try their utmost to stop people inadvertently drinking snails. And so a legal doctrine was born from a biblical quote.

I'd destroyed a book by my wife. And I had no clue why. I began to fumble about to find a place to hide it, to conceal my crime. I opened a cupboard full of brown boxes.

Perfect, I thought.

But as I tore open the top box I was met with many more copies of *Executive X*. Feeling faint, I grabbed the box to steady myself but pulled it down with me, spilling boxes and books, ending up on my back thrashing about on the floor. Once everything had stopped tumbling I sat up and looked around at the boxes spewing out multiple copies of *Executive X* and noticed something else among the chaos – small figures.

They were toys, plastic dolls, figurines packed with detachable organs: lungs, liver, spleen, in bright reds and blues that could be pulled out and popped back like a three-dimensional organic jigsaw. I grasped one and my panic peaked when I peered into its tiny plastic cavities where a little heart and brain should have been. It was missing vital organs. Their absence made me so mad that I tried to compose myself by lying back flat on the floor, arms outstretched. Holding the toy in my right hand I stared at the ceiling, trying to ride the panic back to calm. Very slowly, as my breathing hit a more natural rhythm, I turned my head and looked down the white line of my arm to my clenched fist, the figurine's head poked from one side of my palm and his feet from the other.

I sent a signal to my hand, but it seemed so distant and disconnected that I was faintly surprised when slowly, like a flower in bloom, the fingers opened and from my palm burst the organs – red kidney, purple spaghetti nervous system, deep brown bowel rolled along the wooden floor, and for a moment I simply stared at the imprint they left.

Once I had got a grip of myself I carefully replaced all the tiny organs – this small task filled me with childish contentment – then I repacked the books, hiding the one I'd abused deep down at the bottom of one of the boxes. (My wife would never know.)

I put the little dolls back. As I placed the final figurine on to the top shelf of the cupboard I spotted, right at the back, a small jar, an old Colman's mustard jar. On the label scrawled in childish writing it read – *Leap of Faith!* There was no mustard inside. There was a murky fluid and floating in the centre was a parsnip, no, a bent crayon, no, a pale asparagus, no, it had a nail on it – *it was a child's little finger*.

Having been floored by a book and a toy, I expected that a child's finger would have sent me straight to the nuthouse. It did quite the opposite. I watched it – suspended in fluid – and it brought me a sense of calm; followed by a vivid flush of pride. I sat on the floor and cradled the Colman's mustard jar. Aside from the pride, the finger didn't bring back any specific memories.*

I took an itinerary of 'my search for me'. Needless to say, the clues so far failed to illuminate the dark recesses of my lost personality.

All I had was:

1. A maddening book by my wife.
2. Some weird dolls with detachable organs.
3. And a spare pinkie.

---

* I assumed that I had not kidnapped a child and chopped their little finger off. But, really, who knows? I decided, until I knew more, that it was probably best not to mention the floating finger to my wife.

TERMS & CONDITIONS
OF IMPRESSIONS

It's hard to do an impression of yourself.

Since I had returned from the hospital, my wife and I stuck to a strict routine. The doctor recommended this, advising us that routine was the best route to recovery. So my wife and I would have a proper dinner together every evening.

Pleasant would best describe our dinners. We chatted about small things – her day at work, colleagues, the news – and, yes, occasionally we laughed a little. But the dinners had the quality of a first date – *a perpetual first date* – where each night we tried again to get to know one another. But each night we were frustrated by that grating friction which strangers generate between the rub of forced politeness and mild suspicion.

Sometimes Oscar would join us for dinner and this often made matters worse. I felt an added pressure in his company, as I tried hard to remember details. They tried hard to be as patient with me as possible. I wasn't at all sure that patience was a trait Oscar was familiar with.

Whenever I tried to bring up the question of my *little episode* my wife always answered my question with a question – 'Why do you always ask about that, Franklyn?'

Because it sounds scary, I wanted to say.*

It became obvious that Oscar and my wife had spoken to each other and devised an answer – or a deflection – which was simply, 'You were just tired and stressed before the car crash. Don't worry about it.'

But during one dinner with Oscar and my wife I did hit upon another memory (this time my taste buds were the spark). While eating a slice of cake a detail came to me: a child in a cowboy outfit pointing

---

* But I didn't, as I was conscious of not causing my wife and Oscar more anxiety than I already had.

his gun and screaming at a group of stunned kids, 'Stop eating my cake! You can all just go now!'

I ventured a guess: 'Oscar, you once tried to kick your friends out of your own birthday party . . . because they were eating your cake?'

My wife laughed and said, 'That's right, Franklyn.'

Oscar looked pissed off before admitting, 'Yes, I was a bit of a nightmare as a kid.'

'And it looks like you really like your cake,' I joked, realising too late just how offensive it was to say this to a fat man like Oscar.

They both looked stunned that I had said something so rude.

Clearly Old Frank would never have said this and I felt the heavy disappointment of letting them down. Again I was failing this performance; I was basically doing a very poor impression of myself.

But, after a terribly long pause, Oscar grinned, then guffawed, and this in turn got a laugh from my wife, who smiled sweetly and said, 'You got it, Frank.'*

---

* Maybe I hadn't said the wrong thing after all. I noticed she called me Frank that time. Just Frank. Not Franklyn. Like I got something right enough to be called my old name. This made me uncontrollably happy.*1

*1 Maybe this performance wasn't quite so impossible after all.

TERMS & CONDITIONS OF SEX

It takes two to tango (but both parties need to dance to the same rhythm).

Sex with my wife was a strange affair.*

---

*   Particularly because she was basically still a stranger. Lying in bed, I spied on my wife as she cleaned her teeth. Even below the baggy folds of an old T-shirt the shape of her body was clear, a beautiful but not natural figure, distinctly modern, meticulously developed by cycling, yoga, multiple hours of fitness fads expressed in svelte, defined flesh. Still unaware that I was watching, she pulled off her T-shirt and appraised her body in the mirror.*[1] If her goal was to achieve an androgynous form, which I suspected it might be, she would forever be thwarted by a persistent layer of gentle curves. Atop her toned legs her hips had little fat yet their natural shape remained wide, spread out, wing-like, open and inviting, but their soft invite was mildly undone by her intimidating stomach, which was as hard as it was flat, even slightly concave, a trunk of uptight muscle hiding all suggestion of female organs below, and relief from her hard centre came only when her abdomen broadened outwards to accommodate her ribcage and breasts, which, although in no way large, were just big enough to resist being toned into the tough musculature upon which they so softly sat. Lost in her shape, I failed to see that she was now watching me watch her; she was approaching, saying, 'I didn't tell you this, but Dr Mills said the best way to re-jog your memory was to have sex with your wife as often as possible.'

I felt faint, out of breath, losing lots of blood, as her fast hand, snaking below the sheets, found the very spot where most of it had decided to collect.

I said, 'Um, this might not take long.'

With a disarming grin, she said, 'Don't worry, Mister,*[2] you were never much of an endurance runner. Now you really need to relax a little, Franklyn. Let me do this, just relax.'

At first, all was going well, and then in the middle of a lovely moment, as our breathing became heavy and harmonised, I heard myself say, 'I want to make love to you, Alice.'*[3]

Aside from my mental neurosis, I was also physically struggling to free myself of my clothes as I tried to get my stupid boxer shorts off. Then, having recovered from my embarrassing gaffe, just as our heat and pace built to a new peak, I moved too quickly, causing a jagged pain to shoot across my body, as if one of my loose ribs had sailed

*[1]   Reading a woman's face as she reviews her body would take up more paper than the world has to offer, but I read enough to know that disappointment was at least one part of her critical self-assessment.

*[2]   *Mister?* That was new. Was it a code between us? Something fun and provocative?

*[3]   *Oh dear.* I realised too late what a crap thing that was to say. In the centre of this hot moment I should have growled, *Let's fuck* – no, that's too rude! Possibly something milder, *We need to have sex right now?* I shouldn't have said anything at all. I was muddled between my polite mind and horny body; crude contradictions of love and lust, tangles of pleasure and rage clotted my tongue.

into a nerve. I squealed, kicked out my leg catching my wife in the face with my knee – crack!

She straightened up, shocked, her body taut as if under attack, her expression baffled. I wanted to crawl away and die.

I got on to my knees, brushing her face, 'Oh God, I'm so sorry, I think I just kneed you in the face.'

She touched her cheek gently and said, 'Goodness me.'

I muttered, 'I'm like a fucking schoolboy, I'm sorry, let's just forget this.'*

She looked as if she was just about to accept the offer, roll over, and go to sleep, but instead she got down and helped me struggle to get shot of my boxer shorts and said, 'Stop, Franklyn, calm down,' and she leaned in and kissed my face, and placed her hand gently on my chest as if to bring my heart back to a normal rhythm, 'No need to rush.'

She pulled the sheets free, tossed them off the bed, and I felt horribly exposed, lying naked, my pale, scarred body uninviting next to my wife's finely carved figure. But she seemed not to notice. She looked at me with nonjudgmental eyes. She touched my penis in the way that you might handle a trophy, she made me feel important. My God, my wife was an amazing woman, and somehow she even managed to joke, saying in a sexy tone, 'At least this part of you is still going strong, Mister.' She stopped me as I tried to move again, pushed me back, put a leg over me and straddled my body. With an almost yogic motion she slowly laid her entire body on top of mine in methodical stages.

So calming was this movement that I knew it was something we must have done in the past. For all our awkwardness – trying to get to know each other and work around each other – this moment, her lying flat on top of me, was the closest we had come to true calm. Where our personalities had so far failed to synch, our bodies were perfectly fitted together: her breasts came down first, packed in between us, soft and warm, spreading peacefully over my anxious heart; our shoulders aligned and locked; her concave stomach descended, a hollow filled by my small belly; her hips gently bracketed my own and, with a short practical motion of her hand, she directed me deep into her, as the soft equal sign of our thighs and shins came parallel. For a second, maybe two, I was calm; for the first time since I had woken up in the hospital, I was home.*3

Sex didn't bring back any memories as such, but my body, blood and bones remembered something, remembered enough to release them from the panic that had encased them since my crash.

---

* But although my mouth said, *Let's just forget this*, it was hard to ignore my penis*1 which was saying something altogether more forthright – *Let's fuck!* With both of us kneeling, facing each other, my cock literally looked like a small desperate hand stretching out to touch my wife's vagina.*2

*1 Is cock a better word? Prick? Knob? Dong?

*2 My wife's pussy? Cunt? *Oh I don't know!*

*3 I had been so lost in my mind since the accident and finally I was out of my head and inside my body. I was *feeling*. Momentarily relieved from the unyielding *thinking and thinking and thinking*, I wanted to scream with joy – *Why hadn't we done this earlier!* I felt overpowered by an urgent need for the sort of sex which would pitch me into a state of unthinking abandonment.

Alice kissed me and whispered, 'I love you, Frank.'*

Her hips moved and I was so close to saying, I love you, Alice – I thought the words were literally about to exit my mouth – but what came instead was a light exhale of air and in its wake I felt the build-up, the moment of pressure which precedes relief. The pressure was strong: the many tiny cuts I had in my neck, where the doctors had pushed their drip tubes into me, felt like they might tear and I would squirt like a human sprinkler. As the tension built I waited for the pleasure to come but I realised too late the pressure was panic, radiating out from my groin across my stomach, jangling my ribs, raking against my heart and singeing my brain. Alice misread the sudden jerking of my body – as I tried to disconnect, tried to buck her off me – for some sort of sexual ecstasy and she rose up on her arms like a soldier doing press-ups, biceps tightening, pelvis grinding. My panic attack was in full flush – tears and sweat and sperm rising out of me like a squeezed sponge – as thrashing Alice rode my attack all the way home, clashing hips, her head raised so I could only see the underside of her jaw, clenched and hard like the rest of her primed body; only her breasts gave away any softness in her as she shouted to the ceiling, 'Come on, Mister, that's it, that's it, yes, yes, yes!'

I was crying but didn't want to admit that I was in a state of terror so I gripped on for dear life – the tendons on her neck tightening – hoping she would finish soon. Before I could throw her off she pushed a final brutal shove downwards, her jaw loosened, fell slack like an anchor dragging down the rest of her face – taut wire veins deflated and receded back into her throat – and her head lay heavily on my chest as she moaned and ground the last bits out of me as if at the gym giving her all on a final push-up. I had managed to run my panic back deep into the centre of me somewhere and I smiled and hugged her tight so she couldn't look at my face and read my terror. Her tense body deflated and she moaned, 'Great job, Mister. We'll have you up and running in no time, I'll be your personal sexual trainer.'

'Sounds good, where do we start?' I managed to say, hearing in my voice the flutter of my passing panic. 'Quads then pecs?'

'Let's begin at the core, lots of cock exercises, then up from there. How does that sound?'

'Sounds perfect,' I said, as she curled up into the hollow of my arm.

'You know what,' she whispered, 'I think we're going to be fine, Mister, just fine.'

I still didn't remember or really know my wife but, at that moment, even for all the farce and confusion that we'd just been through, I knew I cared for her. I had put her through hell – the crash, the worry, the anxiety, me returning home like some amnesiac retard – and she had done everything to support and love me. I still didn't really know who she was but I knew enough to know that my wife was a very special woman.

* The returning message of love bubbling up – *I love you too* – got lost somewhere between my heart and my mouth.

TERMS & CONDITIONS
OF MY OFFICE

I'll do anything for a great view.

One man's tragedy is another man's TV show. You see it on the news every week. The eye witness frothing at the mouth describing some atrocious thing that happened to someone else: 'And then, like, the bullet hit his throat and it, like, almost took his whole head off, it was awesome . . .' Realising they're being insensitive they add, 'Um, what I meant was . . . you know, an awesomely terrible tragedy . . . it was terrible, a truly terrible tragedy . . .'

I suspect that this was how my *little episode* was viewed by my colleagues. Who really knows what I did?* So although the staff gave me sympathetic looks, deep down I sensed that many of them had a good chuckle. It was probably a real entertainment to them; anything to cut through the office boredom.

And it turns out I was not just your average employee. The very first thing I saw was a sign on the office door:

Shaw&Sons*
*Lawyers

In a mild twist it turned out I was one of the sons while Oscar, who was both my brother and boss, was the head of the company. He explained that our grandfather had founded the firm; our father then ran it, before Oscar (and I) had taken over.

On my first day back at work, Oscar made a speech to the staff about how I had been through the wars but this was not just a business but a family, and that he was going to make sure I got back to being the brilliant man I once was. It became apparent to me that I had once

---

* For all I knew I had run about with my underpants on my head farting the national anthem.

been brilliant. I felt terrible for disappointing people in my new less-than-brilliant form.*

The first few days ticked along normally. My colleagues were very friendly; they seemed not to mind when I fell asleep at my desk, a little drool on my yellow legal pad. The building was one of those sheer glass shards in the city, a thousand mirrors balanced one atop the other with Shaw&Sons perched high in the top two floors. And at first I found it all very easy; I slipped back in, people were nice, they smiled and asked how I was. I assured everyone I was tickety-boo (and they seemed to believe me).

The only slight problem about the office was a door. In my first week back I tried to ignore it but each day it loomed larger in my peripheral vision. It was like any other door but it was ever so slightly whiter and cleaner. I can't explain fully the effect of it other than to say it scared me. I literally couldn't go within ten feet of it without feeling faint and woozy. I ignored it as best I could but it was like ignoring the sun on a bright summer's day.

One morning I saw three men in suits enter into the office with the white door. I walked near the door but couldn't get too close before sparks swam in my vision and I backed away, leaning against the wall to steady myself. I couldn't go near the door.

So, instead, I figured out that I needed to keep my distance, stay at my desk, and wait for the door to open. That way, as soon as I saw someone come out I'd run after them – *without going too near the door* – question them, and crack the mystery.*1

Unfortunately my desk was tucked in a corner, which meant I couldn't really see the white door from where I sat – not unless I stood behind my desk and leant at an awkward angle like a bent straw. Which is exactly what I did for half an hour until Oscar came over and gently told me that it was kind of freaking people out.

When I asked Oscar who worked in there, he laughed and said, 'No one works in there, buddy, it's just a closet or something.'

---

* I was the elegant butterfly emerging from the chrysalis a fat dumb caterpillar.
*1 I had a plan, brilliant in its simplicity.

I told him I'd just seen men going in there and it was clearly not a closet.

Oscar said, 'Hey, Franklyn, did you take your medicine today?'

'Yes.'*

Instead of standing and leaning, I began to shunt my desk over. It was awkward when I moved so far to the right that my desk touched my colleague's desk.

'Franklyn, can you move your desk back a bit?' she said.

I said, 'Of course I can.'

I didn't.

Instead, when she left for a meeting, I moved *her* desk further away too, and then the desk next to hers and so on, pushing the whole office around in a slow circle.

As soon as people went off for meetings, when I was alone, even for a few seconds, I'd shift the desks slightly. I imagined it all in time-lapse: desks migrating like tectonic continents across the deep green carpet.

One day someone tripped over my taut electrical wire and yelled, 'What the hell!'

I used my lunch hour to run to a store where I bought an extension so I could keep surreptitiously shifting desks.*1

I didn't quite get all the desks far enough around in those first few days back. The white door was still not in view from where I sat. So on the Friday I came in early, before anyone was around, and did an additional shunt; then over lunch, when everyone went out, I finally had enough time to administer one final push of all of the desks and then it happened – *I had the perfect view.*

Keeping my distance, I could simply sit at my desk and stare down the corridor to the white door, and – soon as it opened – I'd be on my

---

* No. (But I'm absolutely fine!) Painkillers killed pain but also killed everything else, including your sense of existence, which was something I was quite keen to cling on to. And my anti-psychotic drugs had dreadful side effects. So I stopped taking those horrid pills (and so far so awesome!).

*1 And still I was convinced that this was in no way an obsession! (Oh no no – *I'm all good!*)

feet, charging down whoever came out, asking what the hell was in there that gave me such a deep sense of doom.

I sat there feeling elated, waiting, focusing my entire being on the door, when I heard a colleague across the room shout, 'Hang on a minute, I used to have a window seat, who the fuck moved my desk?'

There was a meeting held in Oscar's office. I saw them all talking then pointing at me. Oscar came over and very softly told me off for moving the desks and said it wasn't good behaviour for me to get obsessed with things and Dr Mills had said this could happen.

I promised Oscar I'd forget about the door.*

I went straight to the front desk of the building and spoke to the main doorman. I politely explained that there was a shiny white door down the corridor from my office, and I just wanted to know the name of the company; that was all.

The doorman said, 'Opposite Shaw&Sons? A new office? No. Are you saying that I haven't noticed an entirely new office opening in my own building? Are you saying I'm not doing my job properly, sir? Is this a joke? Did Jeff from maintenance put you up to this?'

Taken aback, I said, 'Um?'

He looked at me suspiciously and sneered, 'Nice bloody try, sir.' Then added, 'I don't recognise you. Have you even got authority to be here?'

I fumbled for my ID and muttered, 'I'm a . . . Shaw.'

He didn't look impressed; instead he took an age to study my ID, then said, 'You look sort of different. What's happened to you?'*1

Too baffled to continue the conversation, I said I'd been on holiday, then ran off, deciding to go and stare at my beautiful barista. (Seamlessly shuffling one obsession with another.)

She was even more beautiful than I remembered and I was so smitten that I had to stop myself approaching her, fearful that partway through ordering I might blurt out my undying love.*2

---

* I lied.

*1 I refer my client to the previous 20 pages of confused revelations.

*2 *An espresso with two sugars, you fantastically wonderful example of everything in life that I love and adore.*

22

I noticed that she was chatting to someone on her phone, and then the doorman, who I'd previously argued with, came over, and told me I had to leave the premises, as I was freaking out the young lady.

Overall I wouldn't say that my first week back had been a blinding success.*

---

* Not unless, that is, you compared it to the following week, which turned out to be one of the worst of my life.

TERMS & CONDITIONS OF BEES

They're dying.

I took a few days off, doctor's orders. I'd given up searching for clues in the flat. I accepted that I was looking for someone who wasn't there. I was a junkie who'd forgotten what drug he was addicted to. The need was there but with nothing to sate it, I craved without end, desired without satisfaction. Between being Old Frank and New Franklyn I found I was forever second-guessing myself – saying something but hearing the thing I actually wanted to say echo in my head – like a Russian doll of disappointed versions packed deeper and deeper within. So I made the decision to put myself out of my own misery. I didn't want to find Old Frank. I was happy as I was, and I kept sadness at bay for a while, until I met three people. The first was Sandra, the second was Doug, and the third was the oddest – it was me.

I was watching a programme on television and a presenter was explaining what an essential link the bee is in life's chain. 'Without this little Aphrodite of the flowers, mankind is in danger of following the bees into extinction,' the man said, smiling to camera. It cut to an image of dead bees scattered like gun pellets in a field and I felt warmth on my face. Tears. I was crying. Crying for those damn stupid bees. Tears rolled down my face. I didn't even place the story into the greater context of what it meant for mankind, I just felt incredibly sad about all those poor little dead bees. There was a knock on the door and I waited for Alice to answer it, but remembered she had a yoga away-day with her boss, Valencia. I quickly tidied myself up and when I opened the door there was a lady who said what everyone said to me these days, 'I'm not sure if you remember me, Frank.'

'You're Molly?' I guessed.

'I'm Sandra.'

This woman had the most remarkable nose, like something chiselled from crystal, with so many wonderful angles that I got lost in it. She smiled in a way that filled me with love. I felt as if she were my real wife. I held this rushing sensation of love in place and said, 'Your nose is really beautiful.'

'Thank you,' she said, and blushed. 'I'm a friend of your wife. Well, to be honest, I'm an old friend, maybe an ex-friend. It's been years. But a friend told me about your . . . accident. I miss you, Frank, I'm so sorry about what happened . . .'

Then, before I could stop it, I started to cry again. Without pausing Sandra gathered me up into a hug and deep inside her hair and her cardigan – which released just a whiff of mushroom – I suddenly recalled a detail. 'Is Molly OK? Your mum is Molly.'

Without breaking the hug, Sandra said, 'I'm so sorry to have to tell you this, Frank, but Molly's not well. She's in hospital. She's dying.'

I cried even more loudly and, before I realised what I was saying, I heard myself mutter into Sandra's warm neck, 'Just like all the bees, Sandra, just like all the poor bees.'

She kept hugging me and whispered, 'I know, Frank, I know.'

TERMS & CONDITIONS OF CULLING

Friends are a hindrance.

Since my wife and I had made love – which turned out to be a one-off incident – things had not gone as smoothly as I had hoped. Initially we were fine and our pleasant dinners continued to be pleasant until one night we hit a hurdle. It started when I began to ask questions. Without mentioning the book *Executive X* or the floating finger, I just said vaguely, 'Was I depressed before the crash?'

She stared hard into my eyes as if we were working on a telepathic level, only my receiver was broken and nothing was coming through.

'Why ask that, Franklyn?'

She loved answering questions with questions. I was growing irritated by it.

'I just feel something isn't quite right.' Then I went one further, and said, 'Look, Sandra came to visit me and she told me Molly's sick.'

'I know,' said my wife, with no surprise in her voice.

'You know Molly's sick and you've not been to see her, or even mentioned it to me.'

'You're still sick yourself; I didn't want to stress you.' My wife then looked up and said coldly in a voice I'd not heard before, 'Look, Franklyn, to be honest with you, I dumped them, I culled them.'

'How do you mean?' I asked, confused.

'Did you take your medicine today?' she asked.*

Then my wife said, 'I culled them because I just decided they weren't getting me anywhere.'*1

But this time, before I could stop myself, I heard myself saying, 'Is that what friends are for? To get you places? I'm pretty sure that's what cars are for.'

---

* No (but, as I said, I'm doing really absolutely brilliantly without it).

*1 Now, normally at our little dinners – to keep it all sweet – I would do everything to avoid rocking the boat, and I would have just said, 'OK, I understand, I'm really sorry I asked.'

My wife paused, her fork hit her plate a touch hard and she looked at me.

'I see you're starting to remember what a smartarse you were,' she said.

It was delivered in a particularly caustic tone, yet it suited her and vibrated through me into some past truth.

I said, 'But Sandra told me you were best friends.'

'*Best friends.* You sound like you're six years old, Franklyn,' she said, and smiled a smile so thin it could slice eyeballs.

I raised my voice a little, 'Well, you sound like a bitch.'

We took a moment to accept that I'd said something cruel, but what was worse was a sense that we had finally hit our groove. I felt deep down – in a way that was more powerful and convincing than mere memory – that my wife and I used to argue like this before my crash.

'Franklyn, listen, they're just *old* friends.'

'Old friends are the best ones. They're the ones you've had the longest.'

'What the hell's got into you? What happened to that happy Franklyn that came out of the hospital? Let it go. Molly and Sandra are ancient history.'

'They're a part of our ancient history,' I whispered, suddenly tired.

'I promise I'll see Molly later this week. As for our own discussion, I have to go cycling with Valencia, so let's re-sched, so we can thrash it out later. Sound good?'

'No. It sounds fucking awful,' I said.*

---

* And she looked at me as at a pet which, after years of docile obedience, had turned on her.

From: fuckthis@hotmail.com
To: franklynmydear@hotmail.com
Subject: East Beats West

Frank – hi!

Went to Wat Pho to see the reclining Buddha – a stunning piece of
golden mellowness.

In the West our religious icons hang off crosses, emaciated, bleeding
and in eternal pain.

In the East they have a golden God reclining like the happiest fucking dude
in the universe.

Love and joy,
Malc

PS Reincarnation is real in Thailand. Suzuki cars come back as boat engines.

TERMS & CONDITIONS OF GOD

He had ten of them.

When I returned to the office after my little break, they started me on real work – on terms and conditions. Oscar joked that no one ever read them so I wasn't to worry too much about it. I suspected the contracts I was given were not live ones, just old ones to make me feel useful. At first, the tiny words swam like tadpoles, and sleep pulled me under. But still no one told me off. In fact, Oscar treated me so well that I had a dull sense that he liked New Franklyn more than Old Frank.

He smiled when I came back with a pharmaceutical contract and, checking it over, said, 'Great work, buddy. So you don't have a problem with this?'

'Not at all,' I said, not really understanding the question.

'I love it,' said Oscar. 'You're like the new and improved Franklyn Version 2.0.'

Contracts were in some sense a great comfort. My post-crash life was a chaos of emotions, but fine print allowed me to tie things down with tidy rules. Small print also gave me the first clues about my old self. Reading his contracts, I saw Old Frank was a neurotic ball of fret. I could smell it in the way he wrote terms. I felt privileged to have been him; he was a man who elevated neurosis to an art form. A contract lawyer protects clients by mitigating risk and avoiding responsibility, so no loophole is left unlooped or condition unqualified. And Old Frank was a master at it. A great lawyer does not abide the Rumsfeld rule of *unknowable unknowns*. He insures clients against *all* unknowable unknowns. For instance, the dreamy-sounding *Force Majeure* – colloquially called *Acts of God* – is the ultimate opt-out clause used to ensure that everything from weather to unforeseen incidents will get a client off the hook.*

The strict translation of *Force Majeure* is a *Superior Force*, and I considered the Superior Force in my life to be the people, or possibly entity,

---

*   Beware of romantic-sounding legalese.

which had led to my episode and crash. I wondered if Old Frank believed in God. (I barely believed in myself, so having faith in some all-powerful force was a stretch.) I wasn't sure that Old Frank was a believer but I was convinced that he wielded God-like power for his clients. His contracts, so beautifully drafted, acted like Catholic priests – absolving, forgiving, at times even rewarding clients, no matter the situation. Old Frank was indeed a neurotic master. And if poetry was a raid on the inarticulate, then Frank's terms were a raid on the unforeseen.* His terms tamed the riot of life and he was the master of the thing I most feared – worst-case scenarios.*1

So I knew I was doing particularly well when I spotted another thing that Old Frank had missed.

It was a font irregularity.*2

And I barely noticed but, just before I moved off the page, my eye snagged on it:

Publishing rights shall mean in the Work, which shall mean the right to produce, publish, distribute and sell, perform as permitted un **✱3** electronic form (whether in whole or in part, adapted or abridged, sequentially or non-sequentially, on its own or in combination with anot sounds and images) by any electronic means, method or device (including without limitation any digital optical and magnetic information s limitation floppy disk, dvd, **cd-rom**, d-card, compact disc, integrated circuit), mobile and hand-held **devices**, online and satelli telecommunication) and any other device, **medium** or means for electronic reproduction, publication, dissemination and transmission w Work or any part thereof available for reading. Rights shall mean versions that include the Work, in complete **or** condensed or adapt display in any manner (whether **sequentially or non**-sequentially and together with accompanying sounds and images **if any)** by any c **device'** shall include but not be limited to digital optical and magnetic information storage and retrieval systems, online or satellite transm **publication** or transmission whether **now or** hereafter known or developed but excluding Electronic Book Rights. Or satellite transmiss

---

* Here's Old Frank displaying his power in a term he drafted for a writers' contract for television: 'The writer waives any right to seek injunctive relief for the exploitation of their Work.'

The brutal placement of the word *exploitation* cuts so deep.

In layman's terms: *Bend over, you're about to be exploited (and did we mention, when you're being buggered, you won't even be able to complain about it. Now please sign your life away here, here and here).*

*1 A famous computer company's terms are the best example of worst-case scenario taken to an absurd degree: *You agree that you will not use this MP3 player for any purposes prohibited by US law, including, without limitation, the development, design, and manufacture of nuclear missiles.*

Nuclear missiles! Supremely surreal. A company that produces sublime products and ridiculous fine print.

*2 Shaw&Sons, like all firms, has strict rules governing font size:

The nastier the clause the smaller the font.

The more important the condition, the less visible it must be.

*3 *Mea culpa: I am responsible.*

TERMS & CONDITIONS OF DOUG

We're bound by delicate strings.

'Good to see you back on your feet, Frank,' said Doug.

We were in the corridor, standing in what should have been an awkward moment – two men between places, in transit, nowhere to put their hands, nothing to lean on – but it wasn't awkward, it was calm. I didn't remember much about Doug but I remembered enough to know that I trusted him, he put me at ease. Departed memories leave emotional residues, so even though I couldn't remember any facts about Doug, I felt deep down that I liked him.

'I feel much better, thank you.'

'I'm not sure what you remember but I worked with your father. I'm in insurance, an actuary actually,' and he smiled at this little phrase.

I smiled back but Doug then looked at me very seriously and said, 'Now, Frank, tell me, do you *really* feel better?'

I responded with a knee-jerk, 'Yes of course I do. Tickety-boo.'

'Really?' said Doug.

I thought for a moment and said, 'Well, actually, no, not really, not entirely.'

'That's fine,' said Doug, in no way disappointed. 'It will be tough for a bit. A brain injury like that. It's a big thing. A fundamental thing.'

'Yes, it is,' I said. 'I sort of feel like . . . oh don't worry . . . it's silly.'

'No, Frank, finish the thought, please,' he said, holding my gaze with his warm brown eyes.

'It feels like everything is being kept sweet – you know – superficial, like people think I might break or something, and I can't seem to talk to anyone about anything that, well, that matters,' I said, realising as I spoke that this was exactly what the problem was.

Doug nodded and I sensed he was weighing up a decision, determining whether he should tell me something of importance.

He said, 'Look, Frank, um, I think we may need a little chat, so why don't we go and talk a while? My office is just down the corridor. What do you say? I make a mean green tea.'

I almost agreed. But his smile had an unnatural tension to it – a rope pulled too taut – and for a second I wasn't sure if my initial impression of Doug was right. We were so high up in the building that it seemed as if clouds were brushing past the windows. I felt dizzy with indecision: Doug was trying to help me, I knew he wanted to share something fundamental with me, yet I hesitated and said, 'Thanks for the chat, Doug. It's been great talking, but I've really got to get back to my desk and check . . . some things.'

Doug's head sagged and I felt him give up on me. That feeling, of people giving up on me, that's a physical sensation now. As if we're tied by a million soft strings and, when I disappoint, a few thousand strings stretch and break, as my connection to that person is severed by yet more thin slices of disappointment.*

---

* And as I walked away in a daze, I felt the thousand tiny strings between Doug and me snap.

TERMS & CONDITIONS OF CODES

They only make sense when you have the key.

A few days after my encounter with Doug, I sat nursing an undrunk coffee at the café. Someone had spilled sugar on the table and it caught the sunlight and shone beautifully – a sugary constellation. Partway through proofreading one of Old Frank's contracts, I felt odd, woozy, with an unsettling slush in my belly. All I knew was that I felt something was wrong. Something *felt* wrong. I thought I was about to be sick, so I pushed the policy away and tried to focus on not throwing up. Then I picked it up again and told myself to get a grip, but as I read it this feeling of anxiety filtered back in, and the world tipped sideways.

There were words in the contract that a lawyer would never use. And this time it wasn't just typos or font irregularities. Blurring my eyes caused strange words to bob up to the surface. The first word I spotted was the oddest. It dangled in the middle of a sentence – *may*. Not a legal word; far too ambiguous. I highlighted it.

I went over the page again. The next word – *Warning*. Now this may not seem exceptional, but it's not the sort of word used in a contract. It's far too sensational. The sentence it lurked in was standard: *Warning: all benefits agreed by the insurer will be adjusted in accordance with annual increases in interest rates.* The second part of that sentence is in every contract. But I'd never seen the word *Warning* precede it.

Then this: *the full agreed sum will be paid to the customer, contain, after the amount is fully approved by . . .* I felt overpowered by a vague sense that things around me were connected, that I'd stumbled upon a mysterious pattern drawn from blooming revelations and coincidences. This must be what schizophrenics feel in the lucid seconds of excitable realisation just before they tip into the abyss. The epiphany before lunacy.

The final word bubbled up and it was the most bizarre. And when I combined all the odd words into a sentence, it made me laugh out loud. The sentence read:

Warning: This Contract May Contain Nuts!

It was only after my laughter hit a feverish note that I realised I couldn't stop. There was no brake on my hysteria. I couldn't halt it. People, including my beautiful barista, were looking at me, but the laughter bored deep into a place I hadn't been for a long time. Giggling wildly, I stared at those words and I knew. I knew without a shadow of a doubt that I'd written them; I'd tampered with this contract before my accident. Perhaps I'd tampered with all the contracts. It was as if my old self was screaming up from the bowels of a well, roaring at me from the past – *Wake up! Wake up and smell the putrid coffee, Frank, your life's a fucking disaster!* This message had boomeranged back to me – or even *forward to me* – from Old Frank communicating from the past, shouting over the chasm. As I laughed I remembered. I sat, holding tightly to this tampered contract, and my old memory, my feelings, my personality poured into the empty husk that was me.

I really wish I could say something positive – that returning memories were a million dandelion seeds floating back and sticking to my brain. I cannot. Cockroaches hold hundreds of babies in their wombs and, when squashed, their exploded bodies spew spawn as far and wide as possible to preserve the species; as I laughed I started desperately and frantically trapping all the disgusting scuttling memories before they escaped again. That was how it felt.

My brain filed the returning memories, like the lawyer I was, defining in detail my relationships with everyone around me, and the love and obligations that bound us all together. Hysteria rocked my body, memories burst like the hot gush of saliva before vomit, and the first thing I recalled was brutally simple, all the hatred built to a screech, and at its highest pitch rose one word – *Oscar*.

CONDITION 2

HYPERMNESIA*

TERMS & CONDITIONS
OF KNOWLEDGE

Only after you achieve ultimate knowledge do you gain the final wisdom – that ignorance was bliss.

---

*   Vivid recall of the past.

TERMS & CONDITIONS OF OSCAR

The condition of halitosis is one of stinking denial.

Oscar's face is like a board game in which his eyes, ears, mouth and nose compete to win the prize of 'nastiest feature'. If I were judging, I'd say his eyes take the prize. They're less like eyes, more like hollows left by a departing soul.

In case you're still unsure: I hate him.

I remembered it all so clearly now.

He has repugnant halitosis and was forever saying about other people, 'Man, that guy has rank breath!'

In fact it's just bad-breath rebound. Oscar hasn't sussed out that it's his own breath wafting back at him.

The only positive about Oscar is that he's the one thing left that my wife and I completely agree on. (Yes, turns out I'm not a huge fan of my wife either, but I'll come to that.)

I remembered that my wife and I often played the Who-Hates-Oscar-The-Most game.

I'd say: 'If Oscar was an animal, he'd be a rattlesnake.'

She'd trump this with: 'Oscar is Stalin and Hitler's lovechild.'

I'd double-trump that with: 'Most people are reincarnated as animals. Oscar will be reincarnated as AIDS.'

You get the idea. I won't write what Oscar actually is. It is simply too offensive.*

---

* (Oscar is a cunt.)

TERMS & CONDITIONS
OF MY FAMILY

No need to get personal.

Then the crux of the matter came to me. The source of my rage –
the Will.

My dad's Will stated that Oscar would take over the business, then
I would become partner, and finally my youngest brother, Malcolm,
would too. The contract was specific and fair; we all had to work hard
to earn our partnerships. It was nepotism with a legal shine.

Unfortunately, Dad put one tiny sentence in the Will which stipulated that my election to partner would be determined '*at such a time
as Oscar sees fit*'.

A decade after Dad's death, Oscar hasn't yet *seen fit*. My life ruined
by one sentence.* It will be my epitaph. *Here lies Frank. He died at such
a time as Oscar saw fit.* My dad snapped me into a legal trap. I remembered vividly the day I learned of Dad's Will: a grey lawyer reading a
manila Will in a beige office. The windows had steel bars that bent
outwards and the walls were piled high with red books. The significance of the moment saturated everything with symbolism as I sat in
my legal jail. And Oscar, calm as can be, stretched his fat legs out like
a man sunbathing.

My youngest brother, Malcolm, had his own response. He stood,
said, 'Fuck this,' walked out, got on a plane and never returned. Shrewd
move.

The reading of the Will was a crossroads in my life but I'm still
standing in the centre of it, still undecided, still too chicken-shit to
move. I'm not saying I was my father's favourite or that he loved me the
most. He was egalitarian in his love.*1 But just to stick to tradition and

---

* I warned you about that small print.

*1 His love was equitable and fair. His love would have stood up in a court of law. Legal
love.

give everything to the eldest brother was intolerable. Surely my father, even through paternal eyes, blurry with pride, must have noticed that Oscar was a power-mad twat.

Dad distributed the remaining parts of his estate with King Solomon precision. All funds, such as the money from his house, were ploughed back into the business, so logically all three brothers would ultimately profit from the investment.

His other valuable possessions were then split evenly: his expensive briefcase was gifted to Malcolm, his fountain pen gifted to Oscar, and his antique wind-up watch went to me.*

---

* I had admired it once, when I was a kid, and he promised it to me. But later on I found myself dismissing it. When I was an arrogant teenager I compared it to my own *super amazing digital* watch which did not require winding up. Dad didn't like this, and I suspected he may have reconsidered his offer, but he told me at the time, 'The great thing about my watch, Frank, is that you get out of it exactly what you put into it. There's something rather nice and fair about it. It's a beautiful contract. Every morning I take a few seconds to wind up twenty-four hours' worth of time and every day my watch returns the favour by marking out twenty-four precise hours.'

I smirked at him.

I wish I hadn't, and every morning I wind it up, I regret that smirk.

From: fuckthis@hotmail.com
To: franklynmydear@hotmail.com
Subject: No-News Flash!

Frank – hi,

News Flash: Nothing Happened Today

On an island somewhere in Thailand nothing happened today. No politicians lied, no salesmen sold nothing, no missionary preached no word of no god, no policeman arrested no criminal, no one decided that they needed to have plastic surgery because their boobs seemed saggy, no one beat up no one else because no football teams lost no games, no banker embezzled no money, no one divorced no one else, no CIA conspiracies were hatched (not allegedly nor otherwise), no celebrity was photographed doing nothing to no one, no Starbucks opened on no street, absolutely nothing of any significance happened today. Not a blessed thing.

Love and peace,
Malc

TERMS & CONDITIONS OF
OBJECTIVES MEETINGS

There's nothing objective about them.

Not only had Oscar *seen fit* not to make me a partner, he'd also *seen fit* to keep me in the lowest league of our firm. I'm still, so long after Dad's death, the terms and conditions guy. And Oscar never missed an opportunity to put me down. We had the most painful objectives meetings in which Oscar had the cheek to tell me that I didn't have the gravitas required for the promotion. He loved every minute that I loathed.

'You're a little light, Frank,' Oscar said. 'You need a bit more power. Buy some suits that cost too much, get rid of that stupid Japanese car, buy something imposing, enormous, get a new haircut, start wearing odd-shaped glasses. That's how you achieve gravitas. Any questions?'

'Just one,' I said. 'When did you graduate from being a bit of a knob to a full-blown cock?'

'Funny, buddy. Very funny. This meeting is adjourned. No need to get personal.'

But at this one particular objectives meeting I had come fully armed. For months, Oscar and I had been arguing about putting Shaw&Sons on the stock exchange. Or 'going IPO'* as Oscar so hideously insisted on calling it. I warned Oscar that this went against everything we stood for as a family business and that our dad would turn in his grave. For weeks we'd argued. I even looked through Dad's Will and there, like a sparkling jewel, was a clause which stated: *Shaw&Sons is a family firm, and for as long as my name remains on the business, the partners will not publicly list the business, under any circumstances.*

I smiled when I read this. I knew I was about to triumph over Oscar; Dad's cautious nature had given me the weapon I needed to

---

* Initial Public Offering: the moment when the public buys shares in a listed company and makes people like Oscar (and all the other partners) filthy rich.

ruin Oscar's little plan. *Under any circumstances* – my father tied things up tight.

I'll admit that, even in my thirties, there's nothing quite like getting one over my older brother. So I waited until he'd insulted me, and told me I needed more gravitas, and then when Oscar brought up the idea of the IPO again, I casually unfolded the copy of the Will and said, 'You can't do it, Oscar. Dad included a strict clause against it. Let it go. It's all – right there – in black and white.'

I assumed Oscar's rotten mouth would flop open and he'd accept defeat. He didn't; he smiled as if a worthy warrior had appeared in place of his weakling little brother and said, 'Very good, Frank. This is why you'll always be a better lawyer than me. And why you may even make partner one day. But for now you're not a partner and that means you don't have final say in the IPO decision.'

'There is no IPO decision,' I squeaked.

'We'll see,' said Oscar, and walked off smiling.

I should have been glowing in the afterburn of my victory but instead I was twitchy and uncertain as to exactly what had just happened.

TERMS & CONDITIONS OF DOORS

They don't just appear out of thin air.

After that particularly awful meeting with Oscar, I stood fuming at the photocopier, when I noticed a man walk past, down the corridor, into an office that hadn't been there before. We sometimes shift internal walls in our open-plan office but I'd never seen a brand-new door just appear with a new office behind it. The door gave nothing about itself away. No company name, no number. Its only distinguishing feature was that it was ever so slightly cleaner and whiter than the other doors. I tried to get in but it was locked. I knocked but no one answered, even though I had just seen this guy go in. Against the boredom of office life that new door became an obsession. After days of watching the shiny door, it opened and I saw the new man appear. I ran after him, striding down the corridor, and was just about to catch him when I froze: there was this new man talking to Oscar as if they were old friends. I realised what was happening, what this was: that this secret door was probably a bunch of lawyers and accountants all scheming to find some loophole around Dad's Will and get Shaw&Sons listed on the stock exchange. Oscar the snake.

After the new man left, I went to Oscar and said, 'Who's the guy in the new office?'

'What new office?' asked Oscar.

'The one down the corridor.'

'I didn't really notice.'

'It's right fucking there,' I turned and pointed. Stabbing my finger in the direction of the mystery door.

'All right, calm down, Frank.'

'Is this about the IPO again, because you know you can't break Dad's Will?'

'No, it's nothing to do with the IPO.'

'Is it something illegal?'

'Of course not. I'm a lawyer, for God's sake. Jesus Christ. I'm on the Ethics Committee. It's all completely and perfectly legal.' Oscar smiled as if that was the end of the matter but quickly added, 'It's just best you don't know anything about it.'

From: fuckthis@hotmail.com
To: franklynmydear@hotmail.com
Subject: The King and Oscar

Frank – hi!

I don't actually have anything to write but I guess that's why email was invented.

On a tiny island in Thailand. The eager-to-please man who rents out the huts is called Fon.

When it started to rain this morning Fon ran up to my hut through the downpour and forked lightning, soaked to the skin, and said to me with great shame, 'Um, I'm so sorry for this weather, sometime it rain on Ko Chang.'

He spoke as if he was responsible for the entire weather system.

Poor Fon.

Love and lightning,
Malc

PS The bestselling book in Thailand right now is *The King and My Dog*. It's by the king of Thailand. They love this guy here.

PPS The king of Thailand looks just like Dad.

PPPS The king's dog is a salivating bulldog mutt – he looks just like Oscar.

TERMS & CONDITIONS
OF ORGAN DEALING

Oscar once traded in organs.

By which I mean, when we were kids, I used to collect toy figurines with detachable organs – the heart, lungs, liver, brains – in bright reds and blues. The original toy was called the Invisible Man, due to the fact you could see right through him. That odd toy sparked the start of my obsession with the human body, the seed of my desire to become a doctor. I loved the tidy arrangements of organs, each with their own task, working together to produce something whole and meaningful.

Most people don't notice their bodies until something goes wrong, then suddenly they develop a dramatic interest in their sclerosis-scarred liver or coal-blackened lungs. But I've always been fascinated by all the stuff that pumps and slurps.

One day after school I noticed someone had stolen all the jellybean kidneys, wormy intestines and walnut brains. All gone. The figurines stood hollowed out.

When I confronted Oscar, he said, 'If you want them back you'll need to pay me.'

Even though Oscar was only about ten, he was already a corporate lawyer in the making, an embryonic legal bastard. He pulled out a sheet of A4 with the prices of each organ and a place to sign at the bottom to state that I agreed with the pricing.

He handed it to me with an orange crayon, 'Sign here, here and here, please.'

I snatched the paper and tore it. He grabbed my head and punched me in the face.

I begged, 'Please, Oscar, I just want them back.'

I looked around his room. Where might he have hidden them? It was obvious. Like a good pre-pubescent lawyer, he had asked for a safe for his birthday and there it sat under his desk, grey and impenetrable.

He followed my eyes and said, 'Good, now you know where they are. So go get all your money and maybe we can make a deal.'

I cried.

'Or are you just going to run to Mummy?' sneered Oscar.

I decided this was a decent suggestion and off I went. Unfortunately I met Dad first. He was not the right parent for this particular job. My father agreed it was a predicament but he said that instead of forcing Oscar to return the organs he would broker the deal. I assumed this meant Dad telling Oscar to give them back to me. It didn't. It meant Dad telling me in a gentle voice that possession was nine-tenths of the law. 'Son, this was a precept from old English Common Law and so has to be respected.'

According to my father, negotiation was one of life's most important skills. So Dad took my hand and we sat at Oscar's wooden desk. All of us seated on small chairs, my father's knees sticking up high in front of him, floating near his eyes.

Dad read over the contract, looked impressed and said, 'This is nice work, Oscar. Clear clauses. So, Frank, what do you say?'

I cried.

Dad said, 'My client is gathering his thoughts.'

I said, 'I'll give you a pound per organ and nothing more. Final offer.'

Dad flushed with pride and said, 'Not bad, Frank. Negotiation's the key. But just be aware of making final offers when you may have to back down on them; it weakens you.'

By now Malcolm had entered the room and was silently watching the proceedings.

'Counter-response, Oscar?' said Dad.

'Two pounds, nothing less,' said Oscar.

'Well, that's an intractable position, son,' said Dad to Oscar, a little pride leaking into the reprimand.

'Is that reasonable, Frank?' asked Dad.

'One fifty,' I said.

'One seventy-five,' countered Oscar.

'Is this your best and final offer?' asked Dad.

"'Tis,' said Oscar.

'OK with you, Frank?' Dad asked.

'Suppose so,' I said.

'My client is happy with the resolution,' said Dad.

Oscar handed the contract to me as Dad leaned towards Malcolm and said, 'Malcolm, you can be our independent witness to the signing.'

Malcolm glared back at my father, arms crossed over his chest like a knot, and said, 'Fuck this,' then left the room.

Dad ran after him, shouting, 'Malcolm, come back here right now! Who taught you that word? Malcolm! Malcolm! Where did you hear that word?'

I signed and Oscar sellotaped the contract together, laughed and quickly put it in his safe. He said, 'You may pay in weekly instalments if that suits.'

'I hate you, Oscar.'

'No need to get personal, buddy,' he said.

It took five months to get back most of the organs. Every time I got pocket money it went straight into buying them. I got all of them except for one heart and a brain, which were lost somewhere along the way. That was how my dad went about helping his son; he treated it like a day in court. He was a stickler for details, my father. He loved nothing more than a perfectly worded contract. Some men love Shakespeare. My father loved legal contracts; he read them in his spare time.*

My father not only looked like a lawyer, he looked like the son of a lawyer and the father of lawyers. He was all-lawyer. If you cut him in half he'd be lawyer through and through – a pinstripe onion of layered lawyers.

At eighteen the sons of moneyed men might be bought a car, or given the deposit for a flat. Not me. My dad bought me my first insurance policy. When he presented it to me I gave it the level of fascination

---

* I never stood a chance.

that any eighteen-year-old would give to an insurance policy and said, 'Thanks, Dad, I feel really, well, um, insured, I guess.'

Missing my sarcasm, Dad said, 'That's good, son. There's no better gift a father can give his son than legally binding insurance.'

He loved insurance and he loved law. As you can imagine, he wasn't much of a dare-devil. Once he took so long reading the contract you sign at the fair when Malcolm wanted to bungee jump that Malcolm eventually said, 'Oh, just forget it, Dad!'

Dad, not picking up on Malcolm's irritation,* said, 'Well, that's the best thing to do in this situation, son. This document, this release, is basically asking you to sign your life away. I mean, *legally*, that's just insane.'

---

* In the same way that humans can't hear high pitches that dogs can, my dad couldn't hear nuanced tones such as sarcasm. If it wasn't legal, it wasn't audible.

From: fuckthis@hotmail.com
To: franklynmydear@hotmail.com
Subject: Stefan the Swede

Frank – hi!

Swede called Stefan came to Fon's restaurant. Stefan was very serious: 'The final war will be between Zionists and Chinese, it will be an economic war. I'm running away from Chinisation. Thailand is *freeland*! The last innocent place, but even here television is spreading. TV is evil.'

'*The Cosby Show* is bad, sure, but I wouldn't go as far as to say it was evil,' I said.

'There's hope, though,' Stefan said, not smiling. 'If the magnetic poles reverse, north and south will switch and computers will be useless junk, no internet, no TV, no bombs, no phones. Back to basics.'

'But how will I send email?' I asked.

'A clean beginning,' said Stefan who, like all conspiracy theorists, had perfected talking to the detriment of listening.

'Hey, Stefan, this is all fascinating stuff but do you know if there's any weed on this island?'

'Don't smoke it,' warned Stefan. 'They put in chemicals that make you weird.'

'What, weird like you?' I thought.

Love and paranoia,
Malc

TERMS & CONDITIONS OF ETHICS

Ethics are relative.

I know, I know, that's such a lawyer thing to say.

Oscar, my brother and boss, and the most corrupt lawyer in London – and trust me when I say he's up against some bloody stiff competition – heads up London's Legal Board of Ethics. I'm not entirely sure how he got on the board. He probably, without the faintest sense of impropriety, bribed someone. My moronic brother Oscar decides what the lawyers of London can and cannot do.*

Oscar assures me that being a board member is great for the company and '*great for my profile*'.

Being a member of the Board of Ethics is a prestigious role and has made Oscar a minor celebrity.

He's the lawyer that's pulled on to the BBC if there is some ethical conundrum. (Recently he went on to a current affairs show to discuss the ramifications of taking Tony Blair to court over his decision to invade Iraq.) Most infuriating is that Oscar pulls it off. He belongs on TV, he looks the part, and I sit there watching him, boiling over with anger at the idea that my brother could be the spokesperson for what was right and wrong in this ridiculous world.

Although very thin, Oscar's fame is spread as far as it will go. He secretly hired a PR company to do more profiling for him.*1

Oscar's ability to shock me – even when I think I've grown immune to the shocks – never fails to shock me. So it was when Oscar called me to his office one day, not long after I had discovered the white door. My happiness dimmed when I noticed that he was beaming.*2

---

* The world is suffocating in its own satire.

*1 I know this because the PR people came through to my phone by mistake once and I had to inform them that I was the less relevant brother, Frank.

*2 We've a zero-plus relationship; we fight over a finite chunk of joy: the happier he is, the sadder I am.

He said, 'All right, I can tell you about the new office door now. Contracts have been signed. It's a new client that you must never tell anyone about.'

'I'm confused,' I said.

'That's not news,' joked Oscar. 'So the new client is ####.'*

'They're an inventively cruel weapons manufacturer, aren't they?' I said.

'They sure are, Frankie, and do you know who made the most money last year?'

'Inventively cruel weapons manufacturers,' I said. 'And don't call me Frankie.'

'You're really not as dumb as you look, Frankie,' said Oscar. 'I don't care what everyone else says.'

'Don't you think it's *wrong* working for that sort of a company?'

'Typical Frank, you've no vision,' he said.

'I'm not sure Dad would approve.'

'Don't pull the Dead Dad card,' warned Oscar.

'Not sure the partners will agree,' I said.

'Already have. I showed them the money they'd make and they signed on the dotted line with only one condition – that we tell no one we work for them,' said Oscar.

'What about the IPO and stock market – they won't like this,' I said.

'They love it; it's shot the value of our company through the roof, a huge new client.'

'Well,' I said, pulling out my trump card, 'what would the Board of Ethics say?'

'They'll be fine. But just in case they get all *ethical* about it, I've created a separate company, several companies in fact, a shell within a shell,' said Oscar. 'Hire a load of suits to come in and work the business and we just siphon off the cash. No one needs to know we even work

---

* The reason for the #### in place of the company's actual name is that I legally can't state who they are. Just know that they're an inventively cruel weapons manufacturer.

for them. Legally secure and distant enough not to upset our clients or the Ethics Board. Then, just to be really safe, I build a Chinese Wall topped with a barbed-wire super-injunction.'*

After he'd mentioned the company name only once, Oscar started to omit it, putting a short pause in its place when he spoke: 'When we start with [pause] we'll ensure no one here works on it, except maybe you proofing major contracts that come out of [pause]*2 division.'

'Oh my God, and there I was thinking the door was just a bunch of lawyers and accountants trying to find a way to break Dad's Will and get us on the stock exchange.'

Oscar looked shifty before finally admitting, 'Well, actually we've done that as well. This deal with [pause] puts us onto a new financial level and that means we're all, including non-partners like you, buddy, about to get very rich indeed. We're aiming to go IPO this year.'

'But how can you break Dad's Will? He wanted this to remain in our hands, not some faceless board of shareholders.'

---

* For those not fluent in legalese here's a translation. *Chinese Wall*: fictitious wall built around a client that is a conflict with existing clients. In theory you could work for both Coke and Pepsi if you had a Chinese Wall in place, so no one working on the Pepsi account ever spoke to anyone on the Coke account. Of course this is an extreme example and neither Coke nor Pepsi would allow the same company to represent them, even if – quite literally – the Great Wall of China was rebuilt brick for brick down the middle of the office.

Injunction: a gag that stops the media discussing a corporation. Like name suppression but for a company as opposed to a celebrity flasher. But a *super*-injunction is far more potent than your bog-standard injunction. A run-of-the-mill injunction prevents the press talking about the incident but does allow them to write: *BP is being sued for an undisclosed amount by an undisclosed company over an undisclosed allegation.*

But with a super-injunction that same sentence reads:— is being — for an — by an — over an —.

Not much left in there once the super-injunction has gutted everything but the articles and prepositions. Super-injunctions state that you can't even mention the company name. Can't even hint at it. It's a legal method so powerful that it verges on legal voodoo. It literally, and legally, makes problems vanish into thin air.*1

*1 It's how Oscar lives with himself, by constantly building internal super-injunctions around all of his terrible mistakes, affairs and fuck-ups so he never has to face them.

*2 Such is the power of the super-injunction that our reality had literally been dubbed, as if a swear word was scrubbed from our dialogue.

'Well, Dad's a clever man but he was sloppy and he left a tiny detail in the Will, which we've found a way around. He said and I quote, "As long as my name is on the business it will never under any circumstances go public." So I've decided that we're changing the name. We're rebranding; everyone's doing it these days. It's that simple. I was thinking we call ourselves The Firm or Oscar's Law. I don't know . . . those clever marketing bods will think of something.'

I was opening and closing my mouth but astonishment made me mute.

'Are you OK, buddy? Come on, we'll be rich,' said Oscar.

Finally, words shot out. 'How could you do this to Dad and to Mum and . . .'

He shushed me and said, 'Don't get so emotional. This will benefit all of us. Dad made that Will in different times; we need to move on, buddy. Now, any more questions?'

Accepting that I wouldn't shift him on the IPO, I made a last desperate plea to his moral core. 'Don't you have any ethical qualms about working for a hideous weapons manufacturer?'

Oscar smiled and, revealing his moral core to be as false as his Da Vinci veneers, said, 'No, no. This company doesn't just make missiles or drones and things; they also make medical equipment, they make incredible metal alloys for . . .' Oscar's shallow knowledge ran dry and he waved his hand and said '. . . and other stuff. Come on, cheer the fuck up, will you,' then he punched me on the shoulder and walked off whistling.

TERMS & CONDITIONS OF
#####

Later that day, I was sitting at my desk when this fellow approached me.

'Frank?'

'Hello. Who are you?'

'Your brother hired me. I work in the [pause] division.'

I laughed and said, 'You're the invisible lawyer behind the Chinese Wall barbed by super-injunctions. Pretty ridiculous when you think about it, isn't it?'

He didn't smile when he said, 'I can neither confirm nor deny that it's ridiculous.'

TERMS & CONDITIONS
OF SAVIOURS

Don't be surprised if they turn up in trainers.

Reliving my past was a punishing experience and as I clutched my coffee cup I was aware that everything remained the same – my cold coffee; the *May Contain Nuts* contract; spilled sugar still glittered like a sweet constellation – yet everything was different. I was different – *or the same*. I was Frank again.

My beautiful barista came over and asked if I was OK. She explained that I'd been laughing hysterically and freaking out people in the café. I noticed her hips, so invitingly wide, and her slight belly bent out towards me.

In a daze I heard myself ask, 'Do you know of a place that doesn't have lawyers?'

She looked at me meaningfully and said, 'How do you mean?'

'A place without lawyers, without contracts, a place where people aren't always protecting their own backs, maybe a place where people don't even speak English.'

'Oh, right,' she said. 'Yeah, I know just the place. I went to Majorca last summer and half the bloody people there didn't even speak any English. It was a friggin' nightmare.'

She smiled her sweet smile and left me to my confused thoughts. I looked down at the contract screwed up tight in my fist. Then I let my head hang low, staring blankly at the floor, where I think I would have remained for hours had my peripheral vision not been broken by some strange black trainers. My eyes moved up a pair of dark moleskin trousers, past a crisp white shirt to Doug, who had a look of such terrible concern etched on his face that I said, 'My God, what's wrong, Doug?'*

'Come on, Frank,' he said. 'Let's have a bit of quiet time.'

---

* Before I realised his concern was directed at me. I was what was wrong.

Without saying a word, I followed. In his office Doug made tea, pulled his chair over and sat beside me. He didn't speak, didn't ask questions, he just remained quiet until I said, 'I've started to remember . . . things.'

'That's great news,' Doug said but, reading my expression, added, 'or not?'

I began, 'I hate Oscar, I work for an arms manufacturer and . . .' And then – before I had time to stop it – I started crying. Doug handed me tissues and tears kept coming. He rubbed my shoulder and, for a moment, his hand felt like the only thing anchoring me to reality.* It seemed he understood this because he didn't move for a long time before saying, 'Yes, um . . . that does sound like the old Frank I once knew.'

Snot started to chase the tears running down my face as I said, 'Oscar and Alice didn't tell me any of this when I asked about my old life. They told me everything's fine, that I was just a bit stressed.'

'Listen, Frank. Don't believe everything you hear.'

In a childish weeping jag I gulped down a series of tiny sobs and said, 'Sorry, Doug. I'm a horrible mess . . .'

Men aren't conditioned for emotional encounters so we found ourselves temporarily stuck. I smiled, sipped my drink, and hid my teary face behind the lip of my cup. I gained a little control, cleaned my face, and felt the silence grow around us.

In what I assumed was an attempt to break our awkward moment, Doug suddenly jumped up and said, 'Hey, come on. Want to see something amazing, Frank?'

But after my blaze of revelations, hardened in the kiln of shock, I mumbled, 'Sorry, Doug, but nothing more could amaze me today.'

'Nonsense. Trust me, Frank. You'll love this.'

He walked across his office to a couch that was in keeping with his style: functional, brown, something no-nonsense and Scandinavian about it.

---

* As soon as he moved his hand I feared that I'd drift off into weightless insanity.

'I hear all sorts of silly rumours about myself in this place, Frank. That I spend hours in deep mathematical meditation. But the truth is I just love taking catnaps.'

And with this Doug pulled a lever and the couch folded out into a thin bed. Doug took such delight in this little moment that it made me laugh (and the unexpected sound of my own laughter – so long unheard – made me laugh more).

Doug laughed at me laughing, we relaxed a little, and both stared at how odd the bed looked in such a strict office environment. I didn't feel embarrassed about crying any more. I blew my nose hard. By that stage if the man had run me a bath I'd happily have stripped down and plunged in – such was the harmony of my vulnerability and Doug's reassurance. So, without another word, I walked over and lay on the bed.

Then – just as I started to feel a touch self-conscious about lying there – sleep grabbed me. When I woke Doug was gone but he'd left a note:

Frank – got a short meeting but back soon.
Stay where you are. Relax. I told Oscar you were with me and all's well. Sleep lots.
PS Feel free to raid my 'drinks cabinet' – the green tea is powerful stuff!

I tried to get out of bed fast to establish the fact that I was fine. The room spun so hard I screamed, 'Earthquake!' before realising it was me doing the spinning. The scar on my forehead throbbed like a warning light and I sat down. I got up slowly this time. The world still had a woozy tilt but I was feeling a little better as I walked across the office. Looking out the window – ignoring my ghostly reflection staring back at me – I saw across the way the offices of Shaw&Sons and recalled how I felt about the place I spent most of my life.

TERMS & CONDITIONS
OF MY OFFICE

Institutions that do the most damage are often the dullest.

My office is deathly dull. We all hate each other but – given the terms and conditions of office life – we all pretend to get along. After the revelations about #### I began to look around, to evaluate the company I worked for – this place that bore my name – and started to see it for what it was. A place of dull bureaucratic evil. Though you wouldn't know it to see it. We disguise our dealing well. The walls are painted bright colours in some lame attempt to distract from the blackness all around. Some of the meeting rooms have purple sofas and oversized lampshades, which makes them look like the set of a kids' TV show. We even have a green shag carpet (the fluff sticks to the soles of my shoes so at the end of the day it looks like I kicked a Muppet to death). The sofas, carpets and bright colours are trendy, apparently; they're trying to make the office seem fun and innocent. It doesn't work.*

There was a time when I loved work, when this tightly controlled world of contracts made sense to me. I once loved terms and conditions; they were the meticulously written rules by which I ran my perfectly controlled professional life. But long before my *little episode*, I recalled that work had started to repulse me. The way we talked to clients as if they were gods briefly descended from heaven to grace us with their sneers. The way we danced around to the beat of false reverence. If you happened upon our office, and had no idea what we did, you'd assume from our grave tone that we were on the edge of cracking the cure for cancer. We're not. We're not doing any good to anyone.*1

---

* It makes it more depressing. Like painting rainbows and fairies on the walls of children's hospitals. It doesn't fool anyone. Especially not children, who instinctively know all life's tragic terms and conditions. They know you can't cover pain and death with fairies. In the same way a jazzy shade of apricot won't disguise the intractable evil of my office.

*1 Quite the opposite. Here's the big secret: I don't actually do anything for a living.

No one in my office does. We all know this. No one says it. It would be like breaking a spell. Cutting the rope that suspends our disbelief. Like an actor shouting to the audience, 'You know what? This is all just made-up crap. I'm not dying and I'm not even a salesman.'

My clients are so similar that I simply copy the last set of contracts and change the company name and then I paste it and send it to my new client. I can cut and paste ten documents and change the company names all in less than twenty minutes. That is a whole day's work done. Then what do I do? I stare into the abyss of the endless hours stretching out before me. There it is. The raw truth. I cut and paste for a living. Monkeys would be bored by my job. I'm a legal chimpanzee. However, although we're monkeys, I still don't want to give the impression that we don't have an effect. We're monkeys that have broken into the nuclear launch station. One day, by random chance, we'll hit the codes and it'll all be over. Maybe it's already too late. (Or maybe I'm being melodramatic again.) We live in corporate times and Ts&Cs are what Dad proudly called the *DNA of life*. You can't always see them but they nonetheless determine everything you do. Here's what happens: companies are lazy so we all cut and paste each other's work. One set of Ts&Cs is cut and copied and pasted on to many other documents. The more often it happens, the more likely it is that anomalies and mistakes creep in (in-breeding is never a good idea). It happens. It happened to me.* And the slightest of errors, the tiniest inaccuracy, is tantamount to a criminal charge at Shaw&Sons. Dad always liked to cite terrible mistakes to remind his sons of the importance of air-tight accuracy.*[1]

---

* I see whole sentences of mine that I wrote ten years ago reappear in another document from another firm. I marvel that a sentence survived, made it through all the cutting and pasting, all the hundreds of documents, travelled from my company to many more companies, and somehow here it is, full, complete, not a comma moved, staring back up at me, my sentence, my baby. It fills me with shameful pride but plagiarism really is the sincerest form of flattery.

*[1] My dad's favourite was 'the Greene comma': on his deathbed Graham Greene added a comma to a clause which sparked decades of legal debate between his estate and his biographer over the rights to Greene's archives.

As a kid I worked a summer job and Dad told me to look over a contract and alter the names. I replaced all the old company names. It was easy.

A synch.

But I made a mistake.

I missed one. One of the *old* company names remained on the *new* contract. Dad went ballistic. He told me if the client signed this agreement it would be null and void; that one mistake, that one word, made the document defunct. He would have lost the contract and the client, and the reputation of the firm would have been in jeopardy.

All that from just one tiny word.

So the offices of Shaw&Sons were far from my favourite place in the world. I remembered once that I noticed dead flies lying in clusters on the floor near my desk. Not swatted into two dimensions but lying dead in circles on the carpet. It was eerie. I wondered how they had died all together like that. My theory was that they'd killed themselves. Upon entering the office they'd simply lost the will to live. They flew to the highest point, turned, folded their wings and dived to the floor, desperate for death.

Ts&Cs are the modern curse.

We live in over-simplified times and lawyers – like me – exploit that to hide, disguise and distil so many life-altering terms and conditions behind two simple statements: *AGREE* or *DISAGREE*.

I don't have the answers but I do know this much – few things in life that are really worth thinking about can ever be reduced down to those two words.

I seemed to have spent my life stuffing the world with fine print. What will I leave behind, what is my legacy to this earth? Am I just the man who makes everything safe for rich nasty men? Is that my sum total?

I imagined an end-of-the-world scenario in which aliens came down to look through the rubble of our earth, but everything and everyone is dead and there's nothing left except piles of corporate contracts, all the rubbish I write. My contracts are the only evidence left of humanity. All the petty arguments between business partners, hideous prenuptials, corporate buy-outs, all the pathetic loopholes that evil men had slipped through, so many short stories of death and disagreement. I reckon those aliens would just flick through a couple of folders, shake their noble green heads and say, *Oh well, no great loss.*

I don't want to change society – I'm not that ambitious – but I would prefer it if my every working hour was not devoted to making this world a slightly worse place to live.

They should put health warnings on our payslips every month.

Just like they do on cigarettes.

The warning should read – *This sort of work is bad for your health. Too much of it may cause cancer of the soul.**

---

* Or more simply – *Work kills.*

TERMS & CONDITIONS
OF MEETINGS

They're never about work.

Memory is not discerning. When your memory returns it simply gushes all the content out at once, from sad memories that make you want to curl up and die to the really dull crap which most, *most*, of all of our days are generally made up of. Without a discerning editor, your memory is just a giant wasteland of everyday disposable scraps with a few diamonds lost in the rough. Staring out of Doug's window, I remembered as much of the boredom, futility and idiocy as I did the amazing, important and incredible.

I particularly remembered spending many fruitless hours in meetings, usually with Oscar parading around like a prat and the rest of us looking on in glum desperation. What I remembered specifically about meetings was that they are never about the work at hand. Meetings – at their most basic – are really all about how everyone in the meeting happens to be feeling at that time.

Two people are worth mentioning in the office. George is a woman. (Only just. Only in gynaecological terms.) In all other terms, she's a man. She has no breasts, she dresses like a man, talks like a man, walks like a man, is uglier and more aggressive than a man. She never laughs. It's her thing. She smiles sometimes but when she does, you wish she hadn't.

And Gary is our office clown. His thing is that he can count pages just by holding them. Give him a stack of paper, he holds it, closes his eyes, and says, 'Twenty-one pages!' Most boring trick in the world.*

Anyway, we had these monthly meetings in which Oscar would crack jokes and try to be the greatest boss on earth.

---

* As I wrote that I realised that Gary wasn't worth mentioning after all (and neither was George).

Without fail the monthly meeting would start the same way.

I settle in and my friend, the office clown, Gary, who works on another floor and who I only ever saw at this monthly meeting, arrives and shouts in the voice of that old Superman narrator, 'Is it a bird? Is it a plane? No! It's Frank, our Terms and Conditions Man!'

Everyone, every month, laughs at Gary's joke.

It is not that it's funny, it's because he shouts it so everyone is forced to laugh.

He must have said it a thousand times but still, each time he says it, they all laugh.

The worst part is that I laugh too. I'm a social coward; too scared not to laugh.

'Terms and Conditions Man to save the day!' Gary* shouts and the meeting begins.

In the monthly meeting we're supposed to discuss major client issues but all we do is use these issues to push our own problems on to other colleagues. 'Client issues' are just Trojan horses carrying our own agendas within them. I remember sitting in these meetings month after month listening, not to what people were saying, but to what they were trying to say, or even trying not to say. In meetings, subtext is all that matters.

Oscar would say, 'So we have to increase our work on the talent-management side of our Contracts Division. Revenue's running low there.'*9

---

* To be honest Gary is not really a *friend*.*1

*1 More of a colleague.*2

*2 Well not really even a colleague; as I've said, he doesn't even work in my division.*3

*3 So he's more like an acquaintance.*4

*4 Even that's a touch strong.*5

*5 When you get down to it, I suppose he's just the guy that makes that one joke again and again.*6

*6 So I guess he's like my set-up guy.*7

*7 Which I suppose makes me his punchline.*8

*8 Anyway, the guy's a prick and, to make matters worse, I'm the prick's punchline.

*9 Which sounds like a perfectly normal thing to say. But what everyone in the room knows is that Oscar is really talking to one person and that is Roger Parks who is responsible for the Talent Division and who has taken to doing drugs with all his clients and slowly driving the department into bankruptcy.

Roger perks up and says, 'Well, tough times for us, losing that EMI deal really kicked us in the guts, but we'll come back stronger. What I'm saying is – we don't need old EMI, we need new media.'*

To which Oscar replies, 'Yes, well, look, I know a lot of your talent these days are pop stars and they are unbalanced assets, always getting wasted and then having to dry out in rehab. But we need to get that business back on its feet, am I right, Roger?'*1 Even in a dense hung-over funk, Roger is still able to read – loud and clear – exactly what Oscar is implying and he slumps back in his chair as Oscar fires his next round. And so the meeting goes on in this vein, cutting people down or bolstering those that have pleased him. But never in an explicit way – he only ever talks in subtext. It's how he avoids conflict, and how he maintains his delusional status as the good guy, *the boss we all love to love.*

Meetings always remind me of those school classes where you expend all your energy trying to talk about anything except for the school subject. In meetings we talk for so long about anything but the clients. We talk about our weekends, what we've watched on TV, what books we've read, the weather, literally anything in order to ignore the long agenda of serious client issues.

In one meeting Gary said to all of us, 'I read about a man who died in his office somewhere in California, I think, and, get this, no one noticed for two days. Two fucking days he was there rotting as every-one worked around him blissfully unaware. It wasn't until he started to reek that they realised the poor bugger was dead.'

Everyone tutted and made incredulous noises and someone said to everyone, 'That's the most tragic story ever. Can you fucking believe that could happen?'*2

Everyone said, 'It's unreal,' and someone said, as if to protect us from the terrible story, 'Shit like that wouldn't happen here, though.'

---

* What I'm saying is, *I'm not drunk, or stoned, and I'm not washed up!*

*1 Translated simply as: *Stop getting wasted all the time or you're fired, Roger.*

*2 Yes, I can believe it. It didn't surprise me in the least. It could happen right here, in fact, it could happen to me. If I don't do something fast, one day it *will* happen to me.

I listen, tuning out of the actual words people are saying and into the gaps between them where a war rages. Anger fills the spaces, disappointment boils between the words, so many banal office insecurities, bored people, ambitious people, people who feel they're long overdue pay increases or promotions, a single meeting contains so many silent victories and defeats. Turning away from a failed joke denotes the losers, while laughter is the trophy the winners campaign for. I remembered, a few days after the white door had been revealed to me, that Oscar didn't specifically talk about our new nefarious weapons client. Even he was wise enough to realise that we couldn't have too many people knowing that we're working for them. But he did say at the end of this meeting, 'And, folks, we've a new company opening down the corridor, really great bunch of chaps, so make them feel at home.'

This seemed far too casual for me. I wouldn't even have mentioned them if I was Oscar, as I was sure there were a number of my colleagues who would have similar ethical problems about the new client as I did. But that was Oscar. He had no issue about mentioning them, he didn't think people would ask or be interested, he didn't believe there were ever any consequences to his actions. He was one of those guys – and I hated to admit he was probably right – who thought he would always get away with everything.*

Our meetings have a ritualistic quality. We begin and end with a joke. We always begin with the joke about me being Terms and Conditions Man. And always end with a joke delivered by Oscar: 'That's it for this month, folks. My door is always open so you're all welcome to walk through it any time – although I'm almost never in so you can bugger off if you think I'm hanging around waiting to listen to you all moaning and complaining. Now go get on with your jobs!'

Oh, how we laughed.

---

* There are two types of people. The Oscars of the world, who assume, through no actual proof, that they naturally know more than everyone else, and therefore will always get away with murder. Then there's me, the type that assumes everyone knows more than I know and I'll always be caught.

TERMS & CONDITIONS OF
REMEMBERING & REGRETTING

Regret is the seed from which bitterness flowers.

I turned away from the window, away from my pale reflection, away from Shaw&Sons, and looked at Doug's bookshelf, which was filled with books whose titles alone could cure insomnia: *Understanding Actuarial Practice*; *Risk is Opportunity and Vice Versa*; *Executive X*; *Advanced Maths and Applied Maths Made Simple* . . .

Executive X.

There it was again. I took it out and looked at the author picture of Alice.

Because so far Old Frank's memory lane was littered with hatred, confusion and anger, I needed something happy to hold on to. I focused my energy on thinking about my wife, hoping to strike a memory well of love and joy.*

---

* Turned out the well had run dry.

CLAUSE 2.1

ALICE

TERMS & CONDITIONS OF LOVE

Falling into it's easy.

Staying in it – that's the tricky part.

TERMS & CONDITIONS OF LOVE

True love is conditional.

Not the most romantic notion but bear with me, I'm a lawyer, not a poet.

Marriage Ts&Cs
My wife married me because I was brilliant.*
I married my wife because she was nice.*1

I'm not entirely sure who came off worse in the deal. We signed a prenuptial. (Something Dad, against my will, absolutely insisted on.) But, beyond our prenuptial, and between the lines of our vows, ours – like all marriages – had unwritten, unspoken terms.

Which were: I stay brilliant; you stay nice: everyone's happy.

It didn't work out. Everyone's miserable.

Alice was so lovely when we first met. I was starting at my father's law firm; she was working in a music shop trying to figure out what to do with her life.

We loved to talk about books, music and all of our friends.

We were young.

We barely went out.

We were enough for each other.*2

---

* Now I'm not.
*1 Now she's not.
*2 That's a big statement when you think about it.

From: fuckthis@hotmail.com
To: franklynmydear@hotmail.com
Subject: Pure Meow

Frank – hi!

Met a slow-talking American called Joe, an anthropologist researching a soon-to-be-extinct tribe in Burma. When I enquired about what he had learned, Joe said, 'Well, like, you know, we just kinda hung out with the tribe for a while.'

After such a comprehensive reply I felt it rude to delve any deeper.

Joe sat all night lovingly staring into the eyes of his new Thai wife, Meow (I kid you not).

'We,' Joe pointed to his new wife for emphasis and then to himself, 'before we got married we got to know each other really well, we communicated a lot by email, didn't we, my love?'

'Wha?' said Meow.

'We,' Joe said again, louder this time, the fingers again pointing to Meow then to him, then typing on an imaginary keyboard, 'emailed a lot before we met. Yes?'

'Wha?' said Meow.

'Communicated,' said Joe, desperately this time, the show not going well. 'We communicated.'

'Wha?' said Meow.

'Oh never-fucking-mind,' snapped Joe.

Rarely have I seen such pure love.

Love and Meow,
Malc

TERMS & CONDITIONS OF CHANGE

They say change is as good as a break. They lied!

I used to adore my wife. It was as if I had sat beside Alice's creator with a little pencil and jotted down, to my exact loving specifications, all the things she would be.

But then Alice got a job in human resources and everything changed. It started with her hair. Once an autumnal muddle of golden-browns, it was, soon after taking the job, dyed a deep wintry black.* They advised her at the company that her hair wasn't serious enough and if she wanted to be taken seriously she had to project seriousness. So she dyed her hair and it's the straightest, blackest bob you've ever seen. It worked. I started to take her very seriously. A serious marriage is no fun. Although, just below the surface, the fine print can be amusing. For example:

My wife says, 'We need to go to the Smiths' tonight.'

I'll say, 'Oh God. Do we really *need* to go?'

'Yes,' she'll reply. 'We *need* to go. He's a partner.'

'Is this like a tennis tournament where if you miss too many games you lose your ranking?' I ask.

My wife looks at me like I'm a moron and says, 'What are you talking about?'

I say, 'I think I'm talking about tennis but I may be wrong.'

'The only thing you're right about is that you're wrong,' says my wife.*1

My wife's job changed her. She works for the human resources department of a management consultancy. Some jobs are just jobs. Some jobs are religions. You have to believe. Her job was one of those.

---

* For days after the dyeing, grey smudges stained her fingers like evidence of some ambiguous crime.

*1 *My wife.* Why do I insist on calling her my wife? Her name's Alice. I think I call her *my wife* because it fits an odd formality that's descended on our marriage. I'll try not to do it any more.

As a general rule, jobs with the least actual work require the most faith. After the hair, more changes arrived. She fixed her teeth. This tiny gap between her front teeth, so slight that only people who knew her well noticed. I loved it but she went ahead and got it *fixed*, got it filled. I miss the gap; it was the chink that let me inside when she smiled. Now when she smiles it's like being hit by a wall.

Then came the hobbies. First of all she took up cycling because her boss Valencia had taken up cycling. My wife would vanish for hours, returning flushed, slurping off her outfit and leaving it on the bathroom floor like a second skin.

Then came the dreadful dinners with her colleagues. Young men whose slim necks left awkward gaps between neck and collar – betraying something of the schoolboy still in them – not yet filled out into the fat businessmen they aspired to be. They all gave iron-grip handshakes and stared unflinchingly into my eyes. The iron grip and the stare were management tricks. They teach you these things at my wife's firm. I know, because they taught my wife. She was coached to look deeply into people's eyes, to shake people's hands with a firmness that suggested there wasn't a problem in the world she couldn't solve. Sometimes over breakfast I'd look up from my cornflakes and catch my wife staring at me and I'd say, 'Can you stop that staring, it's freaking me out.'

'Sorry,' she'd say, 'I was just practising.'

My wife was lovely when we first met. Relaxed, quick-witted. In fact, more than all of that, she was a wonderful mess of a girl. The day I met Alice she was crying into her beer in a pub on the South Bank. I'd spotted her in the audience at the cinema watching Kubrick's *2001*. Afterwards I followed her to the bar. She looked as lonely as I felt, so I followed her. At the bar she started to cry. I leant over and said, 'The film wasn't that bad, was it?'

She seemed confused and I explained, 'Um . . . *2001*, I was at the same showing.'

She wiped her tears and smiled, 'The film was wonderful, my life's the problem.'

After I bought her another beer, the story came out. She'd been kicked out of home. Her parents' Born Again Christian phase clashing with her Born Again Rebel phase. She had a great degree but no job prospects. She told me she wanted to do something useful with her life, make a difference. She's the only person that's said that to me without sounding deeply insincere. At closing time I asked if she had anywhere to go.

She said, 'Well, Sandra, and her mum, Molly, always put me up, but I just feel like such a failure running back there again.'

From that moment my heart opened up and took Alice into it and there she stayed. She was so honest; there she sat, in a cardigan and sneakers, telling a stranger the truth.

When we arrived at the flat, the door opened and there was Molly with huge white hair hovering above her head like a Chinese lantern.

Molly wrapped her arms around Alice, saying, 'Sweetheart?'

'Mum and I had another fight.'

Molly said, 'Well, that's bad news. Come on in, your bed's still made up from last time. Oh, and who's this?'

'This is Frank,' said Alice. 'He's a friend of mine.'

'Well,' said Molly. 'Do you like mushroom soup, Frank?'*

So I said, 'I love it.'*1

This resulted in Molly cooking me mushroom soup every time I went round.

Alice's friend Sandra joined us in the kitchen, kissing Alice and saying hello to me. Sandra had an interesting face, not beautiful but noble. Her nose was incredible. Large but delicate and the end was made up of so many wonderful angles that it looked less like flesh and more like glass. Alice didn't speak about her parents at first; instead we sat and talked about *2001* and Molly admitted she didn't understand a blinking word of it.

---

* As it was the first thing I was going to say to Molly, I didn't want to say something negative.

*1 When, in fact, I loathe it.

I explained, 'It's a statement about man, God, technology . . . man's fight to overcome time and . . .' I faltered. All three women were staring at me seriously, waiting, and I said, 'Actually, Molly, I've no idea either, it just looks pretty.' They laughed at me.

The kitchen was covered in mosaics, and when Molly saw I was looking, she said, 'Love broken crockery, love using broken stuff to make beautiful stuff.' The shattered mosaic formed childish blue and silver clouds swirling across the walls.

After a little more wine, the topic of Alice's argument with her parents was teased out by Molly, who kept saying things like, 'You don't have to talk about it, love, but sometimes it helps to get these things off your chest.'

What was funny was that Alice was reluctant at first and when she finally did open up, her story had shifted a little. But she was so bashful about it that we all laughed when Alice finally said, 'Well, so, they didn't really kick me out, Molly. I . . . Well, I think I sort of pushed all their buttons and, come to think of it, technically, now that I *really* think about it, I suppose, to be honest, I may actually have stormed out.'

Alice sighed as if releasing the slight pressure that had built around the white lie, and Molly rubbed her shoulder and said, 'There we go, that's good, Alice. That's fine. We all storm out of places from time to time.'

'Poor Mum and Dad,' said Alice. 'I really put them through hell sometimes.'

'Yes, you have to be so careful with parents,' I said. 'You only get one set and you have to try not to wear them out too fast.'

This got a laugh from the girls and their laughter made me feel wonderful. I remembered Sandra winked at me at that moment, I'll never forget it.*

---

* It wasn't a flirty wink; it was just a wink that said, *Nice one, Frank.* That's all it was, friendly, an encouragement. It was Sandra saying, *You're doing a good job cheering up my friend.* It seemed such a generous thing to give me, this stranger sitting with her best friend. How lame words are when you put them against a split-second gesture like that.

When I left, Alice gave me a kiss on the cheek and said, 'Sorry I'm in such a state, I'm not usually like this,' and before I could say anything, she added, 'Actually, I'm always like this.'

I wanted to say, '*I love you, Alice.*'

Instead I said something far less memorable but thought, *How can I get her to fall in love with me?* Most of the love falling took place right there in Molly's shattered kitchen.

TERMS & CONDITIONS OF MUSHROOM SOUP

Mushroom soup makes me lie.

Waiting for Alice one day, Molly asked me, 'When are you making your move, Frank?'

'Where am I moving to?' I asked.

'The move between you and Alice, dummy. Week in, week out, you come here, have tea with us, take Alice out, bring her back, nothing happens. I mean, I love you coming over, but trust me when I say a flower like Alice'll be picked soon enough. Fancy some mushroom soup?'

Sandra said, 'Stop giving Frank a hard time, Mum.'

'I'm merely asking him when he's going to make a move,' said Molly. '*Make a move*, is that what you call it these days?'

'The Fonz calls it that, Mum,' said Sandra, with great irritation.

'Well, however you want to put it. I was just helping Frank along.' Molly served soup and said, 'You're the middle child, aren't you, Frank? Lost in the centre of it all, neither the first joyful surprise nor the last lovely baby. Eager to please. One who lets politeness rule your life. If you don't actually tell people what you really think, your life'll be a misery.'

She looked at me for a reaction. I looked deep into my mushroom soup for an escape.*

She sighed and said, 'How's the soup?'

'Lovely,' I lied.

'Jesus, Frank,' said Sandra. 'Tell Mum you hate it. Alice told me you told her you hate mushrooms! Just tell Mum you hate it.'

Molly looked upset as she said, 'Is that true, Frank?'

'Actually . . . Molly, sorry, I hate it but, if it helps, I'm getting used to it . . .'

---

* Her pop psychology wasn't just embarrassing, it was also accurate.

'Stop eating it, Frank!' said Sandra, laughing. 'You're still eating it as you're telling Mum you hate it. You're hopeless.'

Molly shook her head. 'You're a lost cause, Frank. You'd apologise to your torturer for splattering blood on his shirt.'*

Later that day Alice did exactly what I'd failed to muster the courage to do: she faced me, kissed me, and that was that. We were together.

I loved Alice for all her messiness. Felt privileged knowing her. Back then she was everything I didn't have the nerve to be. Living by her wits, taking part-time jobs, her highs so much higher, her lows so much lower than the meandering stroll of my own life. That Alice, that bewildering, thrilling Alice, that's the Alice I fell in love with, that's the Alice I miss, that's the Alice I pine for when I look across the table and see my wife.

---

* By the way, I hope Molly is not coming over as too much of a wise old woman. She was also a belligerent drunk and had a terrible habit of farting and blaming me for it. But I don't want to be mean; she was also a lovely woman (when she wasn't drinking or farting, that is).

TERMS & CONDITIONS
OF SIGN LANGUAGE

In the right hands it can be a martial art.
And Alice was a black belt.

Initially Alice and I understood each other implicitly. We shared codes, telepathy, empathy and understanding. Such was our bond that Sandra named us *the twins*.

When we started to go out I was at the peak of my brilliance. I'd won Shaw&Sons lots of new business and I'd also been responsible for writing contracts which were so well respected that they became the industry standard. Around that time Oscar was forever shouting, 'You'll make partner in no time, buddy.' (Funny how *no time* turned out to be never.)

But where I was brilliant at work life, Alice was brilliant at real life. Her wit was wild and untamed, and she combined it with a social bravery that at times left me breathless.

On one of our first dates a man barged in front of us in the queue to a club.

Of course I did what I always did, which was mumbled indignantly – *but inaudibly* – 'My God, that's so bloody rude.'

Thinking that was the end of that. But then Alice thumped the man on the back.

He swung around and shouted, 'What the fuck? Got something to say?'

I, of course, had nothing to say and assumed Alice was as terrified as I was.

The man shouted, 'Well?'

Alice held her tongue but let her feet do the talking – she kicked him sharply in the shin.*

---

* Now every man knows that the terms and conditions of this situation are explicitly clear. If your girlfriend starts a fight with a man, then you – the innocent boyfriend – will end the fight. Usually with your face being smashed like a plate.

With this in mind I grabbed Alice in order to run away but the man raised both his hands to stop us moving and shouted, 'Fucking bitch.'

People were watching us now, and metres away at the door of the club the bouncers sensed violence; the queue twitched and writhed, warning them to come quickly. But I knew a punch to my face would arrive faster than a couple of slow-moving bouncers. And just as I saw the situation collapse – imagining myself spitting out my own teeth – Alice did something so absurd that the man actually froze mid-punch.

Alice made a gurgling noise in her throat and started to use sign language, pointing to her ears then her mouth, furiously spinning her hands around to signal that she was deaf, punctuating the air with peace signs to stop him hitting me.

It was so outrageous that – just for a second – the man dropped his fist and said, 'What!' buying enough precious time to save me.

Alice gave one more fantastical display of utterly made-up sign language.* But – cringe-factor aside – she still saved my life (or at least she saved me a big dental bill).

Thankfully the bouncers finally appeared, grabbing both the man's arms and dragging him off. Straining against their grip, the baffled man shouted, 'Wait! Stop! She assaulted *me*! She did! That dumb bitch!'

To which Alice shouted back loudly and clearly, 'I'm deaf, not dumb, you prick! Now fuck off and go learn some manners.'

Hearing Alice suddenly talk caused the man to fall mute. It also won a shocked giggle from our small audience, and people in the queue gave Alice a celebratory round of applause, to which she bowed and said, 'Thank you, thank you. Hope you enjoyed the show. I'll be here all week, please tell your friends.'

I'm deaf, not dumb, you prick! Now fuck off and go learn some manners.

That was my Alice – dangerous, fast-witted and with just a pinch of mean stirred into a whole lot of wonderful.

---

* If political incorrectness were illegal, there's no doubt Alice would have been busted.

TERMS & CONDITIONS
OF BREAKING UP

Against all anecdotal and statistical evidence,
marriage remains surprisingly popular.

When did my wife break our marriage terms?

I remember one night in the car, escaping from another boring dinner, my eyes sore from staring, my hand mildly crushed, I said, 'Wow! That guy Phil's a prick. What's with these guys you work with? All they talk about is mergers and acquisitions, like little corporate gods, when they're just accountants and abacus monkeys.'

I laughed. That's what you do when you make a little joke.*

She didn't.

Instead she was silent for a long time, then she said slowly, as if talking to a child, 'They're my colleagues, brilliant men and women. Show them some respect, Frank.'

That's when I knew.

I knew everything had changed.

Inside and out, from her hair to her soul, all of it cut, straightened and dyed black. From that point on our terms were null and void. My wife became the most determined corporate climber. She climbed so high and so hard her calf muscles actually became more toned (though that may have been the cycling).

So there I stood at dull corporate dinners, looking and sounding interested. When all I wanted to do was kill myself.*1

---

* And the terms stipulate that your wife laughs too and says something like, 'I know — what a doofus.'

*1 You can't tell people that though.*2

*2 They'll think you want to kill yourself.

From: fuckthis@hotmail.com
To: franklynmydear@hotmail.com
Subject: 'Dam Pizza

Frank – hi!

Remember that time we were in Amsterdam?

So stoned, so hungry we decided to call out for pizza but, as I picked up the phone, you suddenly said, 'No, wait, wait, that's far too obvious. We won't call out for pizza; let's wait for the pizza people to call us.'

Suffice it to say we were generally disappointed by the pizza people's complete lack of effort.

Love and munchies,
Malc

PS I am not sure if you know this, but emails work both ways. How do I explain this? I guess the best thing to do is to think about it like a two-way street: I send you emails but you can also send emails back to me. It's a brilliant new technology; you should try it some time.

PPS Sorry, that's just my facetious way of saying – *Write to me, Frank! What the fuck's going on in your life?*

TERMS & CONDITIONS OF WHITE

It's not a colour – it's a shade.

When things were particularly bad between us, my wife decided we needed a fresh start. In her world this meant the two of us painting the flat together: a 'bonding project' she called it. Which meant replacing white with a slightly different shade of white. (It didn't freshen the flat and it certainly didn't help our relationship.) Instead of painting over the cracks, it merely highlighted them. Preposterous though it may sound, we actually spent – wasted! – two whole weeks deciding – arguing! – about what type of white to paint the already white flat.

It was a big deal to my wife.

At one point our argument got so intense, so out of control, that I shouted, 'Do you love this flat more than you love me?'*

'Oh, don't be so dramatic,' she said (but she still didn't answer my question).

We looked through lots of swatches and analysed all the different whites with their wonderful names. The Half Villa Whites, the Quarter Tea Whites, the Eighth Thornton, the Half Supernova.*[1]

I bought test pots and painted patches on different walls and I sat there staring at three types of identical white saying, 'I can't really see the difference,' which made my wife shout, 'You're just colour blind, that's your problem!'

'I don't think white is technically a colour,' I said. 'It's a shade.'

'You're a fucking shade,' she screamed.

Yes, we actually argued over what white was the right white.

---

* She paused just a beat too long.

*[1] Like fantastic-sounding designer drugs, *'Can I have a tab of Supernova and a gram of Thornton White, please?'*

Then, after weeks of deliberation, we finally decided on a white; we received the full pots, and a label on the bottom read, *Production batches may differ from the colour in the test pot.**

When I told my wife about this in an incredulous voice, she accused me of not taking the *process* seriously enough.*[1]

---

* What! How could that be? How could we spend two weeks deciding on an infinitesimal difference in colour spectrum only to be told at the end that the final colour may vary?

*[1] Sometimes she was more observant than she seemed.

TERMS & CONDITIONS
OF MY WIFE'S JOB

Couriers lose hearts all the time.

My wife profiles humans for a living.

She writes psychometric tests to tell companies what people are like. Apparently we can't tell any more. There was a time when we trusted our instincts. Now we pay people like my wife to slice instinct out of the whole flabby human equation.*

There's something so sad about the process, about this human evaluation, that often I have to stop myself thinking about it as it makes me want to weep.

My wife gets me to do the tests. I'm her guinea pig. I've no idea how I score on them and I don't care. But she does. She'll have a spreadsheet somewhere – she loves spreadsheets – or some graph with a swan-diving line indicating my devolution. I wonder when I started to fall from grace. I can't pinpoint the moment I slipped from brilliant to average to ungradable, although I'm sure my wife could tell me down to the exact day.

At university I was a straight-A student, wildly, effortlessly ambitious, incorrigibly intelligent. I loved tests; they made me feel as if I was accomplishing things. My wife met me when I was at the peak of my brilliance, destined for greatness. She picked a beauty in me, she really did. I couldn't sustain it, of course. Brilliance is brittle. It's such a clear and hard thing that when I failed to live up to my brilliance, I cracked. My brilliance was a fragile academic type rather than a worldly brilliance. I was a pure academic who soon found the scope of clean white examination papers muddied by real people and ethical conundrums.

So I take her tests and she never tells me my scores and I pretend I don't care. She says it's not like an exam where you need to get high scores. It's about something else.*1

---

* We've made a science of everything we're too scared to do for ourselves.
*1 What?

She's so different now. I barely know her. She used to be like every-one else. She'd meet someone she didn't like and she'd say, 'Man, that guy's an arsehole.'

I got that. *Arsehole*. Everyone gets that. But now she leaves a party and says something like, 'That guy's such an EFTJ, with rather worry-ing F tendencies.'

I guess what I'm trying to say is this: I don't understand my wife any more. And I'm not talking emotionally. I'm not saying I don't understand my wife because men are from Mars and women are from Venus. I mean: *I actually don't understand what she's saying.* And the more she talks in this corporate gibberish, the less she's capable of understanding my own plain English. Often I say something perfectly normal and she'll stare at me quizzically as if I'm speaking Yiddish. At times I understand so little of what she says that I feel as though I'm lodging with an immaculately dressed foreign-exchange student. Then I find myself getting over-excited when we do actually achieve the most basic understanding.

'Pass the milk,' she'll say.

After frustrated hours of not understanding her, I'll feel giddy that I understood, and pass the milk with a smile, saying, 'Here you go, sweetie, the *milk!*'

She'll take it and, without looking up from her mobile phone, say, 'Stop calling me *sweetie*. When did you start that? It's such a P thing to say.'

Here's an example of one of my wife's test questions:

If I were a garden, I would most resemble:
  a. Wildflower Garden: carefree and enthusiastic.
  b. Japanese Garden: accurate, and detail-oriented.

When she gave me that test question I froze and said, 'I don't feel like either.'

'It's a simple question, why can't you choose?'

'Because I'm not a garden, I'm a person, and I'm fairly sure a garden can't be enthusiastic,' I said.

'Well, don't shout at me. It's symbolic,' she said.

'Well, I still don't feel like a fucking garden, symbolic or otherwise.'

I walked away and pretended to be busy doing something else. I noticed my wife looking at the test, shaking her head slowly. I made a cup of tea and from the kitchen window watched a Renault with *Medical Courier* written on the side. I thought about that car whizzing about the city with a polystyrene box packed with ice in the centre of which sat a dead-still heart, a plump fist of meat waiting to be plugged back in. That this organ can survive without us seems incredible. For a long time I stood staring out the kitchen window, searching for that dead-still part of myself that I had lost.

What do you most resemble?
    a. Japanese garden.
    b. Wildflower garden.
    c. A heart packed in ice in a Renault Clio on the A4.

My wife's boss is called Valencia. I've never met her but I know exactly what Valencia's latest interests and hobbies are because my wife adopts them. Bosses are the new Messiahs. First there was the cycling, then came the Thai boxing. My wife returned from work one night and said, 'We should really take up Thai boxing, it's the new yoga.'

I agreed in the hope that it would bond Alice and me. When you're in a relationship, but no longer having sex, you take up odd and painful hobbies like Thai boxing in the hope that they'll rinse out some frustrations. However, after a month of having my face punched in by a tiny man named Chang, I quit.

When I told her I quit, my wife said, 'But Valencia says it's so good for your core.'

Sometimes Valencia will call on a Saturday to demand my wife comes into the office, and my wife always agrees. 'It's an emergency. I have to deal with this, Frank.'*

My wife thinks I'm having an affair.

---

* What sort of emergency could it be? A doctor I understand. *Someone's dying, I have to go.* But my wife is in HR. She writes psyche tests. What's the emergency? *Come at once, this guy you evaluated as a calm type has just said something a bit mean about my new shoes, we need you to re-test him immediately!*

She reads all my texts and looks through my wallet. I'm not having an affair.*

I admit that I do mourn the death of the person that my wife used to be, but I'd never use that grief to justify being unfaithful to the person my wife has become.

My wife's job involves a lot of role-playing. When my wife first suggested that we role-play together I got very excited, my mind wandering like a naughty teenager into saucy scenarios.

I was to be disappointed.

She meant role-playing really boring and obvious scenes like how to tell an employee they're not performing well at work. My wife and I role-play all the time now. My wife and I have role-played ourselves into the adults we are today. We're role-playing what it would be like if two people who married young and had grown apart still lived together pretending that their marriage was real.*[1]

---

* Yes, I know I have a crush on the beautiful barista but that's just born out of desperation. That's fantasy. I wouldn't have the nerve. I'm not an unreliable narrator. Unhinged, yes; unreliable, no.

[1] I'm sorry, that's actually a terrible thing to say about my marriage.[2]

*[2] I meant every word of it.

From: fuckthis@hotmail.com
To: franklynmydear@hotmail.com
Subject: Cop or Criminal

Frank – hi!

Spotted a sticker on a backpacker yesterday:

Life's a fucking riot, pal! So you best figure out if you're a protester or a policeman!

Ha!

Love and revolution,
Malc

PS I have not the slightest inkling what the hell that means.

TERMS & CONDITIONS
OF EXECUTIVE X

X marks the plonker!

OK, so in the spirit of full disclosure, I should confess that I do know how I score on my wife's tests. I know exactly how I score. The reason I know is because my wife published my results for the world to read. My wife wrote a book called *Executive X*. The cover was black with a giant white X in the middle wearing a collar and tie. It was in that period of the late nineties, before the crash, when everything was working, when there was money everywhere. A time when no one was sure why it was working or who was responsible – until, that is, management consultants were credited with the world's runaway success.*

The Self-Help shelf bulged with corporate tomes such as *The Seven Habits of Highly Effective People*. My wife, a young executive at the time, managed to get in on the act. She published the definitive psychometric book about how to hire the right – or wrong – man for the job. And it made her famous; well, industry famous at least.

It was her friend Sandra, who had become a commissioning editor, who actually published it. Which was all great.

Until I actually read it.

My wife hadn't given me a copy until it was published and when I read it I knew why. *Executive X*, the subject of the book, the man who did all the tests and was analysed like a lab rat, was, yes, you guessed it – me. Muggins.

I remember Sandra phoning me one day just before publication and having the most cryptic chat. Normally when I spoke to Sandra it was fluid, we got on well and laughed, but this conversation was

---

* Proviso: management consultants didn't earn the credit – they took it. They did this by writing books informing the world that management consultants were the reason for the rude health of the world, that they had cracked the code of commerce and in so doing were without question the one and only reason for the unfettered success of the universe.

missing a crucial ingredient that would have bound it all together, which was that Sandra assumed that I'd read the book.

Our discussion went something along the lines of:

'Well, I always knew you were a good guy, Frank. But until I read this book, I never knew just how good you were. You're quite something.'

'Well, thank you,' I replied, thinking I was good in the sense that I made Alice lots of cups of tea when she worked late into the night. 'I just supported her as best I could.'

'You certainly did,' said Sandra. 'I mean, well, to give so much of yourself to her, it is really something, Frank, you're one in a million.'

Right there was the problem. I'm like a child. When people compliment me I blush and lap it all up and in so doing I become completely distracted from the actual content of the words.*

'Well, I love Alice and would give her anything she needed.'

'You can't give her much more than what you gave her for this book. You're a brave man, Frank.'

As friends do, we then went on to chat about other pointless rumours and gossip. Afterwards, that conversation replayed in my head so many times, but I ignored all my instincts and got on with other, less pressing things.

It wasn't until I read the book that I understood what Sandra had been saying; that was when I realised that I had been a monumental idiot. I was Executive X. I was Alice's executive crash-test dummy.

All my answers to tests she had casually given me to do on the kitchen table were there for all to see. And it was not pretty. She didn't paint a nice picture of me, she used me as the basis for who you should *not* hire, as opposed to who you should hire. It made for humiliating reading. At first I fooled myself that no one would make the link between X and myself.[*1]

---

* I miss the fine print.

[*1] What a fool.

But I knew it was obvious that it was me when one day Oscar arrived at work and said, 'Well, if it isn't Executive X himself.'

Oscar has the observational skill of a bat. Utterly blind to anything muddied with nuance, yet even he could see that I was the subject. I knew then that I was screwed. The entire office called me Executive X, or just X. They even began playing tricks on me to see how I'd react to certain situations. In the book Alice had described Executive X as the sort of man who expended huge amounts of energy maintaining a calm and pleasant front. No matter the problem at hand, Executive X was a classic Adaptive Child, bending over backwards to keep everyone happy. So the office would stress-test me; usually – in fact, always – initiated by Oscar. One morning, before I arrived, they put a cup full of coffee upside down on my desk. I picked the cup up and coffee washed over my keyboard, papers, mobile phone and everyone, especially Oscar, who was lingering close by waiting for the punchline, laughed. They laughed, they pointed, they cackled and what did I do?

You guessed it – I did exactly what Executive X does.

I pushed my frustration into the core of my body, I took the joke, I laughed along with everyone, and Oscar, red in the face from the joy of it all, thumped me on the back and shouted, 'X strikes again. Nothing can shake him!'

Alice was on a number of television shows, and the more books she sold, the more famous she became. A *Guardian* reporter asked her if it was based on anyone and she denied it. It was a terrible time. I felt ashamed, that I'd been used, that she'd so accurately nailed down my personality with these ludicrous tests. The book made me look like some snivelling plonker, that's what really hurt, some modern corporate lackey. It was so insulting but, of course, like a good Executive X I took it, I supported her, I said, *Well done, sweetie, I'm so proud of you.*

She loved the fame; she always said: 'This is so good for my profiling, for my career, a published author for the consultancy, it's really great stuff for everyone.'*

---

* Well, not for me, lady, not for me.

She kept popping up as a quote monkey in articles, even in *The Economist* one month, about the surge in dotcoms and the talent search for more and more creative geniuses; it was a time when *Thinking out of the Box* and *Not Reinventing the Wheel* were shoving themselves into everyday speech.*

When I tried to broach the subject with my wife – and explain that I was humiliated by the way she had used me – she denied it. She shrugged and said, 'Frank, X is not you, that's crazy talk, now let's not let our individual personal successes upset each other, that's not what good couples do, now, is it?'*1

---

* And it was a time in which I lost all faith in my wife, in life and, worst of all, in myself.

*1 Many employment contracts have Love Clauses, which disallow employees falling in love at work – *I loathe the way that law thinks it can mitigate love*. It seems my wife and I had developed many of our own Love Clauses. When you find that your Love Clauses outnumber your love, it's time to take a good hard look at what you're doing.

TERMS & CONDITIONS
OF EXECUTIVE X

Unlicensed excerpt – go ahead and sue me!

Executive X is emotionally intuitive. He can empathise with others to a high degree and is extremely ethical. In the context of a modern corporate workplace this can work for, and against, a company employing an X. For instance, the power of empathy can, if left unchecked, result in periods of unrestrained emotional exuberance. X can become unfocused – even distracted – by how everyone 'feels' about what he's doing at work.*

---

* At least I feel something, you cold-hearted bitch.

From: fuckthis@hotmail.com
To: franklynmydear@hotmail.com
Subject: Ignore Signals

Frank – hi!

Vietnam is overrun by scooters. No one pays any notice to traffic lights. They just beep their horns to warn people they're driving behind them.

Driving by sonar!

My Vietnamese driver said: 'Never signal in Saigon – it just confuses people.'

Love and lights,
Malc

PS There are an incredible amount of road deaths in Vietnam.

TERMS & CONDITIONS OF TESTS

**Philosophical debates ('What is the meaning of existence?')
interest me:**
    a. Very much.
    b. Little.
    c. Neither of the above.

I nearly lost my mind when she asked me what sort of garden I was, so you can imagine how hard this question was. I just sat at the table staring at it as if it was the most terrifying question I'd ever faced.

The words in parenthesis ('What is the meaning of existence?') glowed up at me in fierce neon and I realised, as my vision blurred, that I hadn't taken a breath for a long time; I had simply sat there, suspended in my own panic.

I pushed the paper away and said to my wife, who was across the table with her stopwatch, 'I don't want to do these tests any more, sweetie.'

TERMS & CONDITIONS OF KIDS

My wife hates them.

I love them. I want one or two or three or four of them. But my wife is not keen. She's an only child and comes heavily burdened with many of the issues that only children carry.*

Even as an adult she still views other children as a threat to herself, to her time, to her body, to her career, to her parents' attention (to her toys!). When we married she promised that once our careers were sorted we would discuss the *possibility* of having children. And she has stuck to her terms, but I have glibly accepted that 'discussions of the possibility' are as close as we are ever going to get to having kids.

I'm as desperate to have children as she is not. I spend hours negotiating, telling her I'll happily be a house husband, she can return to work as soon as the child is born and I'll raise the child (or children), change nappies, take Sebastian/Polly/Tom/Julie/Amy (yes, I already have names) to the doctor, play with them, love them, cuddle them; I'll make sure my wife's clothes are ironed and that she always has a cooked meal ready for her when she returns to her perfectly clean home.

When I've discussed this with her, she just looks at me and says, 'If you can give birth to the kid too, then we have a deal. I've not worked my body to perfection just to have a kid turn me into some frumpy milky mum. Yuck. And I've not made my way to the top of the career ladder just to sabotage myself with debilitating baby brain. Count me out. I don't want a snotty brat and I don't want a weedy house husband who resents my success.'

'Wow,' I said. 'You should tell me what you really feel some time.'

'Sarcasm doesn't suit you, Frank,' she said. 'You should stop being so EFTP.'

'You should try speaking English.'

---

* In other words, she's a selfish little brat.

To soften her to the idea of children, I once tried to present a well-behaved, good-looking child to my wife, to see if it would melt her cold heart. Desperation led me to agree to babysit Oscar's son, Lucas, one afternoon. I mainly said yes because Oscar's charming French wife, Nina, was at her wits' end, asked for help, and I thought Lucas was the perfect kid to introduce to my wife. Cute, well-mannered, no fuss.

My wife smiled when Lucas came in, she complimented him on his T-shirt, which had something French written on it, and Lucas, being a well-brought-up child, returned the compliment and said what lovely shoes my wife was wearing.*

Then Lucas put his school bag on the table and tipped my wife's glass of red wine all over a report that she was writing.

She grabbed the sodden paper and screamed, 'You clumsy clot, look what you've done.'

Lucas proceeded to cry and demanded to be taken home, and I cleaned up the mess and hugged him while glaring at my wife, who then tried – without effect – to apologise. 'Sorry, Lucas, it's just that I'm writing a very important report and you spilled very expensive wine on it . . . and well, I shouldn't have shouted, I shouldn't have called you that, but I was angry.'

Lucas wiped his eyes and looked at my wife and said, 'You're mean.'

'I'm not really that mean,' said my wife and walked towards him and gave him an awkward rub of the shoulder.

Lucas and I could see that she had the maternal instincts of a scorpion, but Lucas gave me a smile and said to my wife, 'Sorry I spilt your drink on your thing.'

She smiled and they sort of made up but I could see the effort of the moment had annoyed my wife and they never fully recovered after that.

---

* I fell into an imagined future of a house full of our laughing children: Polly playing violin in her bedroom, filling the air with happy music, my son Tom lying on the sofa, his full concentration poured into reading a book, our younger children Amy, Sebastian and Julie splashing about in the bath, and me smiling in the centre of all this life and joy.

My wife went on to ignore Lucas as he and I got down to some colouring-in. I could tell from her huffing and puffing that my wife was upset by how much space his crayons and paper took up on her dining-room table and, after some time had passed, she simply couldn't resist antagonising Lucas. She kept rolling renegade crayons back down the table towards him. Flicking them with her fingers, at first playfully, but then rather aggressively. Together we ignored my wife's darkening mood and got on with making a paper chain of people holding hands. My wife took one look at it, made a face, and said, 'Hmm, it's OK, not great, they don't look like real people.' Who says that to a kid?

Without looking up from the paper, Lucas said, 'You're not great.'

My wife smiled; she had a rival in Lucas, and she liked that.

She said, 'You're an interesting little boy, aren't you, Luke?'

Lucas replied, 'It's Lucas! And you're not good at talking to children.'

She sneered, 'Well, you're not very good with adults,' and stuck out her tongue in what I assume she thought was a playful way but in fact came off as horrid and mean.

I was about to accept this whole thing was a failure and take him off to watch cartoons in the sitting room but he heroically shrugged my hand off his shoulder as if to say he could handle his own battles, pointed his chubby finger at her, squinted his eyes in a serious manner that revealed just a flash of Oscar, and whispered quietly with a hot rush of feeling, 'You make my heart grow small.'*

My wife actually flinched. Something about this odd statement cut deep and, as childish as it was (maybe *because* it was so brutally childish), she could do nothing but snort, stand up and say, 'Well, I think I've had enough of this little experiment, thank you very much.'

I said, 'This is not an experiment, this is a child, this is Lucas, and you shouldn't say things like that to kids, Alice, you know that.'

'Well, research shows that when bringing up kids, unconditional praise is just as detrimental as complete neglect,' she said tartly.

---

* For years I've struggled to describe the withering effect my wife has had on me and in comes this kid and nails it – *You make my heart grow small.*

'Well, research shows that people who only rely on research, and never on their instincts, are generally rather hard to get along with,' I said through clenched teeth, trying not to say anything too obviously rude in front of Lucas.

She waved her hand as if bored of me, before slinking off to open another bottle of wine and chat on her phone to Valencia.

I realised then that my wife and I would never have children together. I saw through little Lucas' clear blue eyes just how ugly and dysfunctional my wife and I had become. I had invited in this little chap to charm my wife and bring warmth and light into our lives, to persuade my wife that children were the answer to our problems, and, through no fault of his own, Lucas had acted as a piercing X-ray, exposing all the fractured bones of our rotten relationship.

With my wife out of earshot, Lucas got back to his colouring-in, and only glanced at me momentarily when he said, 'Why is she your wife?'*

---

* Kids always ask the killer questions.

TERMS & CONDITIONS OF
MY WIFE'S PARENTS

They loved Alice unconditionally.

When my wife and I first met, she was always running away from home and hiding at Molly's house. My wife painted a picture of her parents as difficult people, demanding perfection from a daughter who did nothing but consistently disappoint them.

Which meant that before I met her parents I, naturally, loathed them. I could see they caused their daughter nothing but misery. So it came as no small shock when I met my wife's parents and discovered that I actually loved them. They were kind, they were generous, and it was no act; they loved their only daughter with such unconditional awe and affection that it literally shone out of them whenever they were in her presence. My wife had not given me a slightly skewed version; she had simply lied, blatantly and with malice, about the sort of people her parents were. She had crafted them as evil baddies in order to explain and, at times rationalise, her own increasingly idiotic, selfish and cruel behaviour. We all create baddies as backdrops to make us look like the goodies, and that's exactly the part that my wife elected for her parents. It was a part, however, which they could never convincingly play. They were simply and naturally too good; they were good people.

When I first met them I awaited a couple of ogres, uptight religious creeps who would consistently display their displeasure. In fact what I met was a charming low-key man called Fred, who had a quiff as thick and white as a scoop of cream and always wore soft lumberjack shirts, and a darling lady called Joy – who could have been a model for one of those cheesy mum pictures that advertising men put on biscuit tins to give them a homely feel. They smiled all the time and touched their daughter in the way that believers touch their icons. Their daughter was their life and somehow my wife had taken all that love and twisted it into hate towards her parents.

We had them over for dinner rarely, mainly because my wife never wanted them to come; she was embarrassed by them; so far had she travelled from her parents that she now viewed them as some sort of disposable and disgraceful part of her old life. My wife was the posh Ferrari that lived in shame of the fact that she was originally made in a dirty manufacturing plant. But her parents' campaign to get invited to dinner was relentless. After a while Joy took to calling my mobile, rather than my wife's, to try and arrange a visit. Joy knew I was the weak link.

'Now I know how busy Alice is with her book and her work, and you too, love, I know you're both so busy and we're just old retired frumps, but we'd love to see you guys, happy to come to you, happy to bring a little pot, a stew, so you don't need to fuss.'

I always said, 'Yes of course,' which would cause Joy to yelp, 'Such great news. Fred! Fred! Frank said yes, he said yes, we can see them.'

I could hear Fred, who would shout in the background, 'Tell Frankie I have a new Muddy Waters for him to listen to. Mint condition.'

Fred was the only person to call me Frankie, and from anyone else it might have irritated me, but from him I liked it. Fred and I bonded over a love of the blues; two skinny white men who couldn't stuff enough rural black men into our ears.*

But – again and again – my wife would try and wriggle out of these dinners. If she failed to think of a good excuse in advance, then, at times, she would pull out at the last minute, saying Valencia needed her, and I

---

* A lawyer listening to the blues? Well, I was trying to find something. Trying to find something that wasn't uncovered by my wife's tests, something you couldn't glean from my suit or hairstyle, and music reminded me that when I was young I did have something, something hidden, somewhere deep within the dark spaces between my skin and bones. It was around this time that I understood my character was a conflict waged between inner and outer voices. I was once that brilliant guy you'd meet at a party who'd make you feel witty and relaxed. Then I became the guy you glimpsed behind a pot plant pretending to read texts that weren't there. Every time I said something out loud, my inner voice quietly disagreed. 'I believe we did the right thing in going to war with Iraq,' I'd say, as my inner voice whispered, 'No you don't.' My inner and outer voices, once so melodious, are now battling drunks at a karaoke night. Put simply, I no longer believed a word I said.

would have dinner with her parents but without her. I loved those dinners with them. This is not to say they were a replacement for my own parents, who I loved and respected dearly, but my wife's parents had something that no one in my family could ever fake – and that was an unbridled enthusiasm for life. (Maybe something Malcolm had but not the rest of us.) This could of course go both ways. At times Fred could fall into deep discussions about how a certain guitar sounded, or a single note resonated on an album, and Joy would have to stop herself praising her own daughter, whether she was actually present at the dinner or not. But in the main, Fred and Joy were simply two of life's great enthusiasts.

When my wife did attend these dinners they were – unfortunately – never quite as good.

Joy would forever try and touch my wife – a hug held too long, a pat on the hand – and my wife would flinch and wriggle away. Then Joy would say, 'Now, Allie, I have told the Browns that you're going to pop in to say hello next time you come to visit. Mrs Brown is just so proud of you, sweetie; she has your book in hardback and paperback and no one is allowed to borrow it but she always shows people where you signed it for her.'

Over time Joy had realised that she embarrassed her daughter by praising her all the time and she had hit upon this clever method of using third-party endorsement, such as talking about Mrs Brown, or other friends, and how proud they were of Alice, as a way of continuing to do what she loved most – which was simply to love and adore and encourage her only child.

My wife would smile painfully and say, 'That's sweet, Mum . . . now, I better just check my emails,' and leave the table.

Fred and Joy would give each other just the mildest hurt look then Joy would brighten up and say, 'Goodness me, she is a busy girl. Where did she get that work ethic from, Fred?'

'Not me, sweets,' Fred would say. 'Not me. Now, Frankie, what are your views on the newly polished versions of the Son House album? Why are they messing with perfection, I say. I've got the original record in my bag. We should give it a spin, what do you say?'

'I say let's do it, Fred.'

And Joy would smile, grab my hand a moment as I tried to walk away, and I would know exactly what was coming next, exactly the question which had all night waited to be released from Joy's excitable mind – 'So has Allie talked more about babies, Frank? I know she's a career girl but she is getting older.'

This was always the hardest part of the evening and somehow Joy only ever brought it up with me, as if she knew it was no use pushing her daughter for more commitment.

'I'm keen as mustard,' I said. 'But Alice is really at a key point in her career . . .'

Joy said, 'Say no more, Frank, we know we can rely on you to make it happen.'

And that was it, we were all a team against my wife, and Fred would say, 'Just nick her pills or pop a hole in that rubber there, Frankie, she'll never know!'

Joy would squeal, 'Fred!' then smile, wink, and say, 'But you do what you need to do, Frank, we'll support you. Your secret's safe with us, son.'*

My wife's return to the table would plunge us all into an awkward silence, us three conspirators, and, somehow knowing what we were discussing, she would say, 'Let's not have the bloody grandkids chat tonight, OK? Give it a rest.'

'Whatever you say, dear,' Joy would say, starting to clear up the dishes but catching my eye and winking as she walked off to the kitchen.

There was always a moment at these dinners when the energy my wife exerted trying to be nice to her parents would finally give and she would say something rude.

One night I looked up from my plate and winced at the grating sound of my wife's voice amplified by her third vodka and Coke. She

---

* My own mum and dad never used to call me 'son' so it really got to me when either Joy or Fred tagged that term of endearment on to the end of a sentence – son.

often got drunk in front of her parents, creating a drowsy river of booze between her and them, something to soften the edges of the experience she found so distasteful, and when I asked if she wanted a top-up my wife said loudly, 'I'll 'ave a vodka and Coke, alwight luv.'

She said it in a grinding parody of an East End accent. It was an accent we all recognised immediately.

She was taking the piss out of her own father.

Fred looked so hurt and my wife was not too drunk to see her mistake, and said, 'Only joking with you, Dad, come on, don't be silly. Come on.'

He looked both furious and ashamed and said, 'You – *luv* – used to talk like that too. Remember, before you got all la-di-da.'

This really hurt my wife, who just grimaced like a brat, and her mother quickly patched over the tricky moment by standing up and saying, 'I'll tidy up.'

Then like clockwork as soon as the door was closed behind her departing parents, my wife rolled her eyes and muttered, 'Thank God that's over, they're so embarrassing. Why does Dad insist on wearing those lumberjack shirts? He looks like a fucking builder.'

'He *is* a builder,' I said.

'All the more reason not to bloody look like one,' she replied.

'Goodness me, you are such a snob,' I said.

'Better a snob than a yob,' she replied, trying to make a joke.

I didn't laugh.*

---

* Instead I did that terrible thing that warring couples do: I remembered this moment and filed it away, I stockpiled it among a list of her other mistakes, loading my arsenal to fire back at her later on down the line – when she unleashes upon me a similar stockpile of my own slights and faults. I'm ashamed to admit that I stockpile her mistakes, but I do; it is all I have left to fight her with.

From: fuckthis@hotmail.com
To: franklynmydear@hotmail.com
Subject: Evolutionary Boredom

Frank – hi!

I've been lying in a hammock all week and I've realised something fundamental. Boredom may not seem like much of a motivator but, believe me, boredom is a powerful life force, boredom makes people murder, rape, abuse, it causes insanity, it fuels revolutions, it inspires people to invent, create and discover everything, including art, blood sports, board games, plastic surgery, the internet, mobile phones, money, edible knickers, the stock market, God, pasta, drugs, soap operas, operas, vibrating condoms, books, double-entry billing systems, clothes for small dogs, small dogs without fur that bite people, children, marriage, fights, sex, blowjobs, homosexuality, priests, prostitutes and those small umbrellas for cocktails, perverts, those women who hate men, those men who hate women, lions, giraffes, Bob Geldof, nanotechnology, politicians, the God Particle, lies, secrets, and it makes the world go around and around as we all desperately search for some way of avoiding it, avoiding the hideous boredom of death, the black hole of boredom, searching for places to hide from its vast nothingness, from its eternal and awkwardly unanswerable questions. Boredom is evolution's spark and its fuel, and we all spend our lives desperately trying not to slow down and face the fear that holds in its centre one dull throbbing idea – *That everything is completely pointless.*

Love and boredom,
Malc

PS Having said all that, boredom has not really motivated me to invent or discover anything of any use to anyone so far. Which is not to say I have done nothing. For instance, I have recently perfected a way of expending the least possible energy in order to keep my hammock swinging. Without getting lost in the details, it involves hanging my right foot out of the hammock and swinging it slightly up and down and . . . I'll leave the rest of the explanation for the next email as this may take quite some time. In fact, I may need diagrams to really get the idea across accurately. I assume that you will await my continued explanation with bated breath. Until then.

CLAUSE 2.2

DOUG

TERMS & CONDITIONS OF DOUG

Truth, lies and damn statistics.

TERMS & CONDITIONS
OF CHANCES

You only get half a million of them.

When Doug returned to his office he found me clutching *Executive X*.

'Your lovely wife gave me a signed copy,' explained Doug.

'She's not lovely, though, is she?'

'You may be right there. So a few more memories have arisen.'

'Can you please tell me what I was like before the crash?'

'Well,' said Doug. 'I'm not sure what to say, really.'

'Just give it to me straight,' I pleaded.

'Look,' said Doug. 'I wasn't involved in your life as much as I would like to have been, I don't know everything that was happening to you, but I'll tell you something that I do know. I once lied to you when you were young; it was a small thing, but I think I may have influenced your life detrimentally. And for that, I'm sorry. So now I'm going to tell you something very blunt. To try and make amends, so to speak. Humour me. So here it is. Don't listen to what people are promising you, Frank. Not Oscar, nor Alice, not any of them. All that rubbish about you just being a bit stressed before your little episode. It's untrue. They're revising your history. You see, before the accident, and before your mental breakdown, we spoke, you and I, only briefly, in the lift, and I'll tell you now, take it from me, you were bloody miserable. There were nothing but problems in your life and I don't want to sound bleak but at the time you were very unhappy. You don't want things to get back to being normal, you don't want to be back to the way you were. But the good news is that they say after an accident you get a second chance.'

'You think my accident is a second chance for me?' I asked, hopefully.

'Don't kid yourself, Frank,' said Doug sharply. 'That's all movie clichés. But it's a second chance for me to tell you something. I'm a statistician and let me tell you now; we have half a million chances in life. Every single day we all get up and we could all change the world but we don't, because it is too much hassle, or because our mum's coming to tea. We live until we're about eighty. That's around 30,000 days – that's 30,000 chances. But, in fact, you can change your life at any hour, twenty-four hours, seven days a week for eighty years – with a rough calculation that's half a million chances. So what do we do with these chances – nada. They slip through our fingers like sand. We don't take one of those chances to call our estranged daughter, to help that beggar we ignore on our way to work, to turn to our wife and say, *Honey, I love you.* So forget your accident, forget that cliché about second chances, and believe me when I say that you were miserable. I've seen you since the accident, trying to please everyone, trying to fit back in, am I right? I am. You need to do something else with what's left of your life, Frank. Take it from a man who's done nothing with his own life but calculate death. Life's a gift, so grab it. Oh dear, you've turned awfully pale, are you OK?'

Not an actual word but a squeal escaped from my mouth as I recalled the day when Doug had used all his wit and wisdom to help me.*

'I've remembered who you are,' I said slowly.

Doug smiled. 'Well, now, that's always a nice thing to hear.'

---

* And I, in turn, had employed every ounce of my profound idiocy to dash Doug's attempt.

TERMS & CONDITIONS OF
THE MASTER ACTUARY

Actuary is a science but some consider it an art.

Doug's an actuary. A skilled statistician, which, on the surface, appears to be the most boring job in the world, but you'd be wrong to think this. Doug's a master actuary, a man who weaves together mathematics, statistics, weather, finance, economics and sociopolitical algorithms to determine how insurance companies can maximise profits.

The examinations, tests and experience required to be an actuary are so long, arduous and complicated that it's seen by some as a spiritual quest. Many seek out a master actuary and work under them as apprentices for years before establishing themselves as masters. Sitar players train for a decade before they're allowed their first public performance, so complicated and precise is the instrument. Actuaries have to train for at least twice that long before they become masters, and great actuaries sit in the top offices of the world's skyscrapers, levitating in clouds, determining the essential question – *When will you die?*

How long will you live? And how much will it cost? How much is your life *worth*? Some say you can't put a price on life. Doug disagrees. Doug does it for a living. Doug's the guy who decides how much you should pay for insurance. If you're a thirty-year-old previous smoker with two kids, Doug knows to within a couple of years when you'll die. He also knows to within three or four possibilities what disease will kill you.

Doug has one job: he ensures people pay more money in than companies pay out. The margin between how much insurance companies shell out versus how much they take in is astronomical. You need only look at the major cities in the world to see that margin manifest itself into sparkly skyscrapers owned by insurance companies and banks. And the banks are only that big because the insurance companies keep their profits in them.

If there was ever a real medium, a modern soothsayer, then it's Doug. And he fits the part. Doug is in his late fifties but looks younger than me. According to office folklore he hasn't consumed a grain of sugar for thirty years and he eats only skinless, boneless chicken. He often closes his office door and blinds and is said to spend hours in deep meditation cracking the most complicated advanced maths known to man. I wondered if Doug has calculated his own death date, and is so far away from it that life still seems sweet. Is that why he's so serene? Or is it some sense of godliness that he gleans from his power to see into the future that credits him with this righteous glow?

Doug wears crisp white shirts, no tie, moleskin trousers, with odd shoes that are black and from a distance look like business shoes, but close up transpire to be trainers. No one has ever seen these business-trainers for sale anywhere and they started a whole new myth about the fact that they were specially crafted by men in India who make the perfect soles that are forever pushing essential life-giving, life-extending reflexology points whenever Doug walks. Rumours grow like mould in the Petri dish of office boredom. They're all probably rubbish, but there's something about Doug that validates the hearsay. That makes you think: maybe there's something in it. He doesn't radiate that dull anxiety that so many business people do; he floats around the office in his bouncy trainers, a few rubber inches off the stressful surface of it all.

His office is sparse. Not Philippe Starck sparse, not designer sparse, but sparse in an unused sort of way. White walls, no carpet; Doug got his office floor stripped back to wood. There are theories about this too: the desire to dispel microscopic spores roosting within. Odder still, odder than all the sparseness, is the fact that he has no computer. It makes it seem as though the office is not only deserted, but that the person deserting it stole everything on his way out.

Doug and my dad were associates and their relationship kept my father in business for many years. Although Doug was much younger than my father, they seemed to have a mutual admiration for one another and Doug always ensured that all legal contracts for his insurance company were handled by my father's firm.

When my father ran the company it was a fairly average, medium-sized business. It did terms and conditions and corporate contracts for lots of insurance companies and, yes, some of them were not great companies but overall it was fairly benign stuff. I'm not sure if that was due to some personal decision on my father's behalf or if it was just a slightly gentler era back then. All I know is that in a short time Oscar had brought his own distinctly horrible personality to bear. Suddenly we were working with bad insurance brokers, gambling companies and arms manufacturers.

And I remembered that once it was all out in the open, Oscar and I argued about the weapons manufacturer every single day.

I told him I was appalled and he would just say, 'They'll need legal counsel, buddy; it's just the boring contracts, we're not selling missiles to anyone. Why worry?'

'Because they're death factories,' I said.

'Lighten up,' he said.

That was his advice – *Lighten up*.*

---

* Against his advice I found myself darkening down day by day.

TERMS & CONDITIONS OF DOUG

Effort kills.

I rarely saw Doug.

Few did. He was in his office before everyone and left after every-one. But one night I stepped into the lift and waited for the doors to close – so that I could have a good look at myself in the mirror – but between the closing doors a hand wedged in, the doors breathed open, and there was Doug.

He asked how I was. I said I was fine and was about to enquire how he was, but he looked so radiant that it seemed like a superfluous thing to ask, and Doug was one of those men you didn't want to irritate with obvious questions. Something about his stature – maybe it was just his reputation, the myths – something about him prevented you talking naturally to him. You wanted only to say deep and meaningful things to Doug.

Which made it all the funnier when Doug said, 'Bet you were angry I barged in, Frank. Bet you were just about to give yourself a nice vanity shot with the mirror. In the lift, by yourself, no man or woman can resist it. Am I right?'

'You got me,' I laughed.

'Go ahead – look. We all spend our lives pretending we're not look-ing at things. Not looking at ourselves, not looking at beautiful women. Such an effort. And effort kills.'

As I always did with Doug, I wondered if this statement was coded advice. A suggestion by a man who all day quantifies death and there-fore understood a little more about life. A man who'd conquered fundamental things I'd yet to grasp.

Effort kills.*

Doug said, 'When lifts were first invented they made people feel sick, you know.'

---

* Make your life effortless and live for ever.

Doug hadn't pushed the button yet. The lift wasn't moving. He said, 'So Otis Lifts got engineers to make the ride smoother, faster. Didn't work. People still felt sick. So they hired a philosopher to crack the problem. Some Frenchman, lateral thinker. And he said: we love ourselves. Put mirrors in the lifts, we'll be distracted, and no one will feel sick.'

'Is that true?'

'Sounds true, doesn't it,' said Doug. 'So go ahead, look at yourself.'

'I'm good. I'll give myself a look in the rear-view mirror in the car.'

'Not while you're driving, though,' warned Doug. 'Three per cent of car accidents involving men are due to them looking at themselves in the mirror while driving. I estimate it's around 10 per cent for women. This is counterbalanced, however, when you consider that 30 per cent of men crash leering at women on the street. There's a whole formula I made in the sixties for miniskirts. The Minideath Formula. They killed a lot of men, miniskirts. Even a glance can kill. What can you do? We're all killing ourselves spying on one another.'

'We're a bunch of vain perverts.'

Doug laughed and I made a note to laugh more. Maybe another secret to long life.*

When Doug realised we weren't moving, he hit the basement button.

'Basement, right?' said Doug, and I nodded.

Then we stood, lost in that odd hush which lifts breed – suspended silence – as if the time is too slight to allow for a worthwhile conversation, so you wait it out, waste the moment, mutually agree to experience terse quiet rather than risk dull small talk. But in this instance I'm glad we didn't let the silence stretch unbearably all the way down to the basement.

'How are things in the world of law, Frank?' Doug asked, snapping me out of my trance.

'Not bad,' I said, watching the numbers fall – 31, 30, 29 . . .

'Oscar still running the show?'

---

* Laugh at life and live for ever.

'Yup. He's taking us in an interesting direction.'

'I hear disapproval.'

'It's a direction Dad would never have gone.'

28, 27, 26 . . .

I suddenly wanted to blurt out all my worries to Doug.

I wanted to tell him everything, to cry on his shoulder; he was a channel, a sort of conduit to happier times when my dad was alive and I'd come and play at the offices, and Doug would smile and ruffle my hair. Doug was as close to a friend as my father ever got.*

'You're talking about the weapons contract,' said Doug.

'You know?'

25, 24, 23 . . .

'A dark decision,' said Doug. 'I advised Oscar against it, but you can't tell your brother. There's statistical karma and what your brother's contemplating is statistically incalculable. I don't like incalculable things. Oscar's about to place a big minus sign next to his soul and he'll pay for it, somehow, somewhere down the line, it's unavoidable. You can't play with negative statistics and walk away unharmed. Mathematically impossible.'

It was the most meaningful thing anyone had said to me. I wanted the lift never to stop, to keep descending, to allow us to talk into the night as we dropped through the earth.

11, 10, 9 . . .

'I completely agree, Doug. I mean, I really hate the idea of it but no one else seems to think it's a problem. It's like no one cares.' I stopped myself, as I could hear that I was close to crying.

Doug didn't say anything; he turned slowly and looked at me. I noticed the elevator music, a panpipe version of 'The Girl from Ipanema'.

'You need to make a choice, Frank. You're a nice guy but you need to decide. It's not up to anyone else.'

The hum of the lift, the panpipes, the dull beep of passing floors formed a hypnotic space: 8, 7, 6 . . .

---

* Maybe as close to a friend as I ever got.

'It's so good to talk to you, Doug.'

He looked at me again, not a nice look but hard, as if calculating something.

5, 4, 3 . . .

He said, 'Do you remember when you came to me when you were all of sixteen?'

The memory made me blush. I'd had an argument with Dad. Our first and only real fight.

Over dinner with Oscar, Malcolm, Mum and Dad, I declared that I was going to take biology, chemistry and maths for my A levels. It was my way of telling my father that I wasn't going to do law; that I was going to pursue medicine instead. The table went quiet. Oscar, who was already at law school, let out a dismissive snort.

We all waited as Dad mulled this over, before saying, 'Frank, you're not going to do this. Medicine is a myth perpetuated by the middle classes; it's a horrible job with terrible hours, disgusting sick people and endless training. It doesn't even work. When GPs went on strike the death rate plummeted. You don't want to get involved in all that. Medicine's messy.'

Dad hated messy things, like organs or emotions or hysterical teenage sons. My mother, God bless her, tried to intervene. 'Maybe you should listen to Frank, dear, maybe he would prefer to do medicine.'

Dad patted Mum's hand in a way that made me want to run him through with the carving knife, and he continued, 'You want to be on the legal side of life, Frank, trust me. Your life begins with a birth certificate and ends with a death certificate, and in between all of that are a million documents, insurance policies, employment contracts, mortgages, prenups. Medicine tries and fails to tidy up life's mess after the fact; law ties it all tightly in place *before* the fact. And it's the men who write these documents that run the world.'

It was an old speech. I pretended to listen, then said, 'I disagree, Dad.'

Everyone at the table held their breath. This was not how we spoke; nobody, not even Mum, could say 'I disagree' to my dad.

'Listen here, young man,' said Dad, but I made my fork clash against the plate and shouted, 'Don't you dare call me young man, and stop telling me what to do!'

'I don't want to argue with you,' said Dad.

'Well, I want to fucking argue with you,' I shouted back.

Everyone stopped and, for a second, no one knew how to start again.

Then I heard Mum say, 'Come on now, please, Frank, sit down, don't get upset, we can discuss this, your father is just . . .' As I stood up I heard Oscar sneer, 'Prick,' as Malcolm muttered, 'Fuck yeah, Frank!'

I stormed out. I found myself on the street with nowhere to go. For reasons I cannot really understand – even today – I went to Doug's house. Possibly because it was nearby, possibly because Doug was always honest with me. When I got to his door I was crying.

He poured me a whisky, which made me feel like a man, a person being taken seriously, and we spoke. I assumed Doug was on my side but, as the conversation wore on, it occurred to me that he too was telling me that law was my best option.

Doug said, 'Your father is a highly respected man. You're a boy with an incredible intellect. You're brilliant. And law will allow your brilliance to be both tested and to shine.'

It was the start of people telling me I was brilliant. In my defence, it's hard not to agree with people who are telling you incredibly flattering things. I caved in, Doug drove me home, and eventually I took economics, history, English and, of course, I went to law school. I was ashamed. For a while after, whenever I saw Doug, I was embarrassed that he'd seen me upset, crying like a child. In the descending lift I looked down at the carpeted floor and said, 'I made a fool of myself, sorry, I was young and stupid.'

'Not at all,' said Doug. 'In fact, I made a fool of *myself*. What you don't know is that before you arrived your father called me and told me to support him. I always felt bad about it. I should have supported you more. You never wanted to do law. You were sixteen, yes, but you knew what you wanted, and we all talked you out of a dream. And talking a young man out of a dream – that's intolerable and for that I'm truly sorry.'

I heard the numbers in the lift running down, slowing, we were near the basement, and I was too flustered to answer properly, so I mumbled, 'Don't be silly, Doug. I mean, I was a boy, I needed guidance, I'm sure you did the right thing.'

'I hope you're right. I hope you mean that. I felt bad. Still do. So let me be honest with you now, Frank. You seem unhappy.'

'No, not at all, I'm great.' Why did I say that? It was the first time anyone had noticed how miserable I was but I batted him away.

'Well, OK then, but you look exhausted. Exhaustion will eventually get to you.'*

2, 1, Basement!

Bing!

I was just about to say something, admit to my misery, tell him how lost I was, but the lift whooshed open and the moment seemed to seep out the doors.

'Well, see you soon,' said Doug and walked off on his bouncy trainers.

I stood in the lift so long the doors closed on me. Standing in a box going nowhere, I wondered why I hadn't told Doug how sad I was. How worried I really was about the #### contracts. About the IPO. How messed up my personal, professional and ethical life was.

Why didn't I reach back to him when he was reaching out to me?

Then I realised what it was. It was the dreariness: life's dull days heaped upon me, each day no heavier than dust, yet piled high the weight became hopelessly heavy, and so, when someone said, 'Hey, are you all right, Frank?' all I could do was wave it away with impulsive politeness, saying, 'Oh, yeah sure, I'm fine.'*1

---

* Exhaustion kills.

*1 Then lie back quietly below the density of it all.

TERMS & CONDITIONS OF FEAR

It's hereditary.

Having retracted the bed, we were now both sitting on the couch sipping tea and Doug asked, 'Do you remember Malcolm?'

'I've read his emails. He seems different to the rest of the family, like a wild card.'

'He is different. He wasn't even born in England.'

'Really?' I said.

Doug winced as soon as he said, 'Don't you remember?' Then quickly added, 'Sorry. You must be bored of people asking you that. But, yes, Malcolm was born in Istanbul. Your family went on holiday when your mother was pregnant. Your dad was nervous but your mum wasn't due for two months and so she told him to relax. Then, the way your mum tells it, she said that after the Blue Mosque and a spicy kebab, Malcolm grew restless with the womb and wanted out.'

I laughed at this image of Malcolm in utero: his squashed face grumpy with boredom and his tiny lips mouthing the words, *Fuck this, I'm outta here.*

'It was a complicated birth and your mum and Malcolm nearly died. Your dad told me you were all in this god-awful hospital, he was convinced Malcolm and your mother would die, you and Oscar were wrapped around your dad's ankles crying because you knew something was up, and all your dad could do was accept how powerless he was. Your dad promised himself he'd never put himself in such a position again. Never. After that your dad really tried to batten down all the random hatches of life. Which is probably why your family never went further than Brighton for your holidays.'

Remembering the pitiable and indecisive way I responded to Oscar's news about the arms manufacturer, I confessed quietly to Doug, 'I think that I'm very like Dad was. It seems neurosis is like cancer and baldness – it's hereditary.'

'Rubbish,' Doug said firmly.

TERMS & CONDITIONS OF TESTS

1. If your boss said your new client was an arms manufacturer, would you:

   a. Say, *No problem.*

   b. Say, *Absolutely not, it's against my ethics.*

   c. Dither so much that you did neither until the problem ate you up.

2. If you spotted a man being mugged, would you:

   a. Whip out your mobile phone and call the cops.

   b. Help, risk your life, and have at least some chance of feeling like a member of the human race.

   c. Run away and regret the decision for the rest of your life.

TERMS & CONDITIONS OF DOING SOMETHING

You only regret things you never did.

I remembered that the day Oscar told me about the #### client was one of those days that quickly went from bad to worse. On the way home I was stewing in misery, thinking about Oscar and his hideous new client, when something caught my eye. As I waited at a red light I watched a middle-aged man being surrounded by three younger men who wrapped themselves around him and pushed him into an alley. A young man pulled out a knife and forced the man to hand over his wallet. It was like watching something horrific on television and not being able to change the channel – the rounded window of my car, the brief violent moment suspended in the alleyway, all seemed unreal, and I thought, *What am I doing? I should be helping that man.*

I could have got out of the car, run into the alley and done something, but I didn't. In fact, I slowly pushed down the lock and wound up my window. To make matters worse, once they had the wallet they didn't stop, they punched him and I realised if I ran to help, they'd punch me or kill me. The light changed and I drove off.

I called the police and told them what was happening and where they needed to go, but it would've taken them so long to get there that the man could've been murdered many times over. They say time cures all. They're wrong. Time's a toxin, not a tonic. Every day since then I think a little less of myself. I drive past that alley sometimes, and like a fool, I hope there'll be a re-run of the incident: same man, same muggers, but this time, look – it's me, I'm out of my car, crowbar in hand, jogging towards them, I'm terrified but I don't care, I don't care how it'll end, I don't care if I'm hurt or maimed or killed, I'm just running, sprinting now, laughing like a maniac because I don't feel dead any more, I'm here, I'm doing something, taking part, screaming for dear life as I finally hurtle towards it.

TERMS & CONDITIONS OF TRYING TO GET YOUR WIFE TO LISTEN TO YOU WHEN YOU'RE FALLING APART

You never get a second chance (which is what makes imagination such a cruel gift).

When I got home that night I was desperate to talk to Alice about the mugging and the weapons client but she was fussing with some presentation. I had to set the table for dinner around her, moving her papers out of the way in order to put placemats down.

Finally, after I poured her some wine, I said, 'I had a bad day, Alice.'

It had been so long since I had said it that her name felt funny in my mouth.

'Really,' she said, still looking at her mobile phone.

'Oscar won a new client.'

'That's great, Frank, make sure you get involved.'

'No, the business is with ####' I said.

'Oh, really, well listen . . .' said Alice.*

What she actually said was, 'They do much more than just make weapons.'

'That's exactly what Oscar said. Don't you think it's wrong?'

'Well, it's a bit of an ethical conundrum, sure,' she said, and that was it, like it was some abstract question on one of her tests.

'And, also, I saw a man being beaten up today,' I added.

She tapped something into her phone, and muttered, 'That's terrible.'

'Look at me when I talk to you,' I said.

'What the hell's got into you, Frank?' she said, finally looking at me.

---

*   And, for a moment, I heard her say what she would have said years ago: as the old Alice she would have said, 'You just walk away from that, love, that's terrible, resign and go and open a bookshop or something. No job or money is worth working for those types of companies.'

'I'm trying to tell you something and you're not listening.'

'All right, sorry, I'm all ears, what happened?' she said, pushing her phone slightly aside so it rested near the salt and pepper, but still in reach.

'I saw a man get mugged.'

'That's terrible,' she said again, and added like a punchline, 'But that's just the city.'

'Worse than that, I did nothing.'

'Good,' she said. 'If you had, they could've killed you, people are desperate this time of year. I've written a paper on it. My paper was about executive stress but I'm sure homeless people get stressed too.'

'There were no homeless people involved . . . and that doesn't matter, that's not the point. No, it's not good, and, yes, I should've done something.'

'Well, I'm glad you didn't,' she said, and her hand went to her phone, but I picked it up and threw it hard against the wall. I hoped it would break, smash in a loud dramatic gesture, but it had a rubber cover so it bounced awkwardly, comically, and landed at her feet.

'What the fuck, Frank?'

'It feels as if no one's listening any more . . . I just feel . . . isn't working for an arms manufacturer grotesque? Am I the only one with an ethical fucking problem with this?'

'Oh, Frank, you think you're so fucking ethical, don't you, and the rest of us are all morally devoid gits. Well, listen, Frank, being a boring bastard doesn't make you an ethical pillar. It just makes you a boring bastard. Just because you're too scared and don't even have the balls or imagination to think outside the box, to explore the grey areas, does not make you ethical. It just makes you fucking dull.'

I stood staring in disbelief, not so much at her mean words, but at the fact that we were actually arguing – it was brilliant. I had shocked my flatlining wife back to life.

'Well, I'm glad you're telling me what you think for once,' I said. 'This is great, you shouting at me, actually listening to me . . .'

She nodded and I felt a connection with her as she picked up her phone, cradling it like an injured animal. She turned to look directly at me and I was about to tell her I loved her because in her eyes I saw a rare look of kindness – but before I could talk, she said, 'It's fine, Frank, don't worry, my phone isn't broken after all. Thank God.'

'Bitch,' I whispered under my breath.

She didn't hear, too engrossed in her texting, and when she looked up she said, 'Phil's coming over for a bite; we need to finish off a report.'

Phil was one of my wife's dull identikit colleagues. I could barely distinguish one from the next but I remember Phil because he was incredibly tall. When he arrived I sat at the table smiling at just how tall Phil looked in our flat, folded awkwardly into a seat, sipping red wine. When my wife's colleagues come over I play a game in which I see how long I can go without saying anything, how long I can be completely ignored for, invisible. Above the dining-room table is a clock I bought Alice for her birthday. As Phil and my wife spoke, I watched the clock.*

My wife was chatting about an article Malcolm Gladwell wrote which basically laid the blame of Enron at the foot of Enron's consultancy, McKinsey.

She said, 'Gladwell may be a great writer – sure, no question – but does he know how to hire a staff of two thousand talented people? Could he take those risks? That's what McKinsey did, that's what I do every day of my life; I build companies and it's not easy, not even with the level of science we now bring to bear upon the profiling process.'

'What's Mr Tipping Point know about the real world?' agreed Phil.

I zoned out for a bit, watching the clock and thinking I was doing well – five minutes so far – when I heard Phil ask, 'Is *The Sopranos* really that good?' and my wife explained to Phil how the show captured the 'corrupt essence of America'. 'I'd pay a lot of money to profile the real Tony Soprano. I tell you, most of those top guys would probably hold a lot of the same personality-profile characteristics as our top CEOs.'

---

* My record for the longest silence is fifteen minutes ten seconds.

Phil said, 'You mean they're all fucking psychopaths.'

My wife and Phil both laughed loudly and so did I.*

'Absolutely, very interesting point, Phil,' said my wife.*1

Those were the sort of things Alice used to say to people like Phil. The young Alice had a sharp way of shuffling her intellectual self with her streetwise self – just as she lured someone into a deep conversation about existentialism, she'd throw them off-balance by saying, 'Existentialism is just a bunch of French farts trying to get laid.' I used to love that.

I was clock-watching again: eleven minutes.*2

And, just then, as I basked in the slight elation of minor achievements, my wife said, 'Frank, you listening?'

'Course I am,' I eventually said.*3

'Well?' my wife said.

'Completely agree,' I said.

She gave me that look of infinite disappointment that I had grown accustomed to.

'You weren't listening,' she said, and turned to Phil. 'Frank's company is about to start working for #### and Frank's in a wee ethical conundrum, aren't you, darling?'

I was angry that she was chatting away about something this confidential and personal, and I said, 'I'm just not happy about working for those sorts of companies.'

'Come on,' said Phil, 'death and taxes, old man. Your wife and I work on the tax side of life, you work on the death and insurance part – you'll be set for life.'

They laughed at this but I wasn't sure where the joke lay.

'I don't agree,' I said.

---

* A laugh wasn't counted as talking, so I was still in the game. Seven minutes so far.

*1 Whenever she sucked up, saying crap like, 'Very interesting point, Phil,' I'd hear an echo of what the young Alice would have said to this sort of guy years ago, something along the lines of 'Fuck you, dickface.'

*2 My personal best was in sight!

*3 Damn! So close!

They went quiet. I'd hit too heavy a note for our light chat. This was what happened with my wife and her colleagues; there was simply no conversation that they couldn't ridicule. All of the really big questions were mocked; as if they had seen it all before, they were all so world-weary, too sophisticated to care.

'I'm just concerned that working with those sorts of companies isn't good,' I said.

'Come on, #### do a lot more than just guns and missiles,' Phil said.

'That's like saying Hitler did a lot more than just kill Jews,' I said.

'It's completely different,' my wife protested.

'Is it really?' I said.

She shot me a shut-the-fuck-up look.

'I hear that Hitler did some delightful paintings,' Phil joked.

My wife laughed and said, 'He was also a gifted writer. *Mein Kampf* is a real page-turner. I could barely put it down.'

I cut the laughter short with, 'It feels wrong.'

My wife said, 'Come on, Frank, when did you become such a wet liberal?'

They both laughed so loudly that no one heard me reply, 'When I met you.'

Which was true. I started to be more liberal and caring when I met Alice, who was once the most liberal, intelligent and caring person. I smiled and gave her the peace sign and they laughed.

Phil said, 'You've been reading too much Naomi Klein; time to toughen up, mate.'

Then my wife said, out of nowhere, 'Frank wanted to be a doctor, you know,' and she smiled coldly. 'He wanted to help people but he went to the dark side and became a lawyer so he could legally hurt people.' Drunk and with spite in her eyes, she said, 'Oh God, Frankie, I'm only kidding. You take everything so fucking seriously. Chillax.'

She was no longer the defender of my dreams; my wife would now use a secret that I had shared in confidence as nothing more than a punchline to amuse a colleague.

She added, 'Frank keeps these daft toys from his childhood: gross anatomical figures with plastic organs that pop out. He actually wanted them on display in the flat – can you imagine?'

After Phil had left, I tried to plug her lead into my phone – tried to force the little thing into the socket – but it wouldn't fit.* 'Did you change phones?' I asked.

'Company gave us new ones.'

I said, 'Also, can we talk about something? It's just that I've not been feeling like everything is going too well.'

She looked at me, didn't smile. 'Can you expand?'*1

She sounded irritated, like I was inconveniencing her.

'Never mind,' I said. 'It's just that things don't feel right and . . .'*2

But her phone vibrated and the word *Valencia* appeared.

I handed it to my wife who, as always, started to take the phone to another room.

But as she was leaving, she turned and said coldly, 'We'll talk about this later, Frank.'*3

---

* Even our phones weren't compatible any more.
*1 *Expand.* That's pure management speak.
*2 I was about to say, 'I can't go on like this, Alice, I want a divorce.'
*3 Which is management speak for 'Fuck off, Frank'.*4
*4 We never talked about it again.

TERMS & CONDITIONS
OF FRIENDLY FIRE

Was there ever a more appalling misuse of the word 'friendly'?

Oscar gave me another #### contract. His promise that I wouldn't have to work on them had already slipped. He said he just wanted me to 'look it over', but it was the tenth one I'd just had to 'look over'. As I worked on it I thought about how this contract would be used.

Imagine the scene:

A desert. A man – his face wrapped and covered; only a slit reveals his dark eyes – approaches another man in a suit. The man's suit is dusted in sand, like cinnamon sprinkles. Mr Suit is selling missiles to Mr Headgear. Money is exchanged. Cash (of course). Then, as a brief afterthought, Mr Suit asks Mr Headgear to sign the contract, which says something about the use of the weapons, maybe mentions the Geneva Convention. Mr Headgear sneers at the document. That sneer is as much attention as it merits. He signs with a brutal slash and drives away with his weapons into a swirl of sand and . . .*

Here's the truth:

No desert. No terrorist. In fact, all the dark dealings happen in a brightly lit office. Probably an office just like yours but with more expensive corporate art on the walls and better views. Two men, two lawyers, two accountants transferring obnoxious weapons from one to the other as if selling photocopiers. It's that simple. It's that horrifying. I know all this because I recently sat in on one of those meetings.

So why even bother writing Ts&Cs for weapons? Believe me, you have to. You have to protect the people that make them from the people that will use them and the people who will be blown to smithereens by them. That's what I do.

I protect and serve the sellers; I literally serve Satan. But if there are

---

* Implausible. Sorry. Bit too Tom Clancy.

any less-read words than the terms and conditions on a weapons contract then I've yet to find them.*

It's not the shady underworld you would expect. Want to know the biggest door-to-door weapons salesman? Then Google 'leaders of the free world'. There they all are – Obama, Cameron, Merkel – smiling in front of giant weapons of destruction. In the UK, the defence industry is the second largest, and every time the prime minister pops off on an official visit he adds a less official visit in which he meets leaders and sells them weapons. The world of defence is actually all there to see, barely hidden, almost visible, and it's happening right in front of your eyes. There are entire towns sustained by the economy of weapons, such as Barrow in Cumbria, a place that survives on one industry – the building of nuclear submarines.

Our new client specialised in drones, these small dark inventions that allow leaders to destroy their enemy remotely, to devolve war into some distant video game. The legality of drones is still hanging delicately in the balance and my job, as always, is to assist in ensuring that the drone makers never, under any circumstance, have to take any responsibility. And I did my job. I didn't want to, but I did it, and I did it well.

I won't say that I ever accepted it or that I felt it was right but for a while I did do it. I checked the terms and conditions, the clauses, I made sure all unknowable unknowns were covered, and then one night I switched on the news and I saw my work writ in blood and guts.

It wasn't even a major story, just another news report shoved between the doom and gloom of financial collapse and the horror of paedophiles. But for me that one minute lasted a lifetime. I watched as a reporter stood beside a hospital that looked as if it had been torn open and gutted by Godzilla.

This impoverished hospital in Afghanistan had a hole in the middle of it; it was a Red Cross centre set up in the middle of a war zone to help children caught in the crossfire – only to then be caught in the

---

* Ingredients on ketchup bottles have received more attention.

crossfire. A number of British troops had also been killed in the attack. A British-made drone flown by Americans had killed British troops. An organisation called Dronewatch, interviewed as part of the report, suggested that this particular drone had a well-known design fault, which so far the manufacturer and the government had covered up, and if someone didn't hold the manufacturer accountable, this sort of tragedy would continue to happen and many more innocent people and allied soldiers would be part of the collateral damage. The government, and manufacturer, using a drone that I had written the contract for, had hit soldiers and a civilian target, this hospital which had become hell, with the limbs and organs of children flung far and wide, the souls of the innocent blown to pieces, and the worst part was that no one would pay, no one would be held accountable, no one would be punished, and as I sat there paralysed, staring at the flickering images, I knew I had played my role, I knew I was responsible, not fully and not comprehensively, but I was a part of the machine, the complex, a grim little cog in the fatal machine that killed these children. I had used all my skill, education and experience to protect the people who made this mistake, I'm responsible for the fact that no one is ever held responsible, I'm priest, jury, judge and higher power absolving the rich and powerful to smite the weak and innocent, and, as the report ended and a smiling weatherman told me that sun was on its way, I leaned forward and vomited all over the carpet until nothing but bile dripped from my lips.

TERMS & CONDITIONS
OF WARNINGS

They usually come without warning.

The same evening I accepted that another problem I had been fighting was finally getting the better of me.

I had been having minor attacks with increasing regularity but so far I had hidden them from everyone and convinced myself that I was fine, *absolutely fine*.

But the image of the hospital – all the dead soldiers and children – had pushed me to the edge, and later that evening as I reviewed another #### contract, which I had brought home to work on, I realised what was wrong.

I looked at the #### contract in my hands and I had another panic attack.

My vision blurred. The paper became soggy as it absorbed all of the sweat from my wet palms. I felt sick try to lurch back up from my stomach again.

I looked at the contract and I thought I had figured out where my problem lay – *paper*.

Looking at the disintegrating contract, I whispered, 'Fuck-fuck-fuck-fuck!'

There's a name for it – *papyrophobia*: fear of paper.

To test my theory I walked to the printer and took some blank paper and looked at it but nothing happened, no panic – I could touch it, could smell it, could crunch it into a ball without the slightest sense of fear. It wasn't paper phobia.

But as soon as I looked back at the arms contract and read through the terms I again felt woozy and jittery.

Blank paper wasn't the issue. The problem was not the paper itself.

It was the words on the paper. I had developed a phobia of words and particularly of *warnings*.

Knowing what the problem was didn't help; it only made matters worse. Days later, on my way to get some lunch, someone handed me a small plastic packet of tissues.

I took it and said, 'Thanks.'

But as I looked back at the man I saw he had a cross on his neck and the fixed grin of a God merchant.

When I looked at the tissues I realised there was a bit of paper stuck on the back with a message that read – *Life's hard but resist sin or burn in hell. Jesus Loves You.*

I dropped it and leaned against a building before the pounding in my head stopped and I could breathe properly again.

It was then that I accepted that, since the shock of the hospital tragedy, I had developed a debilitating phobia.

No term exists for my condition.

Closest I came was a word for the phobia of long words: *hippopoto-monstrosesquipedaliophobia.**

From that day on my phobia spun rapidly out of control. Some days were worse than others but it wasn't long before I even stopped looking directly at *Stop* signs or road signs generally, which is an incredibly dangerous habit.

It was a period of great confusion. I had lost my confidence. All I knew at that stage was that the world had never made less sense and, for the first time in my adult life, I was starting to understand what it was like to stand on the chipped edge of madness.

---

* There's something needlessly cruel about labelling the word for the fear of long words with an incredibly long word – thereby inflaming the very people who suffer from it every time you mention their condition to them. I mean, who does that? Probably the same bastards that coined 'dyslexia'.

TERMS & CONDITIONS
OF THE DEAD

It's so hard to get your own back on the dead.

'Still wearing your dad's watch,' Doug said.

I looked at the elegant watch on my wrist and replied, 'It weathered the car crash better than I did. Not a scratch on it.'

'It's a beautiful watch.'

'Yes,' I said. 'But you have to remember to wind it up every morning, it's that old. Bit of a pain really.'

'I actually like the fact it's a wind-up watch,' Doug said. 'Something about winding up a watch makes me think, silly though it is, that the day is like an old toy and when you wind up the watch you're winding up your day. I like that watch, it has such a great tick-tock. Not like those dull digital watches silently swallowing the seconds of your life without the mildest warning that your time is sliding by. No, your dad's watch has a nice tock, like the soft shoe of a blues man tapping out the bittersweet passing of time. I told your dad that once and he looked at me like I was off my head.'

'I can imagine,' I said. 'He wouldn't have understood that at all.'

'He understood more than you think,' said Doug defensively. 'Your dad and I once took that watch to Piccadilly to be fixed by this nutty man who pulled out and replaced the golden cogs. Your dad was like a child, so happy to see it fixed. I suspect that we're the last generation to actually fix stuff, rather than toss it away. He delighted in the fact that you could keep fixing this watch for ever and it would keep going, outliving us all. He was more of a poet than you know, your dad. He was a great lawyer but also a big soul.'

'Oh,' I said, completely floored by this revelation, a little lost in this image of my dad delighting in the golden cogs of his watch.

Doug said, 'I've ordered food. You should eat. I'll pop down and get it. Got you a bacon sandwich and asked the lady downstairs to make your favourite coffee – cappuccino, right?'

Doug left and I lifted Dad's watch to my ear. I took comfort in its gentle tick and tock. From long before I was born this unassuming sound marked out my dad's time and his dad's before him. Now here it was, marking out mine. After Dad's death I was so angry with him and his stipulated condition – *as Oscar sees fit!* – that I'd thrown it in a drawer. I had tried – in only the way a spoiled ungrateful son can – to defy a dead man.

Then, not long before my accident, I took it from the drawer and wore it. Not only was it the start of achieving forgiveness for my father but also it reminded me that time was driving me past some undefined point of no return. In the days before I did what I did, I remembered arriving at work early and, as I rose through the building, I stared at myself in the lift mirror chanting like a maniac, psyching myself up to take action.

TERMS & CONDITIONS OF TIME

It don't wait for no man.

When *is* the time when I will finally sit and read all the books that stack up in my unread pile, when I will go regularly to the gym and become an Olympian; when is the time to step into the garage and throw away all that shit I know I'll never use; when is the time I'll get that suspicious creeping mole checked, spreading sinister like the slowest coffee stain across my shoulder; when is the time when I will go to a club and the music will be perfect and the people lovely and for the first time in a long time I will feel my limbs doing something odd and my head shaking and I will realise I'm dancing again and having a lovely time in a room full of smiling strangers; when is the time when I will sit for a moment, escape the noise of it all, the time when I will stop feeling mildly guilty about what I have settled for; when is the time when I'll finally sit with a guitar and at least try and teach myself just one chord from my favourite song, 'The Devil and the Deep Blue Sea'; when is that time, when is the time when I will call my wife's mum and dad and say to them, *This is hard to say, Joy and Fred, but your daughter, who you love more than life, is ashamed of you, and she will never ever give you grandchildren*; when is the time I will get my wife far enough away from her phone and laptop to sit her down and say, *Sweetie, I'm dying inside and I think you're the acid that's melting me away*; when is the time when I face my brother Oscar, look into his dead eyes, and say, *You've taken our father's company and sullied it with all of your greed and ambition*; when is the time when I stand up at my desk, throw my phone against the wall, and walk out of the office to never return; when is the time that I finally email my brother Malcolm and say, *I miss you and I'm sorry I rarely write but your emails are so full of life I fear if I send you an email that it will reveal how full of death my own life has become*; when will I go and visit Mum and Dad's graves; when is the time when I hear Doug try to help me and, instead of waving him away like the last lifeboat on the *Titanic*, I grab his hand and say, *Yes please, can you help* *me, I think I'm lost, and I just don't know what to do*; when is the time when I'll call Sandra and say, *Sandra, my wife hates you for some reason, but I want to see you, be friends, let's go out for dinner, just the two of us*; when is the time when I accept that most of my day is spent in the service of big men crushing little men; when is the time when I will take control and do something, when is that time?*

---

* It's right now.

TERMS & CONDITIONS
OF ARIAL NINE

Rebellion is only worth it when someone notices.

For days I sat at my desk reading about the hospital bomb and looking for images of it. I tried to desensitise myself to the reality of it, but the more I looked, the more repulsed I became.

In one report I found a photograph of the children standing in a line a few days before the drone hit; they were smiling, looking up at the camera, and a nurse was standing beside them smiling. Many of the children already had war wounds, their small thin limbs wrapped in bandages and splints. One of the children was wearing a Mickey Mouse T-shirt and – awful as it is to admit – this tiny fragment of the West emblazoned on this small child's chest was actually the detail that made me feel a connection with him, made me see that this child was like any child, not some distant foreign entity, not some *other*, but a child who could have been my child, my son, my tragedy. And after staring at the smiling child and the grinning Mickey beaming from his dirty T-shirt, I slowly leaned forward, grabbed my bin, and threw up into it.

As I sat there feeling glum I made a small – some might say tiny – decision. I had to do something. Things with my wife and I were getting worse, our role-play rotting like actors performing their millionth matinée, and work was no better, ten years after my father's death, ten years of being the terms and conditions boy, ten years of humiliating meetings with Oscar, and now with my hands stained by the blood of distant children, I knew I had to do something. I should have stood up and walked out. Quit my job, told Oscar to go fuck himself, divorced my wife.*

But I did do something. A small thing.

I made a call, a small decision, an infinitesimal decision; I decided, screw the consequences, to make my terms and conditions bigger – to make the font size larger.

---

* But I'm a coward and I didn't. I couldn't. I'm just not built that way.

To blow them up from the standardised Arial Eight to the more aggressive and readable non-standard Arial Nine.

I completed the document, I made sure no one was looking, I 'selected all' of my small print and I did it.

I enlarged them from eight to nine.

Wow!

I considered going to ten but, easy now, that was too radical.

My heart beat hard, my mouse ran wet with sweat, I admired the larger font. I'd done it.

At last my words were just that little bit harder to ignore.*

---

*   Disclaimer: I know it's silly and juvenile. What's the point of a rebellion fought in such tiny font? Well, all I can say is it was a start at least.[*1]

[*1]   Disclaimer to disclaimer: I sounded so pathetic in that last disclaimer. It won't happen again.[*2]

[*2]   Disclaimer to the disclaimed disclaimer: I regret to inform you that I cannot guarantee the previous disclaimer.

TERMS & CONDITIONS
OF DISAPPOINTMENT

It's a bottomless well.

I was elated.

I was finally doing something.

I shouted, 'Night, Pam!' to our receptionist as I left. She looked at me funny.

I smiled at strangers. They frowned back.

I had a secret. A power. I'd done *something*.

I went home, listened to Howlin' Wolf, drank whisky; I even danced a little on my own in my study.

But, by the next morning, the revolution was over.

I realised something about my job. I mean, I wasn't completely delusional.

I know that you, the public, never read my fine print, but now I realised that even my boss, my brother, my keeper didn't read it either.

No one read anything I wrote.

I wondered if any of the clients ever read them.

I spent my life writing words no one read.

I was deflated when I left work that night.

I didn't say goodnight to Pam, who didn't even notice me leave.

I sneered at strangers. They sneered back.

I didn't stop there, however.

I felt as if now there were no consequences to any actions. As if I was invisible. There was a certain freedom to it.

Then a big idea formed in my head.

TERMS & CONDITIONS
OF SELF-SABOTAGE

You've only got yourself to blame.

I took my tampering to the next level. I started to sabotage some of the #### contracts. Now don't get me wrong, I wasn't being righteous or unrealistic. I had no hopes of stopping even one arms deal, as I have said; the paperwork is not really a big part of the process. I didn't think tampering with these contracts would prevent a single bullet fulfilling its fatal destiny, but I did think – I hoped – that I stood a chance of at least making the arms company fire us for our sloppiness. I'm not saying I wanted to ruin the company, or Oscar; I just wanted to get rid of this client, and give Oscar a jolt out of his maddening smugness.

So with this in mind, I decided to add a little bit of my own copy into one of our incredibly long weapons contracts. I hid it deep in the jungle of small print at the end of page 99. Few people even make it to page nine. Fewer still make it to page 99. The only person who possibly gets that far is the person being paid a huge amount of money to read it and that person is the in-house lawyer of the arms client. And the only other is me – the lawyer in the agency paid a lot of money to write it. That's all it is. It's just two lawyers – one writing it, me, and one reading it in the arms manufacturer's office – while the rest of the world happily goes about trading missiles and legally blowing each other to bits.

Every missile drags in its terrifying wake entire forests' worth of documentations. Just as behind every new drug, under every tiny white pill, there is a literal mountain of contracts. I knew a few rogue words here and there would get lost in the fine-print sprinkle of hundreds and thousands. Well, they would get lost for a time; until, that is, they were finally spotted by some sharp-eyed legal eagle – then my world would really get interesting.

I'm also the last person to see these contracts before they go to the client, I'm the most accurate proofreader, and although Oscar is supposed to do the final approval, he rarely does, he is too busy being a bastard. So right in the middle of some particularly dull copy about munitions policy and transportation safety issues, I wrote, *Jesus Wept.* Short. Shortest sentence in the Bible. I'm not religious and not sure why I chose that one, it just seemed appropriate. Very slight. Nothing much to it; even the laser eye of a lawyer could miss those words as they scanned one of a thousand documents. I sent it off and guess what happened?

You guessed it.

Not a damn thing.

No one noticed. No one read it. No one fired me or Oscar or the company. We didn't lose the account. Nothing happened. Zilch. So I continued to tamper with the contracts. I got creative. In fact, I started to run riot. I included lyrics and sayings. In the middle of another munitions contract I wrote in the small print, *Sow wind and reap storm.*

Then after a few days of nothing happening, my bravery increased and instead of sprinkling words around – I couldn't stop myself now – I started to write long sentences: *Isn't fighting for peace rather like fucking for virginity?*

It quickly got out of hand. I became a sort of deranged corporate graffiti artist, a lawyer gone rogue, and still no one said a word, still no one was listening. So I did the only thing I could. I carried on. On another contract I wrote:

I'm a missile. But I don't want to explode. Please may I formally request that you just leave me in a deep hole to rot, I promise I won't go off, I'll silently and peacefully disintegrate until there's nothing left but rust and a whiff of sulphur. Yours sincerely, Sir W.M.D. Missile.

I handed it to Oscar, who handed it to an in-house lawyer, and I waited. And nothing happened. When would they notice? When would we be fired? When would I be fired? I thought maybe that even the in-house lawyer couldn't be bothered reading it. It seemed that it was so, because I heard nothing from him. I got more courageous. I started writing little letters and stories. For instance, for a pharmaceutical company I added, in the tiniest teeniest font, the longest one I dared write:

Hi there. I'm a tiny little pill. They call me Viaxton. But my friends just call me Jeff. I seem so white and pure but what you don't know about me is that I'm not really officially tested. I was sort of tested on some monkeys and they sort of went mad and sort of ate their own fingers. But I'm so precious that a few men in suits decided to ignore the men in white coats and here I am, on your hand, ready to enter your body. Look at me, gleaming white on the palm of your hand. And while you're doing that, take a look at your lovely fingers too. It will be the last time you see them. Bon appetit! Love Jeff.

I sat. I waited. I wondered when the first person would notice. I had tampered with so many contracts that I'd lost count. I began printing them and storing copies of them in a box under my bed. And strangely, the more I tampered, the less my phobia flared up. Soon my rebellion spread beyond the office. I went a little crazy, if truth be told. I started vandalising public property. On the tube one day I realised I was the only person in the carriage and I took out a Magic Marker and altered a sign. After I played with it, instead of reading *If you see a suspicious package do not approach it but report it immediately*, it read, *If you see a suspicious package please open and cut the red wire. **Not the blue wire!** The red wire. Thank you.*

Then on the walk home I passed a church and on the board outside there was a message: *When The World Ends Fear Not For God Shall Save Us One And All.*

I got my marker out, added an asterisk at the end and wrote: **Results May Vary.*

TERMS & CONDITIONS
OF DINNER PARTIES

No matter what's on the menu, neurosis
is always the hors d'oeuvre.

I remembered a strange dinner. At that time my wife and I were attempting to act like everything was fine between us. We had taken to throwing dinner parties to hide our own silence with the sounds of our friends. It was one of those dinners that I barely distinguish from so many others – but the passing of time, like fine falling sand, revealed its monumental significance. It was a dinner of Last Times and Only Times. It was the last time Sandra and Alice would ever be in the same room together; the last time Oscar and his wife Nina would be in our house; the only time Doug had been to see us socially. I was forever politely inviting Doug to dinner and Doug was forever politely declining. But this time he said yes and I was slightly thrilled by this fact.

The dinner was at our place but I remember all that week in the build-up to it that Oscar had tried to have it at his place. My wife and I had negotiated hard. We needed it to be at our place. We didn't do it for any reason other than the fact that neither of us could stand going to Oscar's house, which my wife called Oscar's Marvellous Museum of Me, where he spent the whole time showing off his *'lifestyle'*.*

After a few agonising visits to Oscar's, my wife boycotted ever going again, but I would still have to go by myself from time to time. Oscar had one strict term for any poor sods that visited his house, and that was that you had to have a tour, every single time, yet another tour, and you must be unflaggingly enthusiastic about everything that Oscar owned. Here are the basic terms and conditions of me coming to Oscar's house for a quick drink. I arrive and we hug.

Now: *do I go into the living room and sit and relax?*

---

* As he so hideously insisted on calling his *life*.

No. First I have to go on a tour of his house. I've seen his house a million times. That's not the point. He must show me all the new things he has bought since I was last here – *a week ago*. He must show me just how much more wealthy and well-to-do he has become in the seven short days since my last visit.

Some men take up hobbies, such as model aeroplanes or golf. Oscar's hobby is trying to make himself a man of cultural significance. It's a tough stretch for a man like Oscar who knows nothing about art, literature or music. He just likes the whiff of culture, the way it makes him feel, and certainly doesn't have the discipline to learn what it is – no, he simply wishes to buy it, to 'osmose' it. Donating large amounts of tax-deductible company money to museums and people who he thinks might become his friends if he pays them.

Which means I often have to stare at art that makes no sense to me. Stripes of colour on white canvases or bright dots on small postcard-sized pictures that cost more than my car. Objects that seem to me utterly uninteresting but to Oscar are entirely fascinating.

Oscar says, 'Look at this lamp I bought, isn't it amazing. Very pricey.'

*I say, 'It's a lamp. A bloody lamp.'**

No, I say, 'What an amazing lamp, Oscar. I'm not sure if I have ever seen a lamp quite that amazing. How much did it cost? Where can I get such an amazing lamp?'*[1]

Oscar swells with pride, smiles at the lamp as if it is his firstborn child, and says, 'Yah, I know, it's utterly fabulous.'

Then I'm taken to another room where I'll spend some time admiring another object.

Now, this only works one way. We're not both bound by this brotherly contract. It's a one-way road. If I had the *Mona Lisa* on the sitting-room wall and if my coffee table held Damien Hirst's shark, Oscar would simply arrive, plonk himself in a chair, drink a beer,

---

*   Of course I don't say that, no, that is not according to the terms of our brotherly bond.
*[1] Falsifying enthusiasm is exhausting.

and start to tell me about this amazing new lamp he bought the other day.

I desperately want to say, 'Yes, I know, I saw it last week, remember, Oscar!'

Instead I say, 'Oh wow, that sounds like the most incredible lamp I've ever heard of.'

He smiles as if he is without doubt the most fascinating man in the world, 'Yah, it is actually a pretty amazing lamp.'

So there it is. That lamp is not a lamp.*

It's not until I'm well and truly bored to tears that Oscar's wife, Nina, will appear. The most incredible thing in the house is her. She poses a question more profound than all his art combined and that is – *Why? Why did this gorgeous woman marry a plonker like him? Why did this exotic French flower fall for my buttery slob of a brother? My personal theory is that she is French* – it's the only reason I can think of.*1

Nina is everything that Oscar is not. She is caring, she is gentle, she is beautiful, with a face full of the loveliest features jostling for the eyes' attention, all framed with immaculate glossy black hair.

She will appear, my fabulous French saviour, and say, 'Oh Christ, look at you, Frank, you are bored to tears already. What has Oscar done to you? Is he going on about his stupid, ridiculous lamp again?'

This was why my wife and I both resolved to make sure this particular dinner was hosted at our place and not Oscar's. Although partway through dressing up, I realised that it would have been easier to have it at Oscar's place, so my wife and I didn't have to go through all the pre-dinner anxiety, all the host neurosis. We always had pre-dinner chats. As my wife's ambition swelled, our chats took on the characteristics of

---

* Nothing's what it seems. Nothing's anything. Everything's something else.

*1 I don't mean that to sound as xenophobic as it does; I don't mean she's French, therefore stupid enough to fall for Oscar. I mean that for years her English was not great and somehow, somewhere in the courting, enough of Oscar's idiocy was lost in translation that this poor French beauty fell for him.

a work meeting in which she would detail an agenda of conversations and KPIs* for the evening.

'So we need to get Sandra and Oscar talking tonight,' she said.

'Why?' I asked. 'I don't know why we even invited Oscar.'

'Listen, Mister Man, this is not about Oscar, it's about me,' my wife explained. 'It's all about spheres of influence, Frank. I've been reading a book about this, and as much as I detest your feral brother, he is very influential and so we need to gain influence by being close to his sphere of influence. Sandra and her publishing company are dithering about publishing my *Executive X* sequel. Very annoying situation. But I read that joining spheres increases the power of our network. If Sandra knows we have influential people like Oscar in our circle she will feel more inclined to agree to publish my next book.'

'You're publishing another one?'

'Of course I am,' she said, and I turned away so she couldn't see my face.

'Also, try to keep Oscar's wife dry – she's a terrible drunk, really sloppy when she gets going,' warned my wife. 'I really can't stand that woman. All boobs and brashness.'

I made a joke that I was ticking off a meeting agenda saying, *Check, check, and check*, but my wife didn't laugh, she stared at herself hard in the mirror and said, 'Good.'

Realising she was being a bit too business-like, she smiled and said, 'Hey, Mister, if Oscar was a plant he'd be a Venus flytrap.'

I trumped her with, 'Or flesh-eating fungus.'

She double-trumped with, 'Or the *shit* of flesh-eating fungus.'

She kissed me and left the bedroom to get back to arranging the dining table, which was laid out with a meticulousness that reminded me of a polished boardroom table. As our offices were decorated with shag-pile carpets and soft furniture, they came to resemble homes and, by the same token, our home with its white walls and strict Scandinavian design was evolving into a classic office space.

---

* Key Performance Indicators.

I thought about Sandra and felt both excited to see her and somehow also mildly embarrassed about what she would think of my wife and me. We'd not seen Sandra for many months and somehow in that time my wife had really taken her corporate soul to the next level, bringing it into our domestic life in a way I'd not fully noticed recently – until I looked around with the eyes of Sandra – and saw that our sitting room felt like the lobby of a trendy PR agency, our dining room was a boardroom – clean white walls and dark black imposing table – even our tiled bathroom was oddly reminiscent of an office toilet – a Dyson hand dryer on the wall wouldn't have looked out of place. I was mortified that Sandra – who we used to hang out with in Molly's shattered mosaic kitchen – would think that Alice and I had become . . . what? *Executive high climbers? Ambitious corporate rats? Or just wankers.*

I said, 'It'll be lovely to see Sandra again. You two haven't hung out for a while.'

'I can't wait,' said my wife. 'Just hope she doesn't come in one of those god-awful grungy cardigans she insists on wearing.'

'You used to wear those grungy cardigans,' I said.

'*Used* to,' she said. 'Grunge is dead, baby,' she added, as she precisely rolled a lint brush over her black top, reaping a tiny fluff harvest.

The dinner began in flustered fashion. Everyone arrived at once and I found myself juggling small talk with trying to get people the right drinks, but falling short on both tasks. Failing to recall the chat I was having with Oscar's wife, Nina, I handed her a white wine, only to remember as I got back to the kitchen that our chat was about the fact that she loathed white wine. I went back and took the wine off her; she smiled and said, 'Any red will do,' then, white wine in hand, I found myself at the door, where Doug was smiling and holding forth a bottle of red wine.

'Doug! You've arrived with exactly what I need,' I said. 'Red wine.'

'Well, that's a lovely start, glad I can help, it's just a young New Zealand Pinot, Peregrine something or other,' he said, moving towards the sitting room.

As I jogged back to the kitchen, Doug shouted in reply to my question about what he wanted to drink, 'Anything at all so long as it's not alcoholic, thank you, Frank.'

As I poured an apple juice for Doug, I heard him in a perfect French accent converse with Nina and I smiled as I thought, *Of course Doug speaks French.*

All the while I was in the kitchen, Oscar and Alice were entangled in an angry debate. It didn't matter the topic; there was nothing grand or small that my wife and Oscar wouldn't stand on opposite sides of. They agreed on one thing only – that they'd never agree on anything. At times my wife would even sacrifice a long and hard-held belief just so she could stand against Oscar. The bell called me to the door for our final guest and it pleased me that Sandra had on a lovely white blouse but over that wore a grungy cardigan.

'Frank, you look flustered,' said Sandra, hugging me then handing me chocolates. 'I know you like these ones. Something to please your sweet tooth.'

'Not flustered,' I lied. 'Just making sure Alice and Oscar don't murder one another.'

'That sounds like jolly good fun to me,' said Sandra, and went straight to the sitting room where the volume of the room increased as three or four people all said, 'Hi, Sandra!'

I hid in the kitchen pretending to check the roast lamb but really just taking a breather. By the time we were seated I had already noticed that Alice and Sandra weren't talking in the way they once did; something subtle had shifted between them. After that slight conversational lull which happens when people start to eat, there followed a delicious second in which I saw Oscar's unflappable confidence momentarily flap. And the person that flapped him was Sandra.

Oscar boasted, 'So, Sandra, you're in books. I think I may have an idea for a great one.'

'Is that so?' said Sandra.

Oscar said, 'I want to do for ethics in law what Stephen Hawking did for physics. Make it palatable to the layman.'

There was complete silence as everyone at the table stared at Oscar.

'Well, that pitch went well,' said Oscar, propelling his halitosis outwards in reeking waves of laughter.

'You want to write a book on ethics?' I heard myself say, and almost devolved into the little-brother role by adding, 'What a dumb idea. It's like Stalin writing about pacifism.'

'Yes, I am on the Board of Ethics and in the last meeting we agreed it might be good for our profile, and mine of course, if we took the legal black arts and showed them to the world in more transparent terms,' Oscar explained.

My nose involuntarily crinkled in Oscar's stinking slipstream, and I muttered, 'You're unbelievable, Oscar.'

'I even thought of a title, something like *Oscar's Law* or *Shaw Law*,' said Oscar.

'Or *Getting Away With Murder*,' I sneered.

'Interesting, I suppose,' said Sandra. 'I'm not sure people really care much about law unless they're having to defend themselves but we can talk a little more about it.'

'So if I was to get a deal, who writes the book?' Oscar asked, in a way that suggested the entire deal was sewn up and now it was just a question of ticking off a few minor details.

'Well, you do,' said Sandra. 'You write your own book.'

'Oh,' said Oscar, shocked. 'I, um, assumed some ghostwriter did that sort of thing. Some sort of professional would write it for me.'

Nina said, 'Ghostwriter? What is this?' and Doug explained in French what it meant and Nina placed a bejewelled hand on Doug as a friendly but rather intimate *thank you* for the explanation.*

'Well,' explained Sandra gently to Oscar, 'they do if they are terribly famous, but for you it really needs to be your words and your work. You need to write it yourself.'

---

* I had the most wonderfully naughty thought that Doug and Nina would fall in love and topple Oscar's insufferable ego with a hugely public and embarrassing affair. One can but dream.

'I have been on the BBC a few times,' said Oscar, a touch desperately.

By dessert I could see that Oscar was still slightly deflated by his run-in with Sandra. With the sphere of his belly keeping him apart from the table, he kept leaning in to swipe extra chocolates from the box, causing Nina to raise a sculpted eyebrow and warn, 'Not too much chocolate, *chéri*. Your heart can't take what your mouth desires.'

Oscar stole another chocolate and held it near his lips a moment, as if he might not eat it, but then popped it in and swallowed it as Nina once more warned, 'Easy, Oscar!'*

After dessert, as the guests sat back and awaited coffees, Oscar cornered me in the corridor, his halitosis laced with booze, and I suffered under his smell and weight as he tried to hug me and then looked at me very seriously.*1

But all he said was, 'Great night, mate, we should do this shit more often, all we do is work work work, we need to have fun together. We're brothers.'

Oscar didn't seem to notice, or care, that I didn't reply; instead he pushed me a little forward and pointed down the corridor towards Nina, who was talking to Doug. Oscar whispered, 'She's a fucking peach, that wife of mine. God, I love her to death, Frank, in ways that even poets would fail to express, I love that buxom French bird.'

'I'm not sure any poet could best that,' I said. 'Actually, Oscar, that is very sweet,' and I meant it.

Oscar winked at me and said, 'And did you notice Nina's new tits? I know you were looking. It's all right, you get brother's privilege, you can look, buddy. Just look, mind you! What tits! Went to Sweden to get them done. Aren't they brilliant? I tell you, Frank, you should get

---

* Her French accent lent the word *easy* a row of lazy sexy zzzz's – *Eezzzzy Ozzgar.*

*1 My heart sank as I thought he was about to say, 'I fucking know you've been messing with all our client contracts. You're destroying me and the firm. How could you, Frank, how could you do that? You've ruined everything, Frank, and you will go to jail for a long time for what you've done to me and everyone who works there! How could you do this to me, to Dad, to Mum, TO EVERYONE WHO LOVES YOU!'

Alice done. Just look at Nina. She's got new lips, new tits. I love it. Sex with Nina now is like fucking a different woman. Man, it's like I'm having an affair with my own wife.'

'You are truly the least charming man I know,' I said to Oscar, who must have misheard me and said, 'Thanks, mate, I appreciate you saying that,' as we both stumbled into the dining room and returned to the table, where I sat down and Oscar leered at his wife's breasts for a while before stuffing more chocolate into his gob.

'Eeezzy, Ozzgar.'

I experienced a strange moment when Alice – by now a little drunk and smiley – suddenly grinned at Oscar and said, 'So when is the firm going on to the stock market? When are Frank and I going to be rich beyond our wildest dreams?'

Oscar frowned. Even his calm countenance rippled. And I was stunned. Taking the firm to the stock market was probably the most confidential thing happening at that time. Even though I had told Alice about the weapons manufacturer, I had not told her about Oscar's plan to put Shaw&Sons on the stock market. Firstly because I didn't think it would happen but secondly because that sort of thing was top secret, to stop insider trading. I couldn't imagine how Alice would know about it. Oscar looked sheepish and I realised that he must have told her. But when did they talk?

I stared blankly at Oscar and said, 'You shouldn't have told *anyone* about that.'

Oscar regained his composure and, without looking at Alice, said, 'Well, good news is hard to hold, Frank. And it might still be happening, and yes, if it does, it'll make all of us very rich, so cheer the fuck up and let's have another drink, shall we?'

My wife got up and retreated to the kitchen, realising she had made a mistake, and I puzzled over when she and Oscar would have talked about something like this but I too was over the tipsy line and so I filed it away to discuss it with her when everyone had gone.

Nina then became the unofficial star of the evening by asking Doug all the direct questions that none of us ever dared to ask.

Her first was her best. 'Where is your wife, Doug? You did not wish to bring her?'

'I don't have a wife, I'm afraid,' replied Doug.

'No reason to be afraid,' said Nina. 'What of your girlfriend? Man like you, so clean and smart, successful, with the good looks, must have a girlfriend somewhere, or maybe you are French at heart – you have many mistresses?'

Doug smiled in a way that he obviously hoped would put Nina off this particular line of questioning.*

She was French and she wanted an answer.

So again she said, 'So, Doug? Your girlfriend?'

By now intrigue had muted the other conversations around the table, and everyone tuned into Doug and Nina.

Doug smiled and said simply, 'Well, OK, my girlfriend is called Dave and he's a lovely man who I have lived with for many years.'

Nina thought this was hysterical and shouted, 'A girlfriend called Dave. You English are so the funniest.'

I smiled at Doug, who shrugged and added, 'We are rather funny, I suppose, and I promise I'll bring my lovely wife Dave to the next dinner. He too speaks a little French, we are both terrible Francophiles.'

'Well, this is such marvellous news,' Nina said in her high voice, raising a glass to Doug. 'Gay Francophiles are my absolute favourite type of Englishmen.'

Doug raised his glass back and they both said, 'Cheers,' in unison and Doug, slightly embarrassed, said, 'Here's to faggie Francophiles everywhere. Bottoms up!' Which made Nina hoot with delight and shriek, 'Bon Dougie!'

In the wake of this small revelation other conversations re-established themselves but I stayed with Nina and Doug as they chatted away like age-old friends.

---

* But Nina was not polite and English like the rest of us; she didn't read an awkward social moment as something you had immediately to quash with humour or a brisk change in topic.

'And what is it you do?' Nina asked.

'I'm an actuary,' Doug explained.

'Oui, but what are you actually?' asked Nina.

'No, an actuary,' clarified Doug.

'Sorry, that was my attempt at a joke,' said Nina.

'No, I'm sorry,' said Doug quickly. 'That was a failure of my sense of humour.'

'Lost in translation, I think. Actuary, you're the maths man for the insurance, yes?' Nina said.

'Exactly,' said Doug.

'So reply to me this,' Nina said. 'Why do I pay more money than my fat husband for basic health insurance?'

'Ah well, a very astute question,' said Doug, as Oscar shot an ugly look at Nina. 'In insurance terms it's an unfortunate truth that women simply cost more than men.'

'Well, we are certainly a more precious commodity,' said Sandra.

'Indeed,' shrieked Nina.

'I completely agree,' said Doug.

'Even though you like the boys more than the girls,' said Nina.

'I may like being with boys but I like talking to girls more,' said Doug.

'This much I can see,' said Nina, who turned to Sandra and added, 'Why are gay men so much easier to talk to, Sandra?'

Sandra said, 'Something to do with the fact they don't want something from you.'

'Ah oui, le pussy,' said Nina.

'Le pussy!' squealed Sandra. 'Love it.'

I felt that childish flush of drunkenness as I laughed along, and looking around the table I spotted a few tipsy twinkles in people's eyes.

'Time for a cigarette, non?' said Nina, walking over to the window where she tried to determine if my wife's little white bowl – which cost a fortune and was supposed to be art – was an ashtray. My wife was already rushing off to the kitchen and she returned with a grotty lid, to which Nina, crinkling her nose in disgust, said, 'This will do.'

Watching Nina place her hip on the windowsill and smoke that cigarette, I was for a moment consumed by inappropriate fantasies. It must have been the wine mixed with that slight lull that comes after dinner when the food hits the bellies of the guests and everyone slows down, leans back, sated with wine and small talk.

Nina looked immaculate: framed by the window, jet-black hair falling sensationally, milky neckline, and a thin stream of exhaled smoke rising from her lips before being whipped apart by the wind.

I looked at Nina and my wife: Nina was made up of all the soft, voluptuous parts that my wife had worked so hard to whittle away. Nina was a positive to my wife's negative, an expression of my wife's impression, a bust of my wife's relief. Nina was rich in warmth, wit, and a certain wealth of flesh that held a man's eye. When she leaned in to tip her ash, the buttons of her blouse strained to contain the weight, and her cleavage was a fleshy exclamation mark into which I pitched myself . . .*

Doug took his apple juice and sat in a chair as Nina smoked. I pretended to listen to my wife talking about some HR issue, but really I was still eavesdropping on Nina and Doug.

'So how do you sell life insurance, Doug?' asked Nina.

'I simply sell death,' he replied. 'I look at you smoking and I say, 54 per cent more chance of dying before you're fifty.'

Nina moaned and said, 'No, Dougie! You're sucking the one pleasure I get.'

Doug said, 'Your pleasure is going to suck days off your life. Let me tell you a story. A woman. Thirty-six years old. Non-smoker. Good health. Last Tuesday, out with the office on a bonding day, waiting to take her turn on a quad bike. What happens?'

Nina replied, 'Crushed to death by the bike? I am guessing.'

'No no. Such things are for movies, Nina. No, the 36-year-old non-smoker has a stroke. Before she had even turned the bike on. Stroke!

---

* Jesus Christ. I was actually coveting my brother's wife! How horribly clichéd and fucking Freudian. Fuck Freud. And to hell with these dumb fantasies which I'd allowed to creep in. I felt repulsed at the idea of going to a place that Oscar had previously ploughed. Jesus, I was pissed.

Just like that! *Stroke!*' And Doug said *stroke* in a disturbing, almost loving, way.

'Jesus, Doug. Was she OK?' Nina asked.

'Oh, she was fine. I have her covered by the best policy money can buy. Million-pound policy. No problems. All taken care of,' said Doug.

'What a relief,' said Nina. 'She's out of the hospital yet?'

Doug smiled, 'Oh no, she's a vegetable for life.'

'Jesus,' Nina said. 'You are like doom and gloom. Monsieur Death!'

'I think the opposite,' said Doug. 'All the terrible things and sudden deaths, all the statistics remind you that you have still made it through; we, all of us here, at this very dinner, in this room, are still alive and kicking. So enjoy it before you become a statistic too.'

Nina said, 'You're a philosophical insurance man, Mr Doug.'

Doug said, 'So are you going to offer me one of those naughty cigarettes,' and this brought the wickedest smile to Nina's face as she offered Doug a cigarette.

'Are you actually going to smoke a cigarette?' I asked Doug.

'I'm a statistics man, Frank, and I know the risks and I know that there's one statistic that beats all the others which is – *you only live once, my friend*,' and he winked at me and Nina sparked his cigarette and they both cackled like schoolchildren, puffing away.

'And she's always telling me not to eat chocolates as she smokes like a chimney. I tell you, everyone just picks their organ and punishes it. Interesting evening,' said Oscar, and looked at me, whispering, 'Who knew old Doug was a bloody batty boy?'

But he said it slightly too loud and, from the way Doug flinched slightly, it was obvious that he had heard. Oscar had taken all the funny sophistication of the evening and debased it with one sentence. It was a gift of his and I watched as my wife failed to hide her disgust, stood up and started to clear the plates away.

Doug and Nina returned to the table and Doug was talking about me, pointing to me, saying, 'Frank here is the man, a clever man, who writes many of my policies.'

I blushed, warmed by the feeling of a compliment from Doug, and said, 'They're hardly rocket science.'

'Don't put yourself down, Frank,' said Doug. 'You're one of the best in the business.'

Wine and compliments were too much. My face burned with pride and I made sure not to look at Oscar, who I knew was preparing some put-down.

On cue Oscar said, 'Frank's our Contract Killer.'

'How do you mean?' asked Nina.

'He's so good at writing insurance contracts that make people think they're protected when actually they're not,' said Oscar. 'So they pay insurance all their life but the thing they die from is usually not covered. Frank makes things like life so expensive. So people die uninsured. Hence – Contract Killer. Frank's contracts kill.'

Oscar loved this and laughed but Doug looked as if he was about to say something to defend me, furious that Oscar had twisted his small compliment into an insult. Before Doug could reply, Nina did it for him, saying, 'Oh do shut up, Oscar, and use your fat mouth for what it was built for – eating chocolate.'

Oscar looked like a little boy reprimanded and I would have paid all the money in the world for a photograph of that expression.

Nina looked to see if I was OK, and I joked, 'I warned you, every-one – read your contract,' and shrugged my shoulders. 'I'm the king of confusion. Put on this earth to be obtuse.'

Bored of putting me down, Oscar turned his attention to Sandra, who I watched cower politely under what I assumed Oscar thought was a charm assault. Unfortunately, with so much alcohol in his blood, the subtext of Oscar's conversation was embarrassingly obvious.

Oscar grinned and said, 'So I've been asking around after you and people tell me you're the best commissioning editor in the biz,' the booze causing his smile to slip to a leer.

Sandra said, 'No, not at all, I'm one of many.'

'Don't be modest,' protested Oscar. 'Let's be straight:* there aren't many women in this terrible man's world who've done as well as you.'

'Actually, publishing is a female-dominated industry,' corrected Sandra.

'Look, *Sandy*, can I be honest with you?'*¹ asked Oscar. 'I love your blouse.'*²

Later in the evening we scattered to different corners of the sitting room: Oscar and Nina having a low-burning argument on the sofa about how much chocolate he had really eaten and whether he had hidden some in his pocket; Alice talking about gym training with Sandra; Sandra looking bored to death; Doug and myself outside on the small balcony playing a game we enjoyed from time to time.

Called the Fast and Famous, it involved Doug and I determining the lifespan of celebrities. Doug said, 'Look at Brad Pitt. Sure, good-looking, no denying it. But I read he's a smoker, plus he's addicted to coffee, loves it, espressos every day. Him and Clooney always drinking coffee in Italy where the coffee is illegally dosed with lethal amounts of caffeine. Plus, lots of kids, so lots of stress. And the wife, Angie. She's uptight, has problems with food, this difficult time with the mastectomy, so Brad has problems. More stress, more tension. He's coming up to his fifties. I give him fifteen years tops. Then dead.'

I laughed and, looking through the window at Oscar, blobbing on the sofa, his belly testing his shirt buttons, I whispered, 'What do you think, Doug? Oscar? How long?'

Doug smiled and, obviously remembering Oscar's mean 'batty boy' comment, he decided to play along and said, 'Well, overweight, that cuts his years considerably, and all that dairy he pours into his veins, he has a Shaw heart, which is a short heart, as your dad always

---

*   Let's be obscure.
*1 Can I lie to you?
*2 I love your tits.

said, and a French wife, lots of passion but lots of pain, that's enough to keep any man's heart racing. Oscar's a time bomb. He could really go at any minute.'

Not long after that Oscar and Nina, when their argument started to get too loud for a public setting, made a quick exit. I was cleaning up but stopped at the kitchen door when I heard Sandra hissing at my wife, 'You can't do it again, Alice. I refuse to be a part of any book in which you exploit that poor man. Frank has done nothing but help you and that book . . .'

'Get off your high horse,' my wife snapped. 'What I did was fine, Frank doesn't mind at all. He supports me.'

'He says that, but he's just too nice and loves you too much to tell you the truth. You really gutted that man, you embarrassed him by using so much of him in that book,' said Sandra. 'And I for one have had enough of your ambition and we will not be taking on your next book. I love you but this awful business relationship is ruining our friendship so let's end it and just be friends again.'

I waited for my wife to concede but she said, 'Fine, I'll pitch it to another publisher.'

Sandra said, 'Come on, Alice, don't be like that, don't let this come between us.'

My wife said, 'OK, sorry, I'm just pissed off with you. There, I've said it.'

I made a noise and they both spun around and smiled in the way that people do when they are caught talking about you.

'You girls OK?' I asked.

'Great,' said Sandra, loud and unconvincing. 'But so tired I really have to go.'

She gave my wife an awkward hug, which was to be their last, and I took Sandra to the door and she gave me one of her full generous hugs and kissed me on the lips, saying, 'Take care and call me this week, we should have a coffee or something, you and me.'

This was an odd suggestion, certainly not something we had ever done in the past, not without Alice there – as she was really Sandra's friend – but I smiled and said, 'Yes, that's actually a good idea. Let's do that, Sandra. Call me. You know what you and I . . .'

But before I became even more forthright and rambling on the subject of a coffee with Sandra, Doug came and said, 'You're east too, aren't you, Sandra? I can drive you home if you want. You can tell me all about the latest books I should be reading.'

Sandra grabbed Doug's arm and they turned to leave, but Doug stopped just before that and said to me, 'This has been a fun evening, Frank. We should do it again soon.'

TERMS & CONDITIONS OF DARES

Real dares contain real dangers.

Oscar, Malcolm and I used to play together. Never happily and never without a high risk of incident but we were brothers and we still spent a lot of time being boys and being, not friends exactly, but, well, being brothers, I suppose.

Not far from our house was a public park full of things that boys loved: trees to climb, bushes to build dens in, hills to roll down or sleigh down in the winter. There was a safe acre or two of park where paths were cleared and flat, and people would walk their children, and boys played football. And then there was a large area where the park sloped away and dipped into a rambling forest, which grew thick and dark pretty quickly and was riddled with long dangerous drops and high hills – this was where we preferred to play. Far more interesting, forbidden and dangerous. For the most part we were safe; we played there for many years and the most dangerous thing we ever did was tie swinging ropes to the trees so we could fly over the shallow river and back again, squealing and daring each other to swing faster and further.

More than any other place in the world, that forest was where we defined our limits and our personalities. Oscar as the oldest, and most annoying, was in the habit of taking a perfectly lovely time – usually when Malc and I were quietly fishing in the stream – and transforming it into a tense test of brotherhood.

Oscar was the Master of Dares. Most of them were ridiculous, and Malc and I learned to ignore them. But Oscar had one recurrent one that he simply wouldn't let go, and it was a dare in its purest sense – an utterly futile task that took considerable courage.

Oscar even had a name for it – *the Leap of Faith.*

It was simply a jump, a frankly impossible jump, over a ravine.

It was just far enough that through the blurred eyes of bravery you might have thought you could make it, but the drop down the ravine was steep and jagged, with a childish nightmare quality to it. I assumed for many years that my young imagination had filled in a fairly harmless shallow ravine with spikes, depth and jagged ridges, but in fact, returning to it as an adult, I was struck by how frightening it remained. It was a genuinely dangerous gap which, even fully grown, I would think twice about leaping.

Oscar again and again brought it up – 'Do you dare take the Leap of Faith?' he would taunt.

And each time he would up the stakes, offering more and more to get one of us to try it – 'I'll give you my bike, I'll give you all my albums, I'll tidy your room for a month.'

And every time I'd shrug and say, 'No way,' and Malc would say, 'Fuck that shit.'

I can't remember how old we were when Oscar finally took the plunge but maybe Oscar was around fifteen, I was thirteen and Malc was twelve.*

So this time Malc changed his normal script and instead of saying, *Fuck this shit*, he said, 'Why don't you show us how it's done, Oscar?'

Oscar was a little stunned but said, 'Well, OK, what's on the table?'

Malc thought for a second and then said, 'I'll do all your homework for a month.'

Malc was by far the smartest and Oscar the dimmest, so this offer was pure gold.

Oscar looked at us both, then at the gap, and said, 'You have yourself a deal, Malc.'

What followed was a lot of limbering up and Oscar grunting and stretching to prepare; he walked back and forth pacing out the run-up to get it just right, by which time I was saying, 'Let's forget this, this isn't a good idea, this is bad, let's go home,' but Malc remained unemotional and ready to watch Oscar finally put his money where his mouth was.

---

* Although my memory was returning, it was still not refined enough to detail chronology with any real accuracy. But I remember that we were young enough to have that dangerous imbalance of bravery and stupidity.

Oscar stood ready to jump, and he looked at us and said, 'So, Malc, you do my homework for a month if I make it.'

'Deal,' said Malc.

'And what if I don't make it?' said Oscar.

'Then you won't ever have to do homework again,' said Malc.

Oscar smiled at this dark joke and said, 'Very true, very true.'

Malc added, 'We'll call you an ambulance and if we never find your body we will divide your earthly possessions evenly between us.'

'Har, har, har,' said Oscar with a fake laugh, then looked towards the gap, his face tense, his body shaking lightly.

Even back then Oscar had a little extra weight but he was a fit rugby player and for a moment I thought he might just make the jump. It wasn't until he started running that I knew this wasn't going to end well, he wasn't a natural runner, he plodded, and the closer he got to the edge the harder my heart beat. Without knowing it I had stopped breathing and the sounds of the forest pressed in on me – the high pitch of the birds mixed with the earthy rustling of the forest floor – then his body left the earth, but it didn't leave it enough, not nearly enough; like a badly timed long-jumper Oscar two-stepped just at the end, adjusted too late, cutting the speed out of him, blunting his momentum, and he plunged out of sight like a dumb stone. If it wasn't so tense it would have been funny; he didn't leap, he just fell, and I had still not taken a breath by the time I made it to the edge, with Malc by my side, and when we looked over there was nothing there but the river quietly running below like a silver ribbon.

'Oscar!' I screamed and Oscar replied, 'Calm down, Frank,' and there he was, right under us, so close he was hidden underneath us, standing on a small ledge before the final drop, which he had intentionally jumped to and was holding on to some branches so he didn't tip off the ledge into the ravine. It was a trick – he never intended to jump, he knew about the small ledge, the two-step was part of the ploy, and I was relieved and furious.

'You two look fucking terrified,' he said, and he let out that horrible laugh that he saved for moments like this, for times when he had conned us into caring for him.

'You two are a sight. Did you really think I'd try that jump? No way, no one can make that jump.'

'You bastard,' whispered Malc and I could hear how stressed he was too.

After the anger passed I was just relieved, happy not to be sprinting home to call an ambulance to find my dead brother lying buckled like a doll at the bottom of the gap. Malc stormed off and I stretched my hand down to help Oscar back up. Oscar pretended to pull me down with him but he could tell from my pale face that he had taken his joke far enough. Back on the edge he thumped my shoulder and said, 'Thanks, buddy, don't look so worried. I was never going to risk that jump. I'm not crazy.'

I said, 'Let go of me, creep. I thought you were dead.'

By now Malc should have been out of sight, sulking off in the distance, storming off home, but he was actually coming back towards us, in fact he was coming back fast, jogging first then running, sprinting, and his expression was terrible to see.

On his face was described a level of commitment that Oscar could only fake for short periods and that I would never know. Unlike Oscar, Malc was completely committed. I could see from his expression that there was not a molecule in his body that wasn't in accord, not one rogue cell thinking, *Hang on a minute, we might not make this.*

His face was staunch, but it was also scared, as if death himself was slicing at Malc's fast-moving heels. Where Oscar was a lumbering rugby lout, Malc was built to run, slim, unencumbered by fat, his limbs long and elegant but strong enough to pump and push his streamlined body through wind and gravity and to hit speeds that Oscar and I – even as older brothers – could never attain, and just at the moment – when I was going to step in front of Malc to stop him – I saw his face, no longer scared but calm, as if the jump was done, as if the impossible was already achieved and in the past, the face of a boy relaxing at home, but his body remained taut and fast as he zipped past us and took off, not vertically, he knew he couldn't make this jump leaping from feet to feet – he took off horizontally – he knew he had to use all his speed but also every inch of his body – his length – if he was to stand a chance of surviving this jump, of making it, he actually went off hands first like fucking Superman, and to this day I don't know how he technically did it – it's incredibly hard to leap forward from a sprint to a hands-first stretch but he did it – and Oscar and I both watched as he appeared to lay flat in the air, shooting out, suspended over his own certain death – physics and reality pausing to allow Malc access to the impossible – somehow his body travelled far and fast enough that he awkwardly but spectacularly hit the other side, his stretched fingers hitting the dirt of the distant bank and tightening like hooks to cling on as his body caught up, falling and slamming unceremoniously flat against the bank and causing Malc to release a scream as he tried with all his might to scramble up the lip – reality biting back and gravity's heavy hands tugging at his ankles, dragging him into her deadly arms – but with animal panic he tore long lines out of the mud, until he finally gained purchase, a proper hold of a tree root, then he was up, but not standing yet, just lying flat on his belly, panting, taking in the fact that he almost died, and slowly he got to his knees then his feet, and turned to us with a smile. I screamed over the gap, 'You fucking did it, Malcy,' and even Oscar shouted, 'You crazy fuck, you made the Leap of Faith.'

Then Malc looked at his hand, screamed in pain and buckled to his knees.

I ran around the ravine, trying to get to Malc, who by the time I arrived was standing again and smiling, and I assumed it was some sort of joke.

I said, 'Fuck, are you OK, Malc? That was unbelievably fucking amazing, how did you do that?'

'I just took all that anger at Oscar tricking us and I used it to fucking jump,' said Malc. 'But I hit the bank funny and I've a bit of a problem,' and he showed me his left hand.

The little finger on his left hand was so twisted that it looked like a snapped parsnip; it had that grey texture to it and it was bent right back at a grotesque – seemingly impossible – angle and I saw that it had started to swell and the grey was darkening to a blood-purple.

By the time Oscar lumbered over, Malc's finger was huge with swelling and Oscar took one look and just about passed out, folding to the floor like a girl and muttering, 'That's completely disgusting, I think I'm going . . . to spew.'

I didn't have a problem with it, I was fascinated, and I gently took Malc's hand and said, 'I think you've done some serious damage here, Malc.'

Wild with adrenaline and success, Malc said, 'It was worth it.'

Oscar got back to his feet but avoided looking at the snapped finger, and said the only nice thing that I can ever remember him saying to Malc, 'That was the most incredible thing I have ever seen in my whole fucking life.'

Oscar's tune would change but, for a moment, all three of us stood around and took in the awe and amazement of what had happened, of what Malc had just done.

We all looked back across the yawning gap of the ravine and the vertiginous plunge below and without saying anything we started to walk home with Malc cradling his left hand in his right.

We stayed silent and happy all the way home and it wasn't until my mother saw the finger and freaked out with, 'What the hell have you done?' that our tight ranks were split and Oscar stood away from Malc and me, and said, 'It was Malc's idea, he wanted to jump this ridiculous gap and I begged him not to but you can't tell him and . . .'

Malc and I both looked at Oscar with that melting laser glare that teenage boys specialise in. Our mother drove us to the hospital where the doctor explained, 'Nerve damage is really extensive, you have torn everything in there and it's really only the skin that's keeping it on. Now you can keep it on there but it will just be cosmetic, it won't work, we will crack it back into shape but I think you have broken it for ever. We can amputate it if you would prefer but it's your choice. We can just take it off at the knuckle, nothing too extreme, and nothing that will affect your life too detrimentally.'

Malc talked to Mum and then was taken away.

Next time we saw Malc he told us how they literally snapped the finger back into place, with one confident crack.

Malc didn't have tear tracks on his face; he seemed placid throughout, still riding on the experience of that stupid-wonderful thing he'd done.

Today I look back at that moment and – tainted with adult judgment – I think, *That was a ridiculous risk for a young man to take, what a waste that could have been. To risk your precious life for a stupid dare!**

Malc, after much debate with our crying mother, made the decision to cut it off, from the knuckle, telling the doctor he didn't want anything on him that didn't work. That made my mum cry harder than ever and she begged him to keep it. In a very basic way Mum had made that little bit of finger and she had a natural sense of propriety about it. She even tried to call our dad, who was on a work trip in Europe, in order to get him to tell Malc not to cut it off – even Dad would not have changed Malc's mind, though, I knew that; I knew Malc had a strength of conviction that could defy even the might of our all-powerful dad. Malc never seemed to mind, it was cut off and that was that; he just made a joke about giving up flute.

After the surgery we all took a look at the bandaged stump and with Mum in the room Oscar played older brother, telling Malc off to win points with Mum, 'That was a crazy thing you did, Malc, very irresponsible; lucky Dad's on a business trip or he'd be very upset.'

---

* But, more importantly, I remembered what I really felt back then, as a kid. I remembered how pure my heart was; there was nothing sensible in my reaction, nothing judgmental, I just looked at Malc with the deepest clearest admiration and I thought, *My younger brother is made of something special, something I don't have and can't fathom, he is a brave hero and I love him for it.*

Mum said, 'Oscar's right, Malc, you could have lost more than your finger,' and she burst into tears, unable to keep reprimanding him, and hugged Malc to her chest until she calmed down, and Malc said, 'I'm fine, Mum, I know what I'm doing, you don't need to worry about me, honestly.'

Mum smiled at Malc and touched his cheek with the back of her hand in a way that I absolutely knew caused both Oscar and I simultaneously to think, *She never touches us quite like that.**

Mum left us boys in the room for a moment to go talk to the doctor.

Oscar said, 'You prick, Malc.'

Malc looked at Oscar: he stared at him so hard that Oscar broke the stare and looked to the linoleum floor.

Malc waited, his eyes unmoving, trained at the spot where Oscar's eyes would return when he looked up again.

Oscar's eyes returned and Malc said, 'You didn't make it Oscar. You made a joke of it. You went for a trick, not the real thing. You failed. But get this: no matter how many brownie points you try and score, no matter how much you lie to Mum and Dad, always remember that I did it, I actually made it, I did something you could never do, Oscar, and no matter what happens – I will always have done it.'

Oscar tried to think of a reply but I knew that Malc had him; I knew Malc had shaken him. It was the only time I had seen Oscar speechless and defeated.

For years after that if Oscar ever stepped out of line or lied or did anything wrong, Malc would catch Oscar's eye and, keeping his hand low – so that Mum or Dad didn't notice if they were in the room – Malc would point at Oscar with the stub of his finger as if to say, *Don't forget I had you, Oscar, I am braver than you can ever dream.*

---

* Mum, like me, had a special soft spot for Malc, always did; he just seemed different to the rest of the family. He suffered none of the repression and uncertainty that we all did; he was his own man. Even as a boy, he was his own man.

And as much as Oscar tried to shrug it off, I could see that it always freaked him out, it got to him, it kept him in his place. With young boys, especially brothers, before money, women, cars, jobs, before objects and people become ego-currency, there was really only one currency that we traded in and that was courage.

From that day on Oscar never regained his bullying grip. Malc had shifted things too far and Oscar would forever fear Malc's courage and commitment as much as I respected them.*

---

* Yes, I did ask Malc if I could keep his little finger and, yes, I did – in a Colman's mustard jar.

TERMS & CONDITIONS
OF DRAGONS

I've been assured that they are not, in fact, real.

'You've not touched your cappuccino,' said Doug.

'I prefer it when it's stone cold.'

'Fair enough,' said Doug, who I could see was struggling with the fact that his immaculate office now stank of bacon and his desk was littered with wrappers and cups.

I started to clean it all up but Doug said, 'No, no, don't worry about that, you just relax and tell me this. What exactly do you recall about your little episode?'

I thought for a moment and then said the only thing I knew for sure.

'All I remember was a man with ugly ears telling me about dragons.'

CLAUSE 2.3

MY LITTLE EPISODE*

TERMS & CONDITIONS OF EPISODES

You don't realise until you're out of one that you were in one.

---

*   *Little episode:* That's what they call my massive nervous breakdown.

From: fuckthis@hotmail.com
To: franklynmydear@hotmail.com
Subject: Suspicious Molar and Phantom Pinkie

Frank – hi!

Istanbul: saw a tooth of Mohammed the prophet.

Very unconvincing.

Love and enamel,
Malc

PS Also, do you still have my pinkie finger somewhere? Because my 'phantom pinkie' finger is itching like a motherfucker. There is nothing there but I can still feel it twitching and itching as if my little finger is completely intact. *Freakiest thing.* Anyway, please can you dig out my pinkie and give it an itch for me? Much appreciated, brother.

TERMS & CONDITIONS OF BELIEF

When you start to lose your mind, you find that
deciding what you believe is real and what is
not really forms the crux of the matter.

The day of my *little episode* started like any other. The only thing that distinguished the day was that I started to think about my parents.

Don't believe a word of it. That was Dad's philosophy. Some people are believers, some are sceptics. My dad was the sceptic's sceptic. If a fact sounded even slightly suspicious, he dismissed it. If you said, *Camels have three eyelids*, he'd say, *Don't believe it.* Even if you tested him with facts like, *Hey, Dad, they cloned a sheep*, he'd shout, *Rubbish!*

He didn't believe anything. It was his defence mechanism against everything. My dad was the ultimate lawyer. Unless my dad had personally overseen the contract to something, he wasn't completely convinced it existed. Written contracts were his only truth.

Whereas Mum, God bless her, believed the lot. She believed everything, no need for contracts or proof. A pure believer. She loved the silly facts that Dad deplored. She'd say, *Did you know the average person swallows a quart of snot a day?* Or if someone bullied me, she'd pick a fact to cheer me up: *Don't worry, Marilyn Monroe had twelve toes!*

Sometimes she'd randomly shout facts as I was leaving the house, *There's cyanide in apple pips, Frank!*

A small warning to keep me alert.

Watching them watch television was fun. A presenter would say, *And research suggests the average TV remote control is home to ten billion bacteria.*

As Dad mumbled, *What rubbish*, Mum would shout, *Isn't that amazing!*

Somehow, our family housed these opposing forces of belief and disbelief. I was cursed with a little of both, my genes cleaved in two, constantly confused.

As I age I bend more to my father's scepticism but from time to time my mother's amazement overpowers me. One thing I do believe is that a healthy sense of disbelief keeps you alive longer. Dad survived Mum by a few years. Mum died a while ago but not before her illness turned her facts a little sour – *Sharks are immune to cancer, Frank. Lucky bastards. When I die my toenails will keep growing. Which means even if my soul doesn't live on, my toenails will.*

I was there when Mum died, at the shiny white hospice. Dad – who'd been standing guard at her bedside for weeks – had popped home and it was then that she passed away.

I think Mum was too embarrassed to die in front of Dad; she was proud like that.

A heart beats a hundred thousand times a day. Fact. *They all stop.* Fact. The terms of your body's condition are written in blood, coded in the fine print of your DNA.

When I called Dad to tell him Mum had died, he whispered, 'I don't believe it.'

'She didn't feel any pain at the end, Dad. The doctors assured me of that.'

We had just had the hardest year of our life, as my mother, with each passing day, died a little more and my dad and brothers all tried to cope without the one person who usually got us through the tough times. In that hard year there had been few nice moments between us.

So I was pleased when Dad said, 'Thanks, Frank. You've been brave during all of this, thank you.'

It was the nicest thing he'd said to me in a long time.

Had I put the phone down then, it would have been a lovely bitter-sweet moment.

Unfortunately I held on, maybe hoping for something else, greedy for more.

Then he said, 'I'm on my way. I need to look over her death certificate and ensure it's all in order.'*

---

* That was Dad. Even death required the correct paperwork.

TERMS & CONDITIONS
OF SEEKING HELP

It was my wife's idea.

My wife said I seemed lost and some spiritual guidance might help. I was surprised by how perceptive she was. I put this down to her consultancy training. They teach you to notice things in consultancy training. Like when your husband starts to cry uncontrollably over his dinner for no reason. That means something's wrong.

My wife's company approaches business holistically. She says her consultancy is more than just profits and losses, numbers on a balance sheet; she believes that even spiritual elements have to be taken into account when making business decisions. Her boss Valencia had been to see a spiritualist, hence my wife's sudden interest in it. I imagine my wife's 'spiritual' office to be draped in white veils with men and women wafting from one pale area to another. In fact her office is the same as mine. Their interior designer studied at the same kindergarten school of design. Obnoxiously coloured walls, one room with a sunken area full of rubber balls printed with inspirational words. Ridiculously named meeting rooms – *Earth*, *Wind*, *Fire*, *Inspiration* and *Paradigm*. It's like a Disney office filled with people dressed in black suits; a sort of sick playschool populated by funeral directors.

I think mediums and spirituality are complete rubbish. (I also, with no apparent sense of contradiction, think mediums and spirituality are real.) Different day, different belief. Some days I think like Dad and believe nothing; some days like Mum and believe the lot.

Desperate, and quickly running out of options, I quietly agreed to my wife's suggestion. What I knew for sure was that I had seen a doctor recently who wanted to prescribe me Prozac. After I read the side effects I decided that I'd rather be depressed.*

---

* Drugs have terms and conditions – side effects are often worse than effects.

So I was willing to try something a little different. Hence the fact that the day of my little episode began with me seeking out a medium. My wife assured me this particular medium was the most famous one around. He had done a lot of celebrities and he was the 'must-go-to guy for all things spiritual'.*

---

* That's how she talked these days – *must-go-to guy*.

TERMS & CONDITIONS OF MEDIUMS

They know too much.

I'd been talking to Greg for ten minutes before I noticed his ears. Once noticed, they were all I saw: his swollen tumorous ears.

Seeing I was staring, Greg explained, 'I played rugby. Semi-professional.'

'Seems sort of strange a man tuned into the delicate world of spirits has such, um, mangled ears,' I said.

'You sound disappointed. In me, I mean.'

I was. Greg wasn't living up to his terms. For a start his name was lame. *Greg.* Not very spiritual. As a medium to the stars, Greg should have been called *Shine* or *Rainbow*. Greg should really have been a stoned hippie half-swallowed by a beanbag. Greg wasn't any of these things. He was a thick-set rugby player in ironed jeans. His flat was an exclusive property. There were no crystals, love beads, not even a Che Guevara poster. The guy wasn't even trying. When things aren't according to the terms and conditions, I get nervous. I take after my dad in that respect.*

'Ready?' Greg asked.

I braced myself for a wash of vagaries, for all the chanting, eyeball rolling and silly voices. So when Greg didn't close his eyes or talk in tongues I was disappointed. He just said, 'Your dad's Edward Shaw, a successful corporate lawyer. Now dead.'

'Google could tell me that,' I said, with the irritating smugness of a sceptic disproving something.

'OK, I see,' said Greg with a weary smile.

Feeling bad about being smug, I softened it by adding, 'Although I'll give you points for that because I've literally spent all morning thinking about my mum and dad.'

'Good. And your brother is Oscar Shaw; he has a huge influence over your life.'

---

* I need people to play their part, to fulfil the contractual obligations of their character.

Before I could stop myself, I defensively said, 'Again, he's my boss and Google, or even our company website, could tell you that, so yes, you're right but no, I'm not impressed.'

'Well, then, let's see if I can impress you, shall I?' said Greg archly. 'For reasons that even you're not sure about you have started to graffiti public property. Worse still, you're trying to sabotage your brother and your own business, and your father's business, by writing rubbish on very important arms and drugs contracts. You're losing your way, Frank. You're completely and utterly lost in the emptiness of your own life, set adrift with no ability to connect to those you once loved. Oh, and your wife's a total bitch.'

If I hadn't already been sitting, I'd probably have passed out. I felt like a boxer who'd been sucker-punched by the referee. Dazed and queasy, I leaned low so that my head almost rested on my knees.

How could Greg possibly know about the graffiti, about the contract tampering?

My brain glowed hot with confusion. There was no way this guy could know this about me.

No one, not a soul knew, about my corporate graffiti – that was my dirty little secret.

I tried to figure out how Greg could possibly know this.

For a moment, I thought like my mother: *Maybe there are people who can hear spirits. I don't know everything, why should I have to be able to explain everything away, why can't there be spirits and things I simply don't understand?**

---

* *Because* – I heard myself respond in the reasoning tone of my father – *I'm an intelligent man who runs his life along a spine of explanation. I need it to stand up straight in the morning, to function, not to just lie around flaccid, freaking out that the universe is an unexplainable mess full of gossiping dead people.*

TERMS & CONDITIONS OF DENIAL

*Denial is a treadmill – you can run for
ever but you'll never escape.*

'You OK?' asked Greg.

'Fine,' I lied, draining my face of any expression, hoping it would make me look more in control.

'Gosh, you've gone very pale,' said Greg. 'I'll make some tea.'

'How could you possibly know about the contracts?' I asked. 'No one knows.'

'I hear things,' he said casually. He was so nonchalant; bored of plundering people's secrets.

'Who from?' I asked.

'Your dad,' he said.

Oh dear. The thought of my father knowing I was tampering with sacred legal contracts brought a tear to my eye. The idea of my dead dad knowing I was trying to bring down a company he – and *his* father – spent generations building. I started to sob. He would be so disappointed in me and my unforgivable, intolerable behaviour.

'Want me to carry on?' Greg asked.

'Prefer if you didn't,' I said.

'Fair enough. But I'll say this much. Your wife's unhappy. Alice. Right? Unhappy. You knew that already, though. Right?'

'No,' I lied.*

'Come on.'

'Yes, yes, OK, fine, I guess I did.'

We fell into silence again. I was sort of angry. He was sort of bored.

'Life is a disappointment to you. You're haunted by an incident in which you didn't help a poor old man who was assaulted. You have an ethical problem working for an arms manufacturer and your brother's

---

* Keep denying – keep running.

attempt to put the firm on the stock market is the straw that broke the—'

'OK! OK! Stop right there, you've impressed me, all right, Greg, I believe.'

'Fair enough,' said Greg. 'Just wanted to make sure I impressed you.'

We slumped into another silence and Greg sighed, then got up, and popped on the kettle. He stared at it for a moment then said, 'Funny thing about kettles. I used to tell my son a dragon lived in the kettle and released this jet of steam to signal when the water was boiled.'

When the boiling water grumbled Greg poured it, saying, 'It was a cute story until I caught him one morning dismantling the kettle. He'd broken it into pieces, literally unscrewed it all, then hammered the crap out of it. When I asked what he was doing, he said, *Looking for the dragon, Dad.* He was suspicious of me for a long time after that. Milk and sugar?'

'Maybe something a little stronger than tea.'

Greg abandoned the tea and poured two thick shots of Scotch.

'Cheers,' he said.

Deep in thought, I took my drink and walked over to a telescope* at the window.

Greg's telescope was adhering to its terms. It wasn't pointed heavenwards awaiting the glory of the cosmos. I looked through it and it was pointed into someone's bedroom. It seems that even the spiritual like to see a naked bottom.

I swallowed my Scotch and asked, 'Is she really that unhappy?'

'Who?'

'My wife.'

'Don't need a medium to tell you that.'

'True,' I said.

---

* Telescopes have terms. Telescopic terms. They're never used to observe stars; they're always used to spy on neighbours – to spot a little faraway flesh.

When Greg went to the bathroom I did something completely out of character. I mean, I couldn't even believe it as I was actually doing it. I took Greg's bottle of Scotch – which turned out to be the same brand that I always bought – shoved it under my arm, and walked out of the house.

The terms of the ego are universal. Deep down we all cradle the illusion we're so wonderfully mysterious – our profound self tucked deep in the core of an impenetrable labyrinth – but a few minutes with Greg made me feel like one of my anatomical figurines, my insides outside, not even a thin skin to cover my bright, embarrassed self.*

---

*   Run for your fucking life.

TERMS & CONDITIONS
OF FACING FACTS

Rewriting your own terms and conditions is hard to do.

They're hardwired into your brain. It's much easier to stick to your terms and deny any conditions that contradict them. So I started to run, I started to deny, I started creating clauses and caveats to make sense of the nonsense. I started to think like Dad. I started to disbelieve anything that was inconvenient.

Here's how I did it. I thought: this is a big city, but the people I mix with comprise a small town really, more a village-worth of people. Greg might be less a spirit-whisperer and more of a man who brushes against the pollen of hearsay crossing from clique to clique; in other words – he's just a nosy gossip. Yes, this was all easily rationalised. Alice must have told people she was unhappy. In fact, I thought, she recommended this man, so she probably told him directly that I used to be brilliant but was now a little less than average. She probably just sat there telling Greg I was a huge disappointment to her. She would also have told him about the mugging and the arms manufacturer. That was that. Rationalised. Denied.

But! The tampering of contracts. That was a deep secret – the deepest kind – the kind with the darkest consequences. That was something inside, inside me. That was a real secret. That was a problem. How could he know that? No soul knew that one. How could I rationalise that? How could I run from that one? Alcohol seemed the only solution. I sat in the car and guzzled the whisky from the bottle.*

---

* Unlike most other things in life, the terms of booze are ever-changing and fluid, a contract written in Etch-A-Sketch. One good shake is all it takes to wipe it clean. I suddenly felt incredibly tired and wished I could lay my head back and have a sleep but my body had recently dispensed of sleep, as if it was some sort of disproved theory, something we no longer needed, like communism or shoulder pads.

I sat there trying to calm down as my body started to freak out.

I wasn't entirely sure of it, and I had spent most of the morning trying to ignore it, but I was gradually becoming convinced that I was being followed around by a bird.*

---

* Not a hawk or a raven or anything ominous, Stephen King-like, just a little sparrow, a brown bird flitting from here to there. I had noticed it when I left the flat. I saw what I assumed was another one later at the car park – which was odd as the car park is underground; now here it was again, flitting around my car.

TERMS & CONDITIONS
OF DEAD VOICES

Dead people really shouldn't keep talking.

I waved the pesky bird away and thumped the windscreen to get it to fly off. It just sat there, cocky as can be, and then I thought I heard something odd. I ignored it and kept trying to get the bird to bugger off, switching the windscreen wipers on to scare it. I heard that something again.* This time I stopped and listened very carefully. I checked that the radio wasn't on. Then something strange happened. I sat still for a long time trying to take it in.

I thought I'd heard my dad.*[1]

I listened. There it was again. Slight, as if shouting from a distance. It was a voice that I still carried in my head every day, the tough, assured accent of a well-educated confident man. He spoke in the way that people on the BBC used to speak before they introduced lots of regional accents. He spoke with clipped Received Pronunciation.

It often sprang unexpectedly out of my muddled internal jukebox, his voice, usually in the form of some advice I was ignoring at that exact moment: *Never, never, sign anything unless you have read it and understood every word, every nuance, every single effect of that contract.*

But to hear his voice *outside* my head . . .

He said, *Hi, Frank.*

Just like that.

Hi, Frank.

It brought an emotional lump to my throat. I leaned against the steering wheel and tried to listen. But I didn't hear any more voices. For a moment I seriously considered that Greg had given me a hallucinogen, spiked my drink. In a delirious moment I convinced myself that

---

* It couldn't be.

*[1] Now – just to emphasise how odd this was – please keep in mind that my dad was long dead.

maybe the whole episode, this entire day, with the spirits and the sparrow, Greg's knowledge of me, all of it was a delirious trip.

A man's word is worth nothing. Get it on paper, Frank. Ink is binding. Ink binds.

That was my dad again.

It sounded like it was coming from Greg's flat. I thought I saw Greg walk past his window. I crept back to his door and peeked through the letterbox. There was just an empty corridor, which looked different to how I remembered. I'm not sure what I expected to see. Maybe my dead dad standing there chatting away to Greg. When I stepped back I realised I was not even at the correct door. I was pretty sure that Greg's door was a red wooden door with a silver number ten on it – but this was a blue door with a different number. I jogged down the street looking for Greg's red door but all the doors were blue and none of them had the number ten. I stopped to catch my breath and shook my head in that same pointless way that you shake or gently bash your phone when it's malfunctioning.

This was ludicrous.

The explanation was simple: I was just half blasted on whisky and shock.

That was all.

Fact.

I sagged with the exhaustion.

I wasn't fit enough for all this denial.*

---

*   Run, run and run some more.

TERMS & CONDITIONS
OF REVELATION

It's not just a chapter in the Bible.

I rang my wife. I realised that I had picked up her phone by accident that morning so I scrolled down the list and called my number, hoping she had picked up my phone by accident.

At first I was going to tell her everything, explain about Greg, confess about the contract tampering, tell her about the bird that was following me, beg her for help, and tell her I was falling apart, but something held me back.

'Hi, Alice,' I said.

'Frank, where the hell are you?' she asked.

'I'm with Greg, the medium you sent me to,' I said.

'What're you on about, Frank? I woke up this morning and you'd disappeared.'

'Don't you remember you sent me to see the guy, the must-go-to guy for all things spiritual,' I said, and – as I waited an eternity for the reply – I felt the world slip a little further away. (I suddenly realised that I had absolutely no recollection of leaving the house this morning or driving here.)

'I don't know any mediums,' she said.

'I think something might be wrong, something might be wrong with me, love, I think something might be happening to me.'

She said, 'Sorry, Frank, can we talk later, I'm literally swamped with deliverables.'

Swamped with deliverables. *

'What does that mean?' I asked.

'It means I'm bloody busy,' she said.

'I was just calling to say . . .' I realised at that moment that I couldn't tell her about hearing my father's voice. 'I'm just so confused,' I confessed.

---

*   What *does* that mean?

'You sound confused, Frank,' she said. Wonderfully perceptive woman. That training again. I waited for her to tell me everything would be all right, I desperately waited for reassurance. She said nothing – and in the long pause that followed I heard a Spanish voice in the phone static shouting – '*Qué?*' Must have been a crossed line.

I said, 'Hey, Alice, if Oscar was a disciple he'd be Judas.'

I really hoped she would joke along with me, try and trump me; I wanted her to play the game we always played, I wanted us to connect, even if it was just over hating Oscar.

With my grip slipping, I needed to gain purchase on something – *anything.*

My wife finally said, 'I really have to go, Frank.'

Before I said goodbye, Alice said, 'You have my phone, Frank, and I have yours. Can you drop mine back? I really need to check my messages. I'm waiting for an important one from Valencia. In fact, thinking about it, if Valencia calls, can you not answer? She'll be annoyed I don't have my phone, she'll think it unprofessional. Don't answer if Valencia calls. Got that?'

I was losing my mind and all my wife was worried about was how her boss would react to the fact she didn't have her mobile phone on her.

I said, 'Fine,' but she'd already cut me off.

I don't know how much time passed – seconds, minutes, possibly an hour – as I ransacked my brain to find any memory of how I left the house, how I drove to Greg's house or why Greg's door had inexplicably vanished – when my wife's phone vibrated and the word *Valencia* appeared on the screen.

I answered it, and this is what I heard – 'Fancy a fuck?'

Fancy a fuck!

It was Oscar. Oscar was on the phone asking for a fuck.

He asked again, 'Fancy a fuck?'

Why is Oscar asking me for a fuck? And why, when Oscar called, did the name *Valencia* appear on my phone? Then I remembered. It wasn't my phone, it was Alice's phone, and I thought, *What's Oscar doing asking Alice for a fuck?*

It takes eight minutes for sunlight to travel ninety-five million miles to earth. That was how this realisation hit me. *Oscar and Alice?* Like something moving at incredible, unimaginable speed but still somehow taking quite a bit of time to actually arrive. *Oscar and Alice sleeping together?* First the idea hit me. I couldn't absorb it. It was ridiculous. Unbelievable. *My wife and brother fucking?* Epiphanies don't come wrapped in dramatic moments like the movies. You're not sitting on the edge of your seat, sunlight striking you at an interesting angle, a deep meaningful soundtrack throbbing. No. Epiphanies arrive with zero fanfare and are all the worse for their lack of frills. They just happen when you're sitting in your car on a dull street with a cocky sparrow flitting about. *Oscar and Alice?*

But as the realisation sank below the shiny surface of logic into the more murky waters of doubt, I could see that it was less fantastical than it sounded. I switched the phone off as Oscar was saying, 'Alice, you there, can you hear me, these fucking phones are . . .'

Could that really happen? *Alice and Oscar?* Behind my back?

A small voice in my head kept patiently answering *yes* to each question.

Was I so stupid that I didn't see this coming?*

Isn't this the stuff of Greek tragedies, or worse, of daytime soap operas?*¹

Have I been a total, complete and utter idiot?*²

I was to realise later that that is the ultimate shame of an affair such as this, of being cuckolded. The terms and conditions of being cuckolded are tantrically slow in being uncovered – they're only ever truly revealed over a long, extended and painful period of time, like the

---

*   Yes.

*¹ Yes and yes.

*² Yes, yes and thrice yes!

exposure of an incredibly slow Polaroid. But, although slow to arrive, their final mark is an indelible tattoo that you will never rub clean.*

But that was all to come. At that moment, as I sat there, I found it difficult to face this fact. This would make my already fairly miserable life seem unbearably miserable. (And *fairly miserable* and *unbearably miserable* are two very different propositions. Believe me.)

I called Oscar back and said, 'You just called Alice and asked her for sex. Why?'

'What! I did not. Was that Alice's phone I called? How come you are calling me on her phone? Anyway, brother, I must have called the wrong number. I was trying to call Nina and talk dirty to her. Those French birds – they can't get enough of all that filthy sex talk,' said Oscar.

I waited to detect the lie but he said it so calmly, so in control. Maybe it was true.

Then Oscar made a joke. He said, 'Alice and I don't exactly get on, you know that. Jesus, no offence, little brother, but I wouldn't touch her with yours.'

'You're a prick,' I said.

But I was actually convinced.

It was exactly as Oscar would have reacted, he was being completely normal; there was no fluster in him at all, he responded with just the right amount of irritation, sexism and idiocy to make me think he was being honest. He was incredulous but not indignant and he was, above all, convincing. And I had to accept that I was just being paranoid.

---

* Yes, the heartache is bad and, yes, you feel betrayed and all of those things. But what you truly grasp over time is that it's the fact that your lover, your wife, and your brother have somehow reduced your life to the tacky sensationalism of a soap opera. That's the final insult. That's the bit that just keeps on smarting, that part where you have to explain to someone what happened and you feel as if you are reading a soap-opera plot. You think your life is so deep and meaningful, that you're this existential man, muddling your way through the rich riddle, when all it takes is for your brother to bonk your wife, and suddenly you're just a bit part in *Neighbours*. That never leaves you. That ridicule sticks like the mortifyingly embarrassing tattoo you got too young. They stained that rubbish plot line into the very flesh of your life.

After all, hadn't I just heard my dead dad talking? Maybe Oscar hadn't said 'Alice' at all?

Of course that would never happen. Not Oscar and Alice. No way.

But – just as I was about to cut him off – Oscar made a mistake; he showed me he was lying.

He said something else – something he would never have said normally – he said, 'I must have hit the wrong button or something, these silly bloody phones, I just don't get them.'*

---

* It was a detail – an unnecessary footnote (something Oscar never dealt in (footnotes were my department)) – it rang untrue and I realised that this was actually happening. But I didn't confront him, not yet. I just said goodbye and laid my head gently back on the seat. First, I had to talk to Alice.

TERMS & CONDITIONS
OF FACING ALICE

You ain't 'role-playing' your way out of this one, sweetheart!

I started the car, put the windscreen wipers on to get the pesky bird off the bonnet, and – drunk and delirious – drove to my wife's office.

'Can I help you?' asked the receptionist.

A giant montage of ethnic children smiled gleefully from the wall behind her.

'I want to see my wife, I mean, I want to see my Alice . . . I mean Alice. I want to see her now.'

'Do you have an appointment?'

'Of sorts. I'm her husband.'

'Please wait here,' she said.

'No, I don't think I will,' I said and walked past the desk and into the office shouting, 'Alice! Alice!'

I barged into the offices named Earth, then into Wind and lots of serious men and women in serious suits said serious things like, 'Excuse me. We are having a meeting here!'

'Well, excuse me; I'm having a fucking crisis. Alice! You here! Alice!'

I spotted her through a glass wall sitting on the edge of a sunken trough of plastic balls. She was still somehow elegant, even though she looked like she'd been swallowed by some children's monster with balls for teeth. She had her head tilted to one side, the way they were taught to listen in a meaningful way.

'Alice,' I screamed.

'Frank. What's wrong? What's going on? You look terrible. Have you been drinking? Did you remember to bring my phone? Did Valencia call? You didn't answer, did you?'

'How could you? With Oscar. With fucking Oscar. My brother. How could you do this to me? How could you fucking sleep with another man? And him, him, him of all fucking people, my brother? Anyone but him. Anyone, Alice, anyone. Even this prick would have been better,' and I randomly pointed to one of the men in the ball pit. The man smiled awkwardly.

I was standing over her as she tried desperately to get out from the trough of balls, spilling them all across the room as her colleagues looked on. A ball hit my foot and on it was printed the word *Slant*. Another followed, *Perpendicular*.

'You're upset,' she said, having finally got out of the hole.

Stating the fucking obvious but making it sound like an astute observation – another consultancy technique. She placed her hands in the air between us – they floated there – and I watched her palms move towards me as she said, 'Now you have to calm down and tell me what's going on. Let's process together.'

More balls rolled by: *Angular*, *September*, *Majestic*. I noticed her two colleagues nodding as they observed Alice try to gain control of the situation. *Epicentre*. They seemed to think this was some sort of drill, a role-play. *Plinth*. They nodded wisely at her as if to say, *That's the right way to deal with this situation, hands up to calm him, voice calm, using the word 'process' a lot, that's nice work.*

Avocado, *Elemental*, *Synchronicity*. I stepped closer to Alice, pushed her hands out of the way and shouted, 'Don't try to calm me down with your consultancy crap.'

Simulation.

'Tell me the problem and we can develop the solution,' she said.

Evolution.

'Don't fucking look at me like that, Alice. Don't you dare think that eye contact will get you out of this. You fucked Oscar and you fucked me. There's the problem. Now develop the fucking solution. Process *that*.'

Distortion. She looked stunned. *Rewind.* Even her colleagues now seemed uncertain. *Blot.* Then I made the situation a little worse. I started to cry.

Inspirationally.

It looked like Alice wanted to hug me; she stepped closer. I held my hand up, warning her to stay away. Then Alice started denying. Alice started running.

Wonderment.

She said, 'Frank, listen, you are in a bad way but you have to believe me, I am not having an affair with Oscar. Whatever made you think that?'

Fantastical.

'I took your phone by mistake, and Oscar called it and asked if you fancied a fuck, and his name came up as Valencia, does Valencia even exist, how long have you been doing this to me, it all makes sense, you and Oscar saying the exact same shit about the weapons manufacturer, using the same crappy phrases like, *It's good for my profile*, Oscar obviously telling you about the IPO when it was highly confidential, and then I asked Oscar about you two and I could tell he was lying and then, another thing happened,' and I really lost my audience when I said, 'I think this sparrow has been following me all day . . .'

And that was when I knew it was all over.

Aspirant.

'What do you mean a sparrow was following you?' she said.

'I mean it's been on my back all fucking day.'

Hypnotic.

She said, 'How can you tell it's the same sparrow, not lots of different sparrows?'

I heard myself say, as if it made complete sense, 'Because this one has a certain attitude about it. The way it flits around, it's the same one, he's sort of cocky but happy.'

A cocky but happy sparrow.

Distil.

It was over.

Effervescent.

I wasn't sure exactly what was over but I sensed that something was over. My grip loosened, my hands opened and I let go of everything.

Atmospheric.

Alice looked at me with pity in her eyes and her colleagues shook their heads as if this role-play had fallen apart because I wasn't acting properly. I'd slipped out of character.

Potent.

'Take a breath and think about what you are saying. Something's wrong,' Alice said.

Recalcitrant.

Something's wrong.

Something *was* wrong.

Opportunity.

She's absolutely right.

Serendipity.

'You're damn right something's wrong,' I shouted.

Equator.

'Something's very wrong,' I shouted louder. 'Everything is wrong.'

'What's wrong?' said Alice. 'Tell me what's wrong. Speak to me.'

I felt faint, I scrambled to find the right words, I saw the eyeballs of my wife and her colleagues floating around me, everything was too hard to explain and then I heard my now quiet voice whisper, 'Alice, the real problem is that you make my heart grow small.'

Lateral.

That's when I ran. I mean physically ran. I ran hard and fast and I bumped into lots of people on the way until finally I got to my car where the sparrow was perched on my boot and as I drove away, I scrolled through Alice's phone messages and there they were, message after message from Oscar – although it was all under the name Valencia – and even suggestive voicemails, 'Hi, Alice, it's me, call me, the eagle has flown the coop, how about a lunch meeting, same place?'

The phone rang. Alice trying to call me. I was crying a lot, steering the car with one hand, scrolling through Alice's messages with the other. A *Stop* sign flashed in front of me; I ignored it and drove on through.

Stop.

The phone rang again.

Give Way.

It was Alice who said, 'Please, Frank, I think something is very wrong with you. Come back and we can talk about it.'

I wasn't concentrating on the road. Something loud with bright flashing lights was screaming towards me – a fast-approaching violence – and the last thing I remember thinking before my car crash was, 'Everything's messed up. My life couldn't get any worse than it is right now.'*

---

* And, of course, I was wrong.

TERMS & CONDITIONS
OF A PERSONALITY

Piecing together a personality is a complicated affair.

Particularly when it's your own and you can't remember who you are.

Which was exactly the dilemma I faced after my car crash.

I lost my personality. More precisely, it was shunted out of me at 100 miles an hour. Car accidents come with conditions. Luckily for the other guy, he was driving a car renowned for being safe. I, however, was driving a car renowned for being crap.

The conditions created by a 100-mile-an-hour collision changed the state of my car from steel to jelly and it wobbled itself to bits.

My personality proved equally flimsy. It imploded, wiping clean the crib notes of my thoughts, memories and ideas, and leaving in its place a stark blank page.

I am that blank page.

My name is . . .*

---

* And you know all about my amnesia, the hospital, and my long walk – *crawl* – back to being me.

CONDITION 3

REALITY

TERMS & CONDITIONS OF REALITY

You can't stir things apart.

If your life became a soap opera and you were the joke character in the centre of it all, would you:
a. Learn your lines and hope for the best.
b. Pray it wasn't a long-running series.
c. Desperately try to get your character killed off.

TERMS & CONDITIONS OF HABITS

They die hard.

I didn't tell Doug all the things I had remembered. I was too ashamed of most of it and too furious about the rest of it.

He threw the remains of his sandwich in the bin and said, 'Let's get you home.'

I raised my hand and muttered, 'Nonsense. I'm actually fine, Doug. Thanks so much for the rest, though, and the chat. This has been the best few hours of my post-crash life and I can't tell you how much I appreciate everything you've done for me.'

'Oh, tosh,' said Doug. 'But, look, even if I'm not here, you're welcome to come and use my secret bed whenever you need, Frank. I mean it. Just let yourself in, close the door, and have a snooze.'

We both stood up and Doug put his right hand out to shake mine but I wrapped my arms around him and he stiffened slightly inside my hug. After we broke apart I thanked Doug another ten times before he gently pushed me out of his office saying, 'Yes, yes, come back and talk whenever you want. I'm usually here meditating.'

I stumbled along the corridor back to work, trying to muddle my way through the many options rolling out before me.

In Sandra's book business they talk about the 'narrative arc' – the gorgeous sweep of a character's development rising up a steep, seemingly intractable problem, hitting an epiphany at the peak, then sliding down the slope to a satisfying solution. Having now remembered all the horrible events that led to my episode and car crash, I felt as if I was at the apex of my arc, looking down, prepared to ride the slide with childish abandon to a gratifying conclusion.*

These moments in life define you but you're also defined by your life in these moments. For instance, if I'd been an American I would probably have taken a gun and shot my wife in the face, shot Oscar in

---

* But it turns out narrative arcs are a little bumpier than they initially seem.

the balls, then strolled to the bright white door, kicked it open, blown away a couple of the lawyers that worked on the #### business to relieve the world of a little more evil, then calmly, amid the mounting chaos, I'd have sighed, sat below a desk, placed the barrel to my head and ended my life with a fatal metal full stop – *bang!*

You see it every week on the news. You even see it in the UK now; I remember someone telling me a lady came into a shop in Chiswick and used a shotgun to blow a hole into a woman who was sleeping with her husband. Before the shock and disgust of the story took hold, I thought – *Wow, that happened in the UK, in Chiswick, no less!*

Like a posh postcode would in some way prevent you being a savage person.

If I were French I would have used that rage to tear Oscar's throat out with a pen and then beaten Alice to death with her bicycle wheel, and would have gone to court smug in the knowledge that I'd be let off because it was merely a *crime passionnel*.

But I'm British. So shooting people wasn't an option. I wouldn't know where to get a gun if my life depended on it. As for allowing my rage to trigger a *crime passionnel*, well, let's be honest, that's far too hot and European for my cold Anglo blood.

I was actually surprised to find that, after only a short time had passed, my anger cooled and my rage slipped into agitated indecision. I couldn't shake the agitation but I overpowered the indecision by making a decision.

First and foremost I wasn't going to tell Oscar or Alice a thing. Partly because I wasn't sure how you approach people and say, *Hey, I just remembered everything – I fucking hate your guts and you both ruined my life by sleeping with each other.*

The other decision I made was to email Malcolm. I opened my laptop, created a new email account – so Alice would never find it – and wrote.

From: frankversion3.0@hotmail.com
To: fuckthis@hotmail.com
Subject: Remember me!

Hello Malcolm,

Don't panic but I've been in a car accident and lost my memory.

The good news is that much of my memory has returned. The bad news is that the good news might be bad news.

By which I mean, I've remembered that I hate my wife and that our brother Oscar might be a twat.

I can't tell you everything that happened; it would take too long.

Can you call me or send me your phone number: I need to talk.

Love,
Frank

I closed my laptop and decided to bide my time. I needed to heed the cliché about revenge being best served cold.

I kept my memories secret and, like a spy, decided to act as if everything was exactly the same until I could figure out an appropriate reaction.

But, of course, everything looked and felt different; my new world was a hard place to live in – as if viewing life through two sets of eyes – and even as I rode the lift for a meeting with Oscar, I nostalgically remembered the bliss of my ignorance.

TERMS & CONDITIONS OF GUILT

Guilt is the gravity that glues the universe together.

Scientists are pondering an elemental dilemma. And it is this. Gravity is not strong enough to hold the world together. They say, in theory, that gravity is in fact too weak to hold a cup to its saucer, to hold us to the earth, to hold the earth to the sun, the galaxy to other galaxies. Gravity is weak glue. We should in theory be flung apart like so many bits of fluff in a storm. Yet here we all are, connected: the cup to the saucer, us on the earth, the earth spinning gleefully around the sun, and galaxies grinding merrily around other galaxies.

So how can this be? Scientists are tangled in the String Theory which suggests that some of the power of gravity's stickiness leaks in from other portals and places. Well, I can tell you the answer right now, I can reveal the mystery of this missing force that holds us in place, so shut down CERN, close the billion-dollar laboratories, and go home.

Here it is:

- Guilt is the missing force.
- It will hold together the most opposing forces of the universe.
- Even my wife and I are stuck together by it.

This is what I realised as I rode the lift. Oscar and Alice had stuck by me, even after their affair. Why? In theory, they should have just gone off with one another into the sunset to screw each other's brains out. They were probably just about to do it too – but then I went all mental and had a car crash.

So what did they do? They realised I had lost my memory and they decided not to tell me anything. Riddled with guilt, they probably thought this was their chance to make amends, so they stuck with me and tried to make it work. Guilt got to them.

As the lift ascended and floor numbers binged – 8, 9, 10 – my brain sizzled with flashbacks of Alice and Oscar sitting nervously at my hospital bed after the crash. I remembered – when my senses were all a-jangle – seeing that seething white light between Oscar and Alice, and thinking it was hatred. In fact, it was the heady cocktail of wild love and filthy guilt. That was my twisted senses trying to tell me something – that bright white light was a warning.

This is all my roundabout way of confessing something, of absolving my own guilt.

I'll confess it here and now – guilt nearly got to me too. I nearly didn't do anything. Floating between floors, I almost took a bad turn. Hypnotised by the soft purr of the rising lift – 11, 12, 13, 14 – I actually thought: *Maybe I'll just let it all go, pretend it never happened; these people have been so kind to me since my accident, have we not all suffered enough?**

---

* Then the opposite thought hit – *Pull yourself together, Frank, and do something with your life!* As this idea took hold my right hand snapped into a tight fist, as if finally snatching one of the half-million chances that usually slipped through my fingers.

TERMS & CONDITIONS
OF THE DEVIL

He's not nearly as bad as his lawyer.

I stepped out of the lift and took a deep breath. The first meeting with Oscar was hard. When I arrived at his office, I spent the entire time chatting calmly to him while imagining myself screaming – *I know what you did, Oscar! You fucked Alice! Now I'm going to fuck you up!**

I heard Oscar say, 'You look pretty pale, pal, do you need to go home? Doug said he found you in the café looking a bit battered and made you lie down. Did you take your meds today?'

'Yes,' I lied.

'Well, look, if you're sure, we have a meeting with a new client, just a small insurance firm. Do you fancy coming in with me and helping me sound impressive?' he said.

I heard my voice, as if from a distance, say, 'Yes, that would be great, Oscar.'

'Nice one, buddy. I'll pitch, and you can pull me up if I say anything too dumb.'

The insurance client was just one chap in a cheap suit and Oscar was on a roll. 'We're big but we're also specialised. We love insurance law, as it's something that's been managed here since the day my grand-dad started this firm. And now his grandsons, myself and the brilliant Franklyn Shaw here, my younger brother, are proud to carry on that work. We know your business, we understand insurance – we get it.'

Oscar – realising he had the guy eating out of the palm of his hand – pulled out his favourite lawyer joke. He gave the man a generous wink and said, 'Franklyn here is the king of fine print, there's not a clause-maker in this city who can seal a contract tighter. You'll never have to pay a customer again once he's drafted you a contract. Franklyn here could make a colander airtight.'

---

* I'm always so assertive in my fantasy life (and I swear a lot more too).

All I managed to squeeze into Oscar's performance was a smile and a nod before Oscar delivered his well-worn set-up line, 'Here at S&S we believe that Ts&Cs stand for *Total Arse Coverage*. We cover your arse against *every* eventuality. And we have the heritage here at S&S. Let me put it this way,' Oscar said, oiling up his laughing gear for the punchline, 'when Robert Johnson sold his soul at the crossroads, we were right there, working for the man with the horns, standing by Satan's side.'

Then, right there in the middle of this dull meeting, I felt faint and had an imagining so vivid it became a vision; my fury flipped inside out and manifested itself as an apparition. Spots floated like pollen, the world tipped at an obtuse angle, I grabbed for the desk, missed, the room rippled, the client and Oscar faded, and in their place here's what I saw:

Robert Johnson, the blues man, stands stick-thin at the crossroads, dust swirls round his old shoes.

Satan, whippet-thin, levers himself from his limousine.

Beside Satan jogs a man in a thousand-dollar suit – a corpulent lawyer with a striking resemblance to Oscar – scroll in hand, muttering, 'Mr Beelzebub, now are you absolutely completely sure you don't want to include Mr Johnson's entire family in this sale? A bulk deal, so to speak. We may as well harvest a sack o' souls while we is at it, Mr B. What do you say? Might as well screw as many souls out of this rusty old blues man as we can?'

Satan himself flinches at his lawyer's unbridled greed, Satan himself feels his sympathy surge towards Robert Johnson, and turning, horns glinting in the southern sun, Satan says, 'Mista lawyer-man, you make me sick.'

Blushing with pride, the lawyer replies, 'Why, thank you, Mr B. We at S&S aim to please. Yes, sir, we do!'

When I emerged from the fit, I was on the floor, flaccid, the world vibrating – the vision still burning the edges of reality – and Oscar was standing over me, slapping my face gently, shouting, 'Franklyn, you OK, Franklyn – *Franklyn!* Someone get some water now.'*

---

* I realised that containing my rage wasn't going to be easy.

TERMS & CONDITIONS OF ACTING

It's easy when you know your motivation.

I was sure that when I saw my wife I would fall apart again but something stranger happened. I opened the door and spotted her in the kitchen making me dinner.

Looking over her shoulder, she said, 'You're home, great. I'm nearly finished cooking spagbol, your favourite.' (My new memory confirmed that it was, in fact, my favourite.)

I said, 'Oh, that's lovely, dear,' as I grabbed a knife and stabbed her in the face . . .*

Before I was fully conscious of my actions, I found myself holding and kissing her. As if I was trying to trick my rage – switch hate to love – so she wouldn't suspect anything. I kissed her and, as she placed her tongue in my mouth, I bit down like it was raw steak, and tore it from the root spitting it out, screaming, *How could you do that to me, you bitch?*[*1]

Then we sat for a pleasant dinner and I told her I'd fainted at work. She placed her hand on mine and said I wasn't to worry, time would heal me.

Our dinner had the woozy sensation of a dream, and I played along, saying, 'Yes I know, I just hope that I remember every single little thing one day, I hope it all comes back to me, I hope I can remember exactly what triggered my little episode, because I feel like I'm letting a lot of people down by not remembering everything.'

She held her expression so tightly I almost laughed.

I pushed the point, 'Yes, one day I just know something will trigger me and it will flood back and we will be together properly again. In love, real love.'

---

* No I didn't.

*1 No – no, I didn't.

She swallowed and said, 'We *are* in love, Franklyn, we are in love, and you don't need to remember everything to know that we are two people very much in love.'

I shouldn't have enjoyed watching her squirm.*

After pudding, the truth of the night came out like an unwelcome dinner guest, the reason for my wife's uncharacteristically happy mood.

Moving the plates aside she said, 'I've got great news. Another publishing house has agreed to publish a follow-up to *Executive X*. Isn't that exciting?'

'Alice, that's such great news, I'm so proud of you.'

'Oh God, thanks, I'm so pleased. I mean, I thought it might not happen but look they said yes and it's going to be amazing.' She took a swig of wine and, without missing a beat, said, 'I'd love if you'd help me with my new test questions. We're really cracking the paradigm, Franklyn, my new approach will revolutionise everything.'

'And I'd just love to help you with your tests, Alice. I could think of nothing better.'

She smiled, turned, and pulled out a test questionnaire from her work bag, laughing and saying in a triumphant voice, 'Well, no time like the present, we should have a little fun with this one, and I promise you sexual favours in return, Mister.'

'Wonderful,' I said. 'Absolutely wonderful.'

---

* But you've got to get your kicks where you can.

TERMS & CONDITIONS OF QUANTIFYING HAPPINESS

On a scale of 0–100, at what capacity are you currently living your life (100% = your personal ideal potential)?
> a. 1–25% of ideal.
> b. 25–50% of ideal.
> c. 50–75% of ideal.
> d. 75–100% of ideal.

I asked my wife why there was no '0%' option.

She smiled and said, 'Very funny, Franklyn.'

My wife's new tests were different; no longer all multiple choice, some now required actual written answers. After pages of the normal inane tosh, I hit the killer question.

What's the worst thing you've done in your life?

I sat there sweating, wondering if my wife could see that I was having another panic attack, wondering if she noticed that I was breathing strangely, the nib of my pen shaking, and the answer formed in my mind:

'Convince myself that everything was fine.'

Instead I wrote, 'Not tell my wife that I love her enough times.'

My wife looked over the test and, when she came to that answer, she looked up and said, 'LOL.'

TERMS & CONDITIONS
OF THE LIVER

Eventually your liver can't keep cleaning up after you.

As we walked down the hospital corridor, Sandra broached the subject of Alice.

She made a joke of it at first. 'Alice joined a cult or something?'

'How do you mean?' I asked.

'I'm being silly,' said Sandra, but she reconsidered, and added, 'Do you know what she did to me the other day? She ignored me. To my face. I spotted her having a drink with some people in a bar in town and I went up to her and she just . . . sort of ignored me. I was incredibly embarrassed. I said hello and finally after saying it a lot of times she turned away from her friends, sighed loudly like it was such an effort, and said, *oh hi, I ike* that, *oh hi.*'

Sandra pulled tissues from her cardigan sleeve, aggressively wiped her tear-soaked eyes, then stuffed the tissues back up her sleeve where they formed an unattractive lump. I looked at Sandra and realised how different she was to Alice.

They used to be the same: Sandra and Alice. Both intelligent, nice-looking girls; both wore cardigans, jeans and trainers, as if they were too intellectual to worry about how they looked. But they had grown so far apart. Sandra still dressed the same; she worked in publishing where you could dress like a messy intellectual, and she carried a little extra weight, but she carried it well. Whereas Alice now dressed like some Italian model, her body thin and hard from cycling and her clothes tailored and immaculate from Gucci.

Sandra caught me looking at her and said, 'It's lovely to see you again, Frank, I missed you.'

I smiled and said, 'Yes, I missed me too.'

'You look different to the last time I saw you. How's your head these days?'

'I've some very interesting things to update you on but let's forget about all that now; I'll tell you after we've seen your mum. Come on now, we need to be cheerful for Molly.'

Sandra reached over and touched my face; her fingers moved up to my scar and she softly felt its outline. With the exception of Dr Mills, no one – not even my wife – had touched my scar and I smiled a little awkwardly and said, 'I just tell people I was attacked by a great white shark.'

Sandra laughed but she didn't move her hand away; instead she caught my fringe and scooped it back, off my forehead so my scar was exposed, and said, 'You look better with your hair like that, that's how you used to wear it.'

When we stepped in, Molly was asleep, pale and thin as death. Her big hair, which used to be piled high like a Chinese lantern, was now deflated, stringy and thinning; her face was hollowed out. The room smelled strongly of mushroom. Sandra and I sat on plastic chairs and watched Molly sleeping as machines purred around us. I noticed she had a red panic button above her bed and it made me feel slightly jumpy and in a strange way rather nostalgic for a time when I was just a pulped amnesiac, a blissfully blank page.

'Will Molly wake up or is she out for the night?' I asked.

'She's on a lot of drugs for the pain so sleep's the best place for her.'

Then Molly stirred and looked straight at me, mumbling, 'Fucking hell, what happened to you, Frank? You've a bloody big scar on your noggin.'

I smiled and replied, 'Car crash. What the hell happened to you, Molly?'

'Life crash,' she joked.

Sandra laughed and leaned over and kissed Molly, who said, 'Where's Alice? Did she not come with Frank?'

'She's really busy at work,' said Sandra.

'Well, I'm really busy dying,' said Molly, and Sandra said, 'Don't say that, Mum.'

'Don't listen to Sandra; she knows it like I do. It's over for me, Frank,' Molly said.

'I know how you feel,' I said.

Anger rippled over Molly's old face as she said, 'Listen here, Frank, grow some balls and put some hair on them, I won't hear you talking like that. I'm all done, but you're just a little broken, like my mosaics. All the best people have a few cracks in them. I know you've had a fright, a bad crash, but your mind is a good one, Frank, it'll come back to you. But me, well, that's different. See this bed, Frank, this shitty NHS bed is the border where death meets life. I'm on the death side; you make sure you stay on the other side, hear me?'

'Yes, Molly,' I said and I was going to say sorry for being a wimp but Molly flipped into sleep in the way that I used to directly after my car accident – like a giant switch had been clicked to OFF. I remember that feeling and all its discombobulating effects. I remember chatting to a nurse one minute then – *splice!* – the nurse would vanish and it would be hours later.*

We sat there a long time and Sandra placed her hand over mine. At first it was a little awkward because of the silence and her hand on mine, but after a bit, a calm sense of exhaustion took over my body and I relaxed.

When I turned to Sandra to say something, to finally tell her about my returning memories, I saw she too had fallen asleep, her head to one side, near my shoulder, her hair falling around my neck and she was snoring.

Even in this room of sleeping, estranged friends, I felt something, a closeness, the like of which I had been so sorely lacking.

Molly woke up again and we had a chat as Sandra slept. She smiled at her sleeping daughter and said, 'She has an incredibly pretty nose, my daughter, but it snores like a bloody tuba. Always has. Even when she was a tiny baby, that honk would wake up the whole house.'

---

* But to me it felt like a split second had passed and the nurse had gone up in a puff of starchy smoke.

I laughed.

Molly said, 'I'll cheat this fucker death yet, just you watch, Frank.'

'I'm right here and I'm watching. Trust me when I say death can be a bit dim; he missed me so there's no reason why you're not nimble enough to skirt around him.'

Molly grinned like a child before sagging back into sleep.

When Sandra woke up I fetched her a coffee and a water for myself, and with Molly now snoring in the background, I told Sandra that I had remembered everything.

'What? Have you got all your memory back?'

'Well, the parts that count,' I said.

'You remember who I am, at least, that's all that matters,' she said and smiled that lovely smile of hers, but then couldn't help adding, 'Which is more than I can say for that wife of yours.'

'And she didn't even get a bash on the head,' I said.

'You look so good, Frank,' Sandra said suddenly.

'Oh.' I was taken aback by how much emphasis she put into that sentence and said, 'Um, thank you.'

The sentence was so strongly laced with emotion that I was lost in the nuance of it; it felt like a thousand little strings stretching, meeting and tying Sandra tightly to me. But as quickly as the flirting flush came, it went, and Sandra and I both sat in silence until the moment was truly torn by Molly farting in her sleep.

'Fancy a drink?' I said.

'Gagging for one,' Sandra said, and she put her arm around my waist and we walked to a nearby bar.

When we sat down with our drinks I told Sandra about the details, about Oscar and Alice screwing each other, my episode, the weapons contracts. In all that time Sandra stared at me gob-smacked. Relating the details of my memory out loud was not a catharsis, it actually made it worse, it made me realise just how ludicrously and irrevocably my life had spun out of control.

When I finished, Sandra took a long drink and said, 'That fucking bitch.'

'Indeed,' I said.

I took a long drink too and finally Sandra, who was lost in thought, turned to me and said, 'So what are you going to do now?'

TERMS & CONDITIONS
OF GLUTEN-FREE

Inspiration can come from the least likely place.

My memory by this stage was incredibly active again. As if the department – which had been shut for many months, its furniture covered in dust cloths – was suddenly back in business, doors flung open, packed with frantic workers desperately filing all the messy piles of thoughts, experiences and memories. As this was happening, I began to do to Alice what she'd done to me for many years. I observed her, stalked her. The day after my total recall I stalked Alice all the way into the arms of Oscar. I followed her when she told me she was going 'cycling with Valencia' and she ended up in a boutique hotel with Oscar; they even had dinner together in the restaurant, in public. I sat a long distance away in the hotel bar watching them. I took photographs with my phone.* I took notes.*[1]

I felt like I had all the ingredients but how best to serve the sour dish? The simplest option: call a meeting with them, calmly lay the photographs on the desk, and watch as they realised that I knew everything, wait to see if they got mad, or tried to lie and squirm their way out of it. But this option seemed unsatisfactory; it lacked something.

Option two hit me as I pretended to read the menu (hiding behind it in case I was spotted) when I noticed that even menus have fine print. It was nothing unusual; it simply had two asterisks that denoted *vegetarian* and *gluten-free* options.

But it triggered something – an idea so simple that it arrived like a beautiful gift. Old Frank had already laid the groundwork for me – the trap was set – I just needed to make it go snap.

---

* I've no idea why.
*1 I've no idea why.

TERMS & CONDITIONS OF REVENGE

It's best served cold (with a side order of humiliation).

Revenge reinvigorated me.

It's a satisfying dish. Don't care what Christians say about turning the other cheek, I'd run out of cheeks to turn.

I've spent my entire existence on this planet mitigating – mitigating risk, mitigating responsibility, mitigating experience, mitigating life, mitigating mitigation. I've mitigated for clients and for myself. I've mitigated and made excuses for the world around me, and finally, I'm all mitigated out, I've mitigated myself into a corner and I can't breathe.

No more mitigation, no more avoidance of responsibility and risk. I now know that those things – the balance of risk and the bravery of taking responsibility – are the bones of life, the flesh of existence. I figured it out. Revenge was risky, exciting and sweet. Like a child with a secret – I plotted and schemed my final moves – I radiated that small glee of having something that was all mine. It was so out of character that I found myself drunk on the covert thrill of it all. That was how happy I was. But when Sandra called, my happiness took a hit, my revenge stalled, and life got in the way of my plot.

TERMS & CONDITIONS OF MOLLY

Sometimes the good die old.

'Frank, Molly passed away last night.'

'Oh, Sandra, I'm so sorry,' I said automatically.

'It was for the best. She really was in an awful lot of pain at the end, and she drifted off during the night, which is probably the best thing. Being Molly, she spent the entire time on her deathbed organising every detail of her funeral. I'd love to see you there.'

'Of course I'll be there,' I said. 'Do you want me to bring Alice?'

'Um,' she left a long pause before she said, 'I'll leave that up to you, Frank. I don't care either way. Sorry if that sounds rude but Alice wasn't there for Molly near the end so I'm not sure if she should be there at the end.'

When I told Alice she looked sad and she acted sad but when I mentioned the funeral date she said, 'Oh bugger, I can't do it, I'm in Scotland for a big meeting I can't get out of.'

I didn't react or even try and talk her out of going to the meeting, I just nodded and said, 'Don't worry, I'll go for both of us. I told Sandra you were crazy-busy at the moment.'

My wife, realising what a crappy thing this was to do, said, 'I'll be sure to send Sandra a beautiful bunch of flowers.'

Slicing all sarcasm from my tone, I said, 'She'll really appreciate that, Alice.'

'Good,' said my wife, 'then I'll do that straight away. Yes, poor Molly, she was a wonderful woman. She really took care of me when I needed it. She was a great woman.'

'So great a woman that you can't even be bothered to go to her funeral, you selfish pathetic excuse for a human being!' I screamed.*

In fact, I did everything I could to make my wife feel that not going

---

* No, no, of course, I didn't.

to the funeral wasn't that big a deal. I didn't want her there to ruin the day; I didn't want her anywhere near Molly or Sandra, or even me for that matter.

Molly's funeral was far from a sad affair.*

The room was one of those dull crematorium chapels, but against its generic backdrop Molly's mourners were dressed in bright, fabulous clothes. Rows of dull brown pews held powdered ladies whose purple hair and nail polish competed with the vibrant colours of their scarves and hats.

A photograph of Molly on the stage showed her smiling, with a fag in her hand, looking into the audience as if to say, *What you lot so glum about?*

It wasn't long before people started smiling as the speeches detailed some of Molly's more outrageous moments; and by the time Molly's coffin was lowered into the ground, I felt happy. She had lived a life I could only dream of. One of those free spirits who scared and impressed me. Walking back to the reception, Sandra caught up with me and I gave her a hug.

'Thanks for coming, Frank,' she said.

'Of course. I think it was one of the funniest funerals I've ever been to,' I said.

'Mum would love that you said that.'

People were gently touching Sandra's back as they walked past us or whispering, 'Lovely service, dear.'

I watched Sandra for a moment, the way the sun caught the amazing angles of her nose, her eyes washed so clear and blue by tears.

She said, 'What are your plans?'

'I thought I might go travelling.'

'Oh,' said Sandra and, with a sad smile, added, 'Off to find yourself?'

---

* Looking at the big colourful turnout of people, I thought: if those who attend your funeral are representative of the sort of person you were in life, then Molly did just fine.

'Definitely not. I've done quite enough of that for one lifetime, thank you very much. I actually thought I might try the exact opposite – and try as hard as possible to lose myself.'

She said, 'Do you think you might need some help losing yourself, Frank?'

'Luckily I have Malcolm for that. I was going to go and join him.'

'No, I meant . . .' Sandra looked tired as she snapped, 'Oh never-fucking-mind.'

'Hey. What's up?'

'For someone who specialises in fine print you're astronomically crap at picking up signals. Here: Molly wanted me to give you this. See you at the reception.'

She walked off and joined a group of ladies who rubbed her back and took her into the building.

In my hand was a sealed envelope that had on the front in red pen – *For Frank's Eyes Only!*

Recipe for Mushroom Soup

Frank — you can't get the mushroom out of mushroom soup, it's in the broth.

So, without getting all bloody 'soup for the soul' on you — but I'm on my deathbed so cut me some slack! — I'll give you this last Molly pearl:

If you don't like something — don't take it, Frank

I have found that death has really tightened my thoughts and I hope that I'm not being too blunt but frankly (ha!) — Stop eating shit you hate!

And remember to kick Alice in the shins for me from time to time. I loved the girl but she got lost in the mix.

Oh, and just one last thing — I know you have rather a lot on your plate at the moment (but that's life, so stop bitching and harden up).

I'll add just one thing, which you can do with what you will (which in your case, let's face it, Frank, will probably be sweet fuck-all).

My Sandra is in love with you and always has been from the moment you appeared in my kitchen that night so long ago.

She, like you, is too submissive to tell the world how she feels, so I thought I'd help you two along.

Love & mushrooms,

Molly x

TERMS & CONDITIONS
OF SNAIL MAIL

It's slower yet more meaningful than email.

After a few days of playing the part of the amnesiac retard – which wasn't too much of a stretch for me – I came across a small parcel on the doormat.

Inside was a matchbox with Thai writing and it had a label attached: *'Might need a new one of these. Love Malc.'*

I slid the matchbox open and there inside was a plastic brain from one of my anatomical figurines. The missing brain.

Under the brain was a note:

Frank – fuck!

Got your email!

But before I could reply the internet went off here, hence old-school snail mail.

Hold on – I'm coming home.

Might take a few weeks as I'm in the middle of the middle of the middle of sweet fuck-all. But I'm coming, Frank, don't worry.

My advice – run for your life and by the time you catch up with it I'll be there to help. In the meantime know this much – I fucking love you.

Love and love,
Malc

PS You're wrong about Oscar – he's not so much a twat – he's more of a cunt.

TERMS & CONDITIONS OF TENSES

Sometimes the future masquerades as the past.

In the final days, in order to keep control of my rage – to stop myself blurting to Oscar and Alice that I remembered everything – and to buy time, I took to running.* In training for the finish, I needed to hold off my anger just long enough to complete my plan of attack.

Every morning I got up early, when the world was still grey – not yet coloured in – and went for a jog in the woods.

The simple sensation of moving through time and space was bliss.

My organs winced if I moved too fast. My ribs remained a little loose, jangling like wind chimes suspended in blood. If I exerted myself, the blood whipped up currents that rushed through them releasing a sharp twinge – warning me to slow down before something popped.

But even at an old man's pace I soon began to feel immortal, running down thin paths bracketed by trees that gave me an artificial sense of speed, a tunnel down which I slipped, branches whipping past, my face cutting through spider webs like a hundred finely spun finish lines driving me on and on.

After a few days of running I felt the change; my body rewarded me with fresh squirts of endorphins, dazzling spells of joy. I smiled as I ran, exhausted and sore as I was, feeling my mind, my body, even my soul, reaching an accord. My organs were no longer battered and dysfunctional, no longer anchors dragging me down. Now they were working together, environmental conditions harmonising with hereditary terms in a silent pact which, for the first time in a long time, meant that I was ready.

---

* When I say *running*, that is a considerable exaggeration. I tried to jog but it was more of a lumbering limp with brief jags of jogging and occasionally ill-advised sprinting spurts. For the most part, at the top end of my performance I was attempting a sort of running-walk – *ralking*, if you will – and down at the low end of my performance, I was doing a sort of running-stroll – I was *rolling*. And though I accept that I looked like an asthmatic cripple, nonetheless this ralking and rolling made me feel like magic.

One morning I was jogging over the pine needles, feeling good, when suddenly I experienced an extreme memory. Unrevealing and not necessarily nice, it was like being poked in the eye. I stopped and grabbed my knees to gather my breath. The image was hard to grasp, slippery, unclear: a door, a safe door possibly, so thick it seemed like a submarine hatch opening slowly into a hazy landscape with a terrifying plunge, and before I could identify anything, the heat and light burnt the image like celluloid melting to a frazzled black.

Showering after my run, all the good endorphins washed away to reveal the neurosis below and I decided that my body might be giving in on me, that this sharp vision was a preview to a sudden death.

Was it my body signalling to me that I was about to die? Just as I smelt the clean scent of hope, my body collapses and dies. Just my bloody luck.

I wondered if these visions were my final memories worming their way out. All the others had squirted out all over the place and now this was the final one, squeezed out of my exhausted, deflated brain like the measly smears of toothpaste wrestled from an abused tube.

But what was I remembering?

The next day on my run, the world again grey and silent and mine, only a few friendly sparrows and frightened squirrels as companions, and again, just as I hit a comfortable speed, just as my body flushed with that warm sense of runner's joy, I was hit by the vision.

I leaned forward and grabbed my knees as I tried to capture my breath, and as I did I muttered a prayer, not to God, or anything like that, but to my organs, to my body I prayed, I appealed, I begged, I asked it not to give up just yet, not when I was so close to the end, not when my lungs and my blood were full of hope and freedom and I muttered, 'Not yet, not yet, not yet, sorry brain for filling you with nothing but confusion, sorry bladder and bowel for all the bad piss and shit I put you through, sorry lungs for all my safe, shallow breaths, sorry heart for the endless sludge of processed foods and dread, and to my long-lost spleen, well, I was never sure what you did, but sorry anyway, I miss your sweet silent ways.'

I didn't want any more memories. I didn't want to remember any more of me. (I'd remembered enough of me to know that I didn't want to remember all of me.) But the vision persisted: the thick door opening, pressure released around me as if escaping a tight hug, but this time an angel with the perfect smile and starched wings – or were those wings simply collars? – and all around me smiling people pointing for me to walk out the door, to drop to my certain death – and I prayed that I would survive this heart attack, this blood clot or whatever it was – and this time the moment didn't pass, it simply clarified itself and I saw what it was.

It was me with Sandra, who was holding my hand, and a smiling air hostess directing me out of an aeroplane door into the warmth of tropical paradise.

It was not the past, and it was not organ failure. I stood up straight, stared up through the canopy of trees, the morning light finding its way in like thousands of flickering fingers, and I understood. It was simply my mind, which had for so long traded only in bleak memories, suddenly shunting to a stop, twisting 180 degrees, and considering something it hadn't dared to for many months – *a bright future.*

From: frankversion3.0@hotmail.com
To: fuckthis@hotmail.com
Subject: Catching up . . .

Malcolm,

I took your advice and I'm just about to catch up with my life.

Don't move.

Don't come home.

Wherever you are, stay there, I'm coming.

Send me an email and tell me where you've got to.

Can't wait to tell you what's been happening. It's been rather an interesting ride.

Love,
Frank

PS I'm bringing a friend.

CLAUSE 3.1

REVENGE

TERMS & CONDITIONS OF ENDINGS

More often than not, they're badly disguised beginnings.

TERMS & CONDITIONS OF CONNING A CON MAN

It's all about timing.

Today I rewrote my own employment contract with a tiny addendum. Which was that if I left the company, regardless of the reason, I would continue to receive my full salary for five years. Getting Oscar to sign was simple. For a start he was willing to do anything for me at the moment. Since I had passed out in our meeting, he had gone into overdrive, as if there was nothing he would not do for me. I took a stack of contracts so that he was in the rhythm of signing when I sprung the trick. I timed it so that my employment contract was placed in front of him right at the moment when the beautiful barista arrived in his office. (Simple distraction technique. Oldest trick in the book.)

'What's this?' he asked.

'My employment contract. HR brought it to my attention yesterday. It's out of date. I told them it didn't matter but they insisted. They're such sticklers.'*

He looked up at me for a moment, unsure, but it was wiped clean off his face when the barista appeared, opening the door with a nudge of her soft hip, holding a cardboard tray of coffees and saying, 'Cappuccino?'

Oscar smiled and said, 'I didn't order one, love,*1 but I'll take it.'

My beautiful barista placed two cups on the desk, and Oscar stole a long, obvious look down her cleavage saying, 'Lovely.'

'So can you just sign,' I said.

I knew that the idea of Oscar signing something, looking important, would be more than enough for him not to read the contract.

---

* Keep your lie trim and taut (any extra fat will weaken it).

*1 Oscar called anyone who had an accent that wasn't as posh as his own *love*. He thought it was a term of endearment that the lower classes used with one another. He'd heard a few cabbies calling his wife that and so he used it now.

He never read them anyway; he left that to his underlings. To me.

The barista waited for the money and Oscar with a flourish took Dad's fountain pen* and scribed a large florid signature across my tampered contract.

'All I do is sign sign sign,' said Oscar, screwing the top of Dad's fountain pen back and standing up straight so the barista could see he was tall and powerful, so she could take in his full impressive fatness.

'That's five quid,' she said.

'Oh right, um, I'm like the Queen, love, I never carry money, filthy stuff, sure my little brother can sort you out,' said Oscar.

Little brother. The comment about the Queen. Another *love* thrown in.*[1]

I asked the beautiful barista to come to my desk where I had money. As I rummaged through my drawer looking for the cash, the sweet scent of her breath hit me like the chocolate sprinkles on a mocha.

She pointed to something in the drawer and said, 'Oh yeah, going anywhere nice?'

She was pointing at my passport, which I had placed in my drawer in preparation.

I thought about lying and saying, 'Off to Majorca actually. You told me you loved it there, didn't you?'

But that sounded creepy and it was also another lie. And since my memory had returned I had decided to live a more straight life; I had self-imposed a new honesty policy.

So I said, 'Well, I'm off on an adventure.'

She said, 'Where you off to, then?'

I didn't want to lie or be too specific so I said, 'A special place.'

'Special how?'

'Well, special in the sense that it's uncorporate and unsophisticated, special in the sense that it doesn't have anyone that's like me there.'

---

* Sorry, Dad, you wouldn't approve of this moment.

*[1] It all slid off me. I had the contract, I felt wonderful, I'd found a loophole all of my own to slip through.

She laughed, 'You're odd, aren't you?'

I handed her the money and said, 'Thank you, I'm trying. All I want to do is try and tell the truth for a change.'

'Well, best of luck with that,' she said. 'Got any truth for me?'

She said it in a flirty way that made my heart race. I could have said so much. I could have confessed my silly crush, told her how much happiness she brought to my bleak days, but then I realised the only thing I could honestly say to her was – 'I really hate coffee.'

TERMS & CONDITIONS OF A
PRENUPTIAL AGREEMENT

It's just a postnuptial disagreement waiting to happen.

My prenuptial agreement made me smile. When we married I never even read it but now it made me so happy. It had an almost magical quality. Before our wedding it had been a sore point between my father, Alice and me. Dad was adamant that it be signed; I was even more adamant that it be torn up. Alice was polite enough to step in and, for the sake of all of us – to stop a family imploding – graciously sign it.

I'm not a spiritual man and it's a strange sensation for a dry contract to work as a channel to the spiritual world. But that's exactly what happened. It may just as well have been a Ouija board.

With his tight clauses Dad had woven a safety net for me. At a time when I had raged against him – and warned him not to sully my grand emotions with his cynical law – he politely ignored me, and thank God he did. For here in this document was everything I needed. There was the clause which read that in the light of any 'morally dubious' situation by the bride, all financial benefits concerned with Shaw&Sons (including bonuses that I would receive or company dividends) would not be granted to my wife as part of the settlement. And the flat – the thing she loved the most – would be taken from her (as it was in the firm's name). Plus he had ring-fenced all money protected under a trust. Which basically, in layman's terms, meant that she might get half of what we had in our current account – a few hundred pounds at best – and otherwise that was the lot.

I felt my eyes well up. This quiet time alone with an old contract, with my dad, was possibly the most emotional moment we ever shared. Long after his death my dad had done what so many fathers fail to do: he had protected me.

TERMS & CONDITIONS OF DAD

He had his moments.

Dad always warned, *A Shaw heart is a short heart.* And he wasn't wrong. His dad died young from heart complications and my dad died young too. Which meant my own Shaw heart had a relatively short lifespan, beating like a bird's, a tight knot of worry pumping towards its use-by date. It made me think of Doug and the half-million chances and how I probably had to cut twenty years off that formula, which was why I had to make a decision quickly – or I'd end up as the guy slumped in my office chair, dead and rotting, without anyone noticing.

My dad was conscious of his short heart too but as far as I could tell he never grabbed life, he never questioned his destiny. My dad was a study in repression and shelved dreams. He showed us boys so little of himself that it felt at times as if there was simply not much there. But I remember Mum would occasionally give us a glimpse into who he was, beyond the dull lawyer, beyond the dry dad.

My mum was a vessel of love, joy and support and I suppose – without over-simplifying her – that she was everything I could ever hope for in a mother. But remembering my father was a less satisfying experience. For us kids he was a humourless disciplinarian, forever treating fatherhood like some extension of his job, always littering the house with tiny scribbled contracts between us and him – *If I clean Dad's car I'll get extra pocket money* – signed by all the parties. I think Dad thought they were funny but as I got older I found all these contracts – all our childish drawings on the fridge eventually smothered in Post-it note contracts – a little creepy. He was simply not an expressive man, which is not to say he did not feel as deeply or profoundly as any other man, but you would just never know it.

When I was young, I asked Mum what Dad was like as a young man – and she shocked me.

I expected her to say, 'Your dad was just like you, Frank,' or, 'Your dad was like Oscar, very ambitious.'

What she actually said was, 'Your dad was exactly like Malcolm, rebellious and forever striving to push people or ideas.'

'Rubbish,' I said. 'Dad was never like Malcolm. Never. No one's like Malcolm.'

'Well, where do you think Malcolm comes from? He's not from my genes, he's from your dad. You're too young to realise but life changes you. Remember that your dad was forced to take over the law firm from his dad too. And, believe me, your dad didn't want to do it at first either. He wasn't a rebel in the way you use the term now but, back in the sixties, your dad was one of the first people I knew to take environmental issues seriously. He wanted to use his legal training not to do contracts for corporations but to take corporations to court, to hold them responsible for breaking environmental laws, and for years your dad worked nights to push through some of the most fundamental environmental regulations that still exist today. He really cared.'

I had to ask, 'Well, what happened to him?'

'Well, to be blunt,' Mum said, 'you happened, and Malc, and Oscar. Life happened and he had to buckle down and be responsible.'

'I just wish he'd show some of those feelings sometimes, that's all,' I said.

'I know, Frank,' she said. 'I know.'

Which is not to say that my dad never showed himself to me.

He was not always hiding within his pinstripe prison. My father was far from an abundant source of emotional moments. But that's not to say there were not *some*. Being his son was rather like walking across acres of grey concrete only to find that somehow, through a tiny crack, a single poppy had bloomed.

I remember when Dad was older and we were in the car together; I think I was driving him for a hospital check-up, and as usual, having covered client issues and work stories, we were left without a huge amount to say to each other.

I had put the radio on and John Lennon was singing 'Imagine'.

Dad wasn't one to tap his feet to music, so when his hand went to the radio I assumed he was about to turn it down or off, that it was irritating him, but he turned it up and we both listened to the song, and Dad said, 'It's a beautifully simple song about people, Frank. People not relying on religion and ideals that cause so much death and war, but people just getting on with one another. This was your mother's favourite song, you know.'*

After extended emotional droughts, these moments arrived with such a sense of relief that I had to look straight ahead to ensure that Dad didn't see I was welling up when I said, 'I know, Dad, it's a beautiful song.'

---

* I paused, waiting for Dad to do what he so often did, which was to kill the moment with a punchline. Like, for instance, he might suddenly – to the tune of 'All You Need Is Love' – sing 'All you need is Law!'

Thankfully he didn't do it this time.

TERMS & CONDITIONS OF HOPE

There are others like me out there.

Just before I went to see Oscar for the last time, I printed off all my sabotaged contracts. Or at least the ones I was particularly proud of. Everything from my original tiny start, right through to the crazy stuff when I lost control and wrote whole paragraphs all over the arms manufacturers' contracts. And of late, I had really been going to town on a whole slew of new contracts. Holding them all together, they seemed so dull and insignificant but, truth be told, they really were the most fundamental and important thing I had ever done with my life.

I took a pink highlighter and coloured in all my best work, so the reader's eyes were dragged immediately to these terrible little additions.

Now it may have been my broken memory playing tricks with me – and I can never be entirely certain of this (or of anything, for that matter) – but as I highlighted my best work, I reread one of the very first contracts that I ever tampered with and there was something new there – something that I was fairly sure I hadn't written myself.

I read and reread it again and again.

It seemed another lawyer, possibly the in-house lawyer, had added something, had responded to my words, had replied – another lawyer had tampered with my own tampering.

For deep in the forest of fine print, right next to the words that I had added to this contract, *Jesus Wept*, was a small addition from another lawyer, a reply I suppose, which read – *and with good reason*.

With a smile on my face and skip in my step I took the contracts to Oscar and, without saying anything, I placed them on his desk.

TERMS & CONDITIONS OF OSCAR

The reputation of a hundred years can
be lost in the blink of an eye.

Waiting.

Oscar, who was on the phone, winked at me and carried on talking. As he spoke he absentmindedly looked down at the contracts.

The first thing that happened was that Oscar's mouth dropped open. Then he stopped talking. He didn't say goodbye to the person on the phone, he didn't put the phone back on its cradle, he just dropped it on his desk, and violently riffled through the contracts, leaning close to them as if his eyes were lying to him. Redness rising in his face, he said, 'What's this? Is this a joke? What's happening?'

I smiled and a great look of fat relief spread across Oscar's face. He knew nothing of my returning memories.*

'Fuck, Franklyn, you really had me,' said Oscar, clutching his heart, sitting heavily back into his chair. 'That was bloody good. I thought we'd just lost millions of pounds of business. Version 2.0 does jokes too!'

I didn't laugh or smile; I just looked straight at him.

His face changed, rage replaced relief, and I said, 'No joke, brother. It's serious; all these contracts are out there, with clients, being used, all as legally binding as a knot of spaghetti.'

Gasping, trying to suck air in, face red, fists curled like hooks, Oscar's words exploded in barks, 'Why? Why! This? This!'

'Well,' I said in a calm reasoning tone, 'even people who make bombs must have a little poetry in their plutonium souls.'

'But! But!'

'Oh,' I added, as if it were just a trifling detail, 'I know all about you and Alice.'

---

* He safely assumed I was Franklyn Version 2.0, as he had taken to calling me. With no inkling that I was not Old Frank, nor New Franklyn, nor Version 2.0, he had no idea that I was something new, something terrible, coiled and ready to strike.

I thought Oscar might have a heart attack and keel over, but he stepped back, away from me as if I was infected, he twisted his neck around, and screamed out of his door into the office, 'Someone get all these contracts now and fix them, stop sitting around like morons and fix these mistakes.'

'It's too late,' I said, 'the phones will start ringing any time now . . .'*

And they did.

Suddenly lots of people were talking to lots of other people on lots of phones.

A wave of panic rang out from desk to desk until someone stood up and shouted, 'Line six for you, Oscar,' and another added, 'Line three, Oscar.'

Three more people joined the chorus.

Line two, Oscar . . .

Lines seven and nine, Oscar . . .

Line ten, Oscar . . .

Oscar!

Oscar!

Everyone held on to their handsets, waiting to see what Oscar did next. He seemed like he might be about to punch me, then he turned on his heels, ran back into his office, and started to talk rapidly and loudly into his phone. I smiled, waved at my colleagues, who all ignored me, and then I left the office for the last time in my life.

---

* I had, of course, spent the previous half hour highlighting all my crazy additions in the contracts and faxing and emailing them to all our clients under the heading – *Always read the small print!*

TERMS & CONDITIONS OF PACKING

Pack fast and light.

By the time she burst into the flat I was bundling my clothes into a bag. Her hair was a mess, windswept and out of place, her bob misshapen like a clay pot spun out of control on the wheel. It made me feel happy and sad. Happy as it framed Alice's face in a way that reminded me of that lovely messy, chaotic girl I fell in love with, and sad in the sense that, looking at her, I realised that this was it, this was the last time I'd see her.

'What do you want me to say?' Alice asked.

'Well, I'm not giving you the answers any more,' I said slowly. 'I've spent years answering your inane questions. You can figure it out easily enough, you're smart. I'll tell you this much, though, you were wrong about Executive X. Even he, the great capitulator and submissive one, eventually finds his breaking point.'

Alice stumbled slightly and sat on the bed, sitting surprisingly close to me as I threw a couple of shirts into a bag.

'There's so much to process: you were injured, I was exhausted, I was going through so much emotional-change enablement trying to cope with your accident, on top of what was a tough schedule . . .'

Very gently I raised my hand to stop her talking, I looked at her with a lot of love in my eyes, and I said softly, 'Alice, please just shut the fuck up.'

'How dare you.'

'How dare *you*,' I replied quietly.

'You don't know what it's been like since the accident.'

'That I understand. But you fucked Oscar *before* my accident.'

'Oh . . . fuck.'

'Most intelligent thing you've said in years.'

'It just happened. We're two similar types, Oscar and I, both high-achievers, on the alpha spectrum, you must have known how compatible we were and . . .'

'No management speak, please,' I said.

'What I mean is, we, Oscar and I, we're a type,' she said.

'You and Oscar are certainly a type.'

'I don't know what to say,' she said.

'Well, that's certainly a first,' I said. 'Did you not role-play this scenario, Alice? Very disappointing. I'd have thought this was one meeting you'd come prepared for. Or did you arrogantly think this day would never come back to bite you, did you assume that you and Oscar were the masters of the universe and that all you did would be acceptable?'

'OK, hold on, Frank, can we just stop, refresh, and regroup.'

'I tell you what. Let's make this role-play a little more interesting.' I walked into the bathroom, grabbed my toothbrush and razor, and threw them into the bag. 'Let's add a couple of parameters. Some conditions, clauses. Let's say that just for once you're only allowed to talk in English. Plain old English. It was your first language, after all, long before you became fluent in this corporate cant you so adore. Can you manage that? No buzzwords. Those are my terms, will you accept them?'

I checked my bag and there really was not much in there. It's incredible what you can reduce your life to.

Alice stood there, as if trying to recollect her normal English vocabulary, and I said, 'Remember all those words you used to use. It's called English. Everyone's talking it these days. Well, all those people who aren't talking in Chinese at least.'

'Stop being so cruel,' she said, and she started to cry.

She could still cry. And I'll admit that I felt part of me want to hug her.* I had intended to be so cool; now I was the one behaving like a child.

'Frank, why are you being so terrible? This isn't like you,' she said.

---

* I preface that by confessing that another part of me wanted to punch her in the face so hard that the little filled-in veneered gap between her two front teeth popped out and I'd see the old Alice just one last time.

'Oh, really, Alice, and what am I like exactly?' I asked.

'You're a lovely man, Frank, you're sweet and kind and generous and you would do anything for anyone.'

'So who am I?' I said.

'You are the man I love,' she said.

'Who am I?'

'What do you mean, Frank? Why do you keep asking me the same question?'

'Who am I, Alice?'

'You're Frank.'

'Otherwise known as?'

'What are you getting at?'

'Otherwise known as Executive X,' I said.

'Not this again, Frank, I told you that was nothing to do with you,' she said.

'Stop lying to me. The tests, all the tests, all the scores, they were all mine, it was me, you made a mockery of me, you did and you loved every minute of it. How could you, how could you do that to me, Alice?'

'I used bits of you, sure, because you were brilliant, you were a high achiever.'

'*Were* being the main word there; I'm such a disappointment to you, aren't I?'

'No, you're not, Frank.'

'I am,' I said, and I sat next to her and took her hand in mine as she wept so hard that the bed moved.

'You're not, Frank, I'm the one that messed up,' she said, and leaned in slightly so that we almost touched. 'I'm so sorry, Frank. Can you ever forgive me?'

I looked into her eyes and softly said, 'No chance.'

'I've sacrificed so much for you,' she said, leaning away again. 'Do you know how hard that level of commitment is? Do you know what I've done for you? I'm a motivated, creative person. I've made it while you've stagnated like a child. I've made something of myself.'

'Making yourself into a cow is not an achievement you should be proud of.'

'I'm not a cow, I'm a brilliant HR person and a change enabler,' snapped Alice.

'Sorry, Alice,' I said, slinging my bag over my shoulder. 'You've used the words "change enabler". You were warned.'

Her face changed, something shifted, and she stood up and tried to palm her hair back into a bob shape and brushed down her skirt, rebuilding her calmness and control.

I stood close to her and she wiped away her tears and said, 'Well, Frank, you can go fuck yourself for all I care.'

'I'll take your advice into consideration,' I replied.

'Oh shut up,' she said. 'I'm about to take you to the cleaners. The flat is mine, don't even try to fight it, you don't even care about it, I put my heart and soul into it, and I will take your money too, and all your shares of the business, which in about a month's time when it goes on to the stock exchange will make me a very rich woman.'

'Yes, about all that,' I said. 'It may come as a slight shock to you but none of those things will happen. The flat is mine, it's tied to the business, all of my money is in a trust, which is also tied to the business, and as for the IPO, well, I am sorry to say that will no longer be happening. Oscar will explain the ins and outs to you when he has time.'

Then I took out the folded prenuptial contract and placed it on the bed beside her. 'You probably don't remember this document but you signed a prenuptial. My dad, God bless his soul, insisted. And to be honest, it leaves you with pretty much no more than the shirt on your back. It's a lovely shirt, though.'

Like a controlled demolition she collapsed in on herself: her back bent, her head sagged to her chest, her hair fell forward as she read over the prenuptial agreement, her eyes darting, failing to focus, until her fist flopped forward, opened, and the prenuptial agreement swished rather gracefully to the ground.

'Well, feel free to read it in your own time,' I said. 'It really is my father's finest work. He was a poet. He understood human nature better than most.'

She looked up at me and I realised I had not really considered my final parting words; I had failed to rehearse my exit from her life.

I thought it should be something profound and memorable, but then I simply smiled and said, 'Well then. Toodlepip.'

CLAUSE 3.2

A SUICIDE*

TERMS & CONDITIONS OF
TERMS & CONDITIONS

*Like an infinite loop, even terms and
conditions have terms and conditions.*

---

* Οφ σορτς

TERMS & CONDITIONS
OF CASSANDRA

Those Greeks knew a thing or two.

I'm just one of many unheard oracles.

Modern life is packed with warnings, whether they be legal – *Terms and conditions apply!* – biblical – *Thou shall not kill* – or cliché – *A stitch in time saves nine*. And what do we do with all this truth and counsel? We completely ignore it.

They say *Don't Speed!* but we just fast forward through it because *Life's too short to worry about the details.*

Stop!

Life is the details. As you age, the wording changes but life's fine print is essentially saying the same thing – *You're a short time living and a long time dead.*

So stop for a second and think about it.

You're shot out of the void, and as a baby the details are simple – *don't lick electrical sockets, don't choke, keep breathing* – as a teenager the messages blare loud and clear – *don't smoke, don't die young, and listen to your parents (they actually know things that you don't)* – you're ageing now and, as you hit the middle, the messages get fuzzy – *easy as you go, seize the day, appreciate the small things, tell your wife you love her* – but by now time is tumbling over itself, and just as you start to take note, just as you stretch to grasp life's simple truths, you're rudely shunted out the other end into more eternal zilch.

Please Give Way!

From: frankversion3.0@hotmail.com
To: oscar@shaw.sons.com
CC: ninashaw@hotmail.com
Subject: Give me back my spleen!

Hi Oscar – my brother, my keeper, my boss and my betrayer

I can't be sure if my contract sabotage will lose you *all* your clients but, at the very least, I can rest assured that it will lose you *some* clients, which will make your life a nightmare as you desperately try and explain what happened – why millions of pounds of client money resulted in worthless contracts riddled with lame jokes. Which means you can kiss your precious stock-market money goodbye. The market doesn't like it when you lose vast chunks of money in a day. Accountants frown on that sort of thing. I sabotaged – tampered with, *improved*? – an awful lot of contracts. So prepare yourself for a whole glut of angry clients.*

In case you've not grasped it yet – this is a suicide note.

Not a standard suicide. I'm not committing mortal suicide. Just corporate suicide, modern suicide, document suicide. I'm erasing myself from the page and hopefully living in a more real world. Of one thing I'm sure, no one will ever hire me as a lawyer again. This is a certainty that fills me with a warm sense of wellbeing. Once settled I may even use all that lovely salary that you signed off to start doing what I have always really wanted to – practise medicine and try to offset some of the bad that I've done with a touch of good. Do you even remember the day I got you to sign my new contract?

I know I misrepresented a little, and I assume that you'll appeal for rescission as you signed it under unfair circumstances. However, I think, were we to debate unfair circumstances, that you certainly made mine intolerably unfair. I therefore appeal to

---

* As a small footnote I'll admit that I didn't send *all* of my best work out; there are still some little gremlins lurking in the terms and conditions, out there in the wild, some that I didn't highlight; I can but hope that they'll keep biting you on the bum for many years to come.

your sense of natural justice, and ask that you look upon that salary as indemnity. I hope you'll honour my new contract in an attempt to balance the fact that you so blatantly dishonoured my life. I may be overestimating you, Oscar, but why don't you surprise me, why don't you prove me wrong? Don't lawyer up, don't fight me, just think about what you've done, pack up your rage, and do something decent for a change.

I'll also be committing suicide in the sense that I will from now be dead to Alice and yourself. Dead in the sense that you'll never see or hear from me ever again. Which I suppose is really what death is. I suspect that I'll rather enjoy being dead. So consider this my final Will and Testament. I'm doing my best to shed all my paper parts, all the documents that make me official. I've already lost my driving licence so that's a good start. (Well, it was taken away from me after the accident.) My legal licence is gone too. For the moment I'll hold on to my passport until such a time as I find the final place I'll stay, rest and eventually die and decay.

Rest assured that this is not – as our American attorney cousins would say – *a cease and desist order*. In fact, it's a *proceed and permit order*. I hereby state that you, Oscar, and Alice are granted legal, ethical and emotional permission to continue to conduct your affair. Go forth with my blessing and bonk my wife's brains out. Oh, and I should probably mention that I've CCed your lovely wife, Nina – *I just imagined your eyeballs desperately shooting up to the CC line on this email and then back again* – yes, that's right, I did really CC her.

Hi Nina!

Finally, I have left you a small gift, Oscar, a memento; it's in a Colman's jar. It's not a pickled onion so don't eat it. Whenever your ego gets too inflated, take a moment to look at it, and remember this – *From deep down in your soul all the way up to your shiny surface, you're nothing more than a fat fraud.*

Bye bye, big brother.

From: frankversion3.0@hotmail.com
To: actualactuary@actuaryinc.com
Subject: Thank you

Dear Doug,

What can I say, other than to thank you half a million times over and more.

You once told me that life's a gift. It's an accurate saying. Accurate in the sense that gifts are usually discarded the moment they're opened. All those gifts you got for birthdays, Christmases. Where are they now? You threw them out because they were crap.

After my car crash – just as the afterglow of my recovery had begun to flicker out – I was doing that: wasting days, disposing of the gift of life. Doing exactly what you pleaded with me not to do, I slipped right back into my old life, or an approximation of it, like wearing an old suit reeking of regret. The human nose is an amazing thing that can adjust to some truly repugnant smells and, for a brief time, adjust I did. Well, no more, Doug. Even though you're a desk-bound soul, you still remain a man of action and you taught me enough to know that life doesn't care, you have to make it care.

I know now that I've spent years waiting for the bridge I was standing on to burn down, willing it to fall apart in order to force me to jump.

Well, I've struck the match, Doug, and for better or worse I'm burning my own bridge, and I'm going to deal with whatever comes next.

I will miss you terribly, Doug, and I wish you the best of luck, or maybe I should say – I wish you the best possible statistical odds that life is willing to offer.

I have gifted you Dad's watch.

Love, Frank

Dear Alice,

Short questionnaire. (Answers below.)

1. How did we fall so far apart?*
   a. I changed.
   b. You changed.
   c. We changed.

2. What will I miss the most?*¹
   a. Your smile.
   b. Your questionnaires.
   c. Both of the above.

3. Do I still love you?*²
   a. He loves me.
   b. He loves me not.

I hope you get this note. I left it on all the boxes of your stuff that the removal men will be taking out of the flat today.

   So I'm on my way to a place called *Anywhere But Here*, accompanied by a woman who really loves me for me, to see a man who really

---

* Answer: c. There's a man called Jerry who every day rides his bike up a hill to the McDonald Observatory in West Texas to fire lasers at the moon, measuring how far away it is from the earth. After thirty-seven years of this, Jerry has realised that the moon is very slowly moving away from the earth. That's exactly what's happened with us. Over time, at an imperceptible speed, we drifted millions of miles apart.

*¹ This is a trick question. The truth is that leaving you for ever will not make me miss you any more than I already have for so many years. I miss the soft curves you carved away with exercise, I miss the warm wit you froze with corporate cynicism, I miss the intimate gap between your teeth. I have missed you for longer than I can bear. I do hope that over time you remember yourself, Alice, and remember what an incredible person you once were.

*² Answer: a. I still love a small part of you – I love the faint echo of that riotous girl I fell in love with so long ago. Sometimes when I listen carefully to you talk, I can still hear her and she makes me laugh.

knows when to say something I should have said so many long years ago – *Fuck this!*

I wish you the best of luck and lots of love.*

Now, if you'll excuse me, it's time for me to begin again.

Frank

ACKNOWLEDGEMENTS

Special thanks to Jemma, Lily, George and all my family for supporting (and at times suffering) my compulsive writing habit. Thank you to all my friends who were forced to read far too many drafts. Bob Gilhooly – you are brilliant; Charmaine Hunt – I'll put more sex in the next one; Dominic Smith – who rightly demanded more Doug; and Alison Burford – you went well beyond your neighbourly duty. To Stan for opening my email and for everything you have done for me since, I'm indebted to you. And thanks to the wise and lovely Helen and all the brilliant double-barrelled Bloomsbury people who took a leap of faith with me.

A NOTE ON THE AUTHOR

Robert Glancy was born in Zambia and raised in Malawi. At fourteen he moved from Africa to Edinburgh and then went on to study history at Cambridge. He currently lives in New Zealand with his wife and children.

@RobertGlancy
#TermsandConditions

A NOTE ON THE TYPE

The text of this book is set Adobe Garamond. It is one of several versions of Garamond based on the designs of Claude Garamond. It is thought that Garamond based his font on Bembo, cut in 1495 by Francesco Griffo in collaboration with the Italian printer Aldus Manutius. Garamond types were first used in books printed in Paris around 1532. Many of the present-day versions of this type are based on the *Typi Academiae* of Jean Jannon cut in Sedan in 1615.